GODS

of

WAR

KING'S BANE
BOOK TWO

C.R.MAY

For Shelby

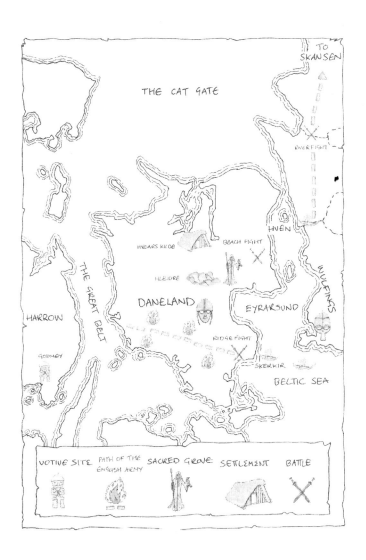

THE CAT GATE

TO
SKANSEN

RIVER FIGHT

HVEN

HXOARS KILOE   BEACH FIGHT

HLEIDRE

DANELAND   EYRARSUND

WULFINGS

HARROW

RIDGE FIGHT

THE GREAT BELT

GODMEY

SKERKIR

BELTIC SEA

| VOTIVE SITE | PATH OF THE ENGLISH ARMY | SACRED GROVE | SETTLEMENT | BATTLE |

GLOSSARY

Duguth – Doughty men, veteran fighters.

Ealdorman – A provincial governor.

Eorle – A hero.

Fiend – The enemy.

Folctoga – A leader in war, the ancient English equivalent to a General or Field Marshal.

Gesith– The king's closest companions, a bodyguard.

Guda – A male priest/holy man.

Huscarls - Literally House Men or Inside Men. A force of warriors, permanently attached to a lord. The Danish equivalent of the English Hearth Troop.

Scegth – A light warship.

Scop/Skjald – A poet/word smith, usually itinerant.

Snaca – Snake, a larger warship, forerunner of the later Viking period dragon ship, the 'Drakkar'.

Thegn – A nobleman with military obligations.

Volva - A priestess.

Wyrd- Fate.

Har the Hard-gripper,
Hrolf the bowman,
good men of noble lineage,
who never flee.
I wake you not for wine
nor for women's mysteries;
rather I wake you for the hard game of war.

The Saga of King Hrolf Kraki.

ONE

The Jute shuffled forward as the line moved on. Ahead, yet another man turned his face aside to gush yellow bile onto the grassy hillside as they drew ever closer to the blood letting. The fool behind him was still repeating the same plea to his lord, over and over, and Garulf's face twisted into a snarl as he turned and snapped out through gritted teeth. 'Your lord can't help you now. If you don't stop that, I will gut you myself.'

Vacant eyes moved to focus on him for an instant as the man's mind came back from his thoughts, and although the voice came in a whisper, they still carried weight as they asked the age-old question: 'why us?'

Garulf shrugged, irritated by the man's weakness. 'Because we are here and the gods willed it. There is no need to bother them now, they have already decided our wyrd is to die here.' Despite the grimness of the situation he surprised himself as a snort of amusement escaped into the cool morning air. He recognised the man from the muster, he was the one with the strange name. 'You can ask this lord yourself in a short while, Thomas.'

The man was idly fingering a silver pendant between his thumb and forefinger, and Garulf saw to his surprise that it was not the hammer of the thunder god as he had expected, but the equal-armed cross of the Christ. His new-found charge flinched as the staccato thrum made by thousands of English spears on shields redoubled in intensity, rising and falling in time.

Clack...clack-clack...clack.

Clack...clack-clack...clack.

His neighbour hung on his every word, and Garulf's antagonism evaporated as he realised that the distraction was helping him to cope with his own impending death. He forced a smile, despite the terror he felt at the goings on up ahead as he nodded down at the trinket. 'My cousin went to Cent. Is that where you got that?'

The man pulled a thin smile and pressed the pendant to his lips, grateful for the distraction as he answered with enthusiasm. 'I was born there, as was my father. My family settled in Cent when Hengest was king.' He gave a snort of irony. 'I only returned to Juteland to arrange a wife for my son. It looks as if he will have to find one for himself.' Thomas continued as the English spearmen chivvied the prisoners along with the points of their weapons, grateful for the unexpected chance of a last conversation. 'Where did your kinsman settle? I may know him.'

Garulf shrugged. 'Who knows, we never saw nor heard from him again. Either he got lucky and found a patch of land to work or the Britons got him.' He paused and forced a watery smile: 'or the Saxons, or the Franks or the Engles. There are always plenty of folk willing to stick a spear into a man without kin nearby, nor a lord to back him up.' He looked about and shook his head. 'Not that it's done us much good!'

The crack of a whip cut through their conversation as the driver of a team of oxen huckled his charges away. The Jutish pair looked across as the big wheels began to turn and the cart pitched and rolled down the slope. Thomas chewed his lip as they watched it go. 'How many is that now? Where do you think they are taking them?'

Garulf shrugged as the next wagon was hauled into place, and he flicked a look along the line as he made a quick calculation. Each cart held about a score or so of the bloody husks which had so recently been living, breathing men, and his body gave an involuntary shudder as he realised that the gore soaked planking before him would very soon contain his own. Thomas was repeating his question, and Garulf shook his head to clear the thought as he replied. 'I don't know Tom, but it can't be far or they would not be able to reuse the same wagons.'

'And the horses, earlier?' Thomas added fearfully. 'What in God's name are they doing?'

Garulf thought back to the time of the first sacrifices. The stallions taken from the king and his horse thegns after the fighting at The Crossing had been led to the brow of the hill as the first glimmer of light had drawn a line on the eastern horizon. Their worst fears had soon been realised as the guda, ash white and antlered, had left the great hall to perform their rituals. Soon the side of the hill had been thick with gore, slick with blood, as entrails as thick as ship's hawser washed knee deep across the grass. He gave a sad shrug as he attempted to answer his friend's question. 'We are being sacrificed to the gods, does it matter why? Perhaps they are returning to Juteland to lay waste to the North. We just saw King Osea and his leading men killed before us, who is left to stop them?'

Thomas persevered. 'So why sacrifice us? We are nothing to your gods.'

Garulf surprised himself as a chuckle escaped his lips, despite the horror of their surroundings. 'The gods have a hearty appetite, Thomas.'

The conversation was becoming gloomy and their future was already short and grim. He moved on quickly. 'You said that they were my gods just then, and you wear that cross at your neck. So this lord you were asking to help you was the Christ lord that the southerners worship, not your natural lord?'

The ghost of a smile flickered onto the Jute's face at the mention of the name, and he answered with pride and confidence. 'There is only one Lord, Garulf, and his name is Iesus.'

Garulf chuckled again. He was glad that Thunor had sent this fool to take his mind off the end that the norns had planned for them. They were edging closer to the bloodletting and the stench was becoming overpowering. His breath was coming in rapid, shallow snorts as he tried to shut out the sour odour of loosened bladders and bowels from his final moments on Middle-earth. It made conversation difficult but he carried on regardless, intrigued despite himself. He was a farmer, of middling stock. He had answered the war horn and fought for Jarl Heorogar when the English attacked, but there was to be no place in Woden's hall for the likes of him, nor his kin. No great cry of recognition would resound as he strode to take his seat at the family bench, feasting among his great ancestors as they whet their swords and awaited the last great battle of wyrd. That was reserved for his betters, men like Heorogar and the Engle who had tossed him the gallon of ale the night before as he stood penned in with the others. Like sheep on market day he snorted in disgust. Like he was doing him a great favour, the bastard. He had heard tales of the strange God, and pressed his new friend for more. 'A man once told me that your God welcomes all men into his kingdom, kings, jarls and common folk alike.' Garulf chuckled at the absurdity of the idea but, to his surprise, he found that a small part of him wished it to be true. He had always been a devout follower of the hammer god, but even the sacrifice of his only milk cow had failed to prevent the sheep being wiped out by scrapie. They had lost the bairn, his only son, thinking themselves lucky that the little waif had been the only one to succumb to the man cull they had come to call the hunger summer.

Thomas inhaled deeply, his chest swelling with pride. Garulf could sense the man strengthen as he thought of his God and the sight impressed him. 'It's true,' he replied firmly. 'The Lord welcomes all those who turn to him. Noble or base, we are all his children.'

Garulf grimaced as a new smell, far worse than the smell of soiled clothing and puke reached his nostrils. A memory of blood month, the annual slaughter of livestock in autumn came, and a shudder ran through him as he recalled the sights and throat clawing odours as hot offal and guts slid steaming to the ground. A spark of hope kindled within the Jute and he pressed Thomas again. 'And there is no work there and all men are equals in the eye of your God?' he continued, hardly daring to hope that the absurdity could be true. Thomas smiled in reply, and Garulf recognised in it the action of a man whose fears had been driven away by the strength of his devotion.

Caught up in their conversation Garulf had not noticed that they were still shuffling forward, and he flinched as a blood chilling scream pierced the air only feet away. He glanced down the slope of the hill to his right, to the place where the pitiful cries of those whose courage had deserted them at the last carried up to haunt the column. Hacked about the legs and arms by the English warriors, they had been left to suffer their agonies as a warning to others that escape was not only impossible, their deaths would be long drawn out, humiliating and painful. The very worst of deaths, the death of a *nithing*.

A dove grey cloud slid from the face of the sun, bathing the ghastly scene in its soft spring light as Garulf seized on this unexpected glimpse of salvation. Reaching out to pluck at his new friend's sleeve, the words had left his lips before he was aware that they were even there. 'You say that the Christ takes all, however base. Will he take me?'

Thomas' eyes widened in surprise, but he quickly slipped the leather thong over his head and draped the small cross of silver around Garulf's neck as strong arms gripped his friend and began to tug him away.

'Do you repent your sins and open your heart to the Lord?' he cried.

Garulf opened his mouth to reply, but the breath was forced from him as he was swung to face the priests. Before him the sacrificial stone was slick with gore and rough hands gripped his shoulders, forcing him to his knees in the slime. Up close, the English guda looked even more terrifying than they had from distance. One in particular, tall and slim beneath a circlet of stag horns, his hide-clad body a mass of runic charms, stood to one side, his face a mask of undisguised joy.

As the priest moved before him and began to raise a long blade, the thrum of English ash shafts on shields increased to a crescendo. Garulf's mind swam but a strong voice cut through, its urgent tone setting it apart from the din. 'Turn your face to the Lord, Garulf. Ask his forgiveness for your sins. Call his name and enter his kingdom.'

Garulf fumbled for the cross, clenching it tightly as his bladder loosened and he started to shake. The voice of Thomas came again, and the Jute dimly recognised that his friend was reciting from the Christian God-spell as English war horns blared.

'Ure Fæder, þu eart on heofonum...'

Garulf raised his chin, his cry cut short as steel flashed in the dawn.

*

'What you got?' Osbeorn tried to sound lackadaisical but nobody was fooled.

Octa shrugged, playing along with the game: 'sausage.'

'Where did you get it, Oct'?'

Octa took a bite and closed his eyes as he savoured the taste: 'The Barley Mow.'

Osbeorn tried to remain calm but he licked his lips instinctively and his eyes widened for a heartbeat, giving him away. The Barley Mow made the best sausage in Sleyswic, firm and meaty with a hint of crow garlic, harvested over the winter from beneath the hedgerows which grew out back. 'You got any more?'

Octa took another bite as Eofer forced down a snigger. Laughter danced behind the eyes of his troop and, although Osbeorn knew that he was being played like a straw whistle, it was a small price to pay for the chance of a bite of one of Ena's finest. Finally he cracked. He had to ask, the longing dripping from every word. 'Give us a bit.'

Octa looked at the gnawed remains and pulled a face. 'It's my last one mate.' Finally he relented with a sigh and tossed the thing across. Osbeorn's look of triumph was quickly replaced by a mask of horror as the sausage sailed high through the air. Despite a desperate lunge, it spun end-over-end to land in the waters of the Sley with a pathetic plop. Osbeorn looked back at his hearth mate, but the pain and disbelief on his features changed to a wry smile and an uttered curse as he saw that most of his troop had produced sausages of their own and were happily munching away.

Eofer laughed along with the others as his duguth ducked into a shower of the things, and he made his way aft to the steering platform as Osbeorn's voice came down the ship: 'ho bloody ho. What funny bastards you lot are!'

The eorle's smile was cut short as another roar rose into the air above the nearby hillside, and he exchanged a look with the *scipthegn* and pulled a pained smile, all the humour of the moment lost in an instant. 'There are not many people laughing in Sleyswic this morning,' he said with a frown.

Eadward shrugged. 'If you had spent the best part of your life chasing away Jutish raiders from Harrow you would not be so concerned Eofer. Think on it,' he added,

8

awestruck. 'To sacrifice a king to the gods; that's powerful spell-work.'

The snake ship coasted down the great inland waterway with gentle strokes of the oars, each pull carrying her and the men who crewed her a pace further from the mayhem at the burh. A chill wind gusted in from the West, and a shaft of sunlight broke through as the blanket of grey which had shrouded the town since dawn finally cleared away. Even at this distance the banks of the Sley were lined with ships, and the crews stood and watched as the snaca swept by, hearty cheers and cries for gods-luck rolling across the icy waters as the proud men aboard grinned like cats and waved in return.

Eofer turned away and forced his mind to other things as the clatter of weapons on lime wood boards grew fainter, and he reflected with pride on his send off that morning. Despite the duties of the day, King Eomær had shown him honour by coming to the dockside in person. Attended by his own father, Wonred, and the latest member of the king's bodyguard his own brother Wulf, Eomær had wished them well and told the gathering of his confidence in them as the crew had visibly swelled with pride. Now they were off to bait the Danes, and the thegn recalled his final instructions as they moved slowly towards the waters of The Belts: '*Burn the East, Eofer,*' the king had said as the flames of war shone in his eyes. '*Move among the Danes like a wildcat, draw their army away from the landing grounds and we shall repay them a hundredfold for their depredations in our own lands.*'

The sun peeped through as they cleared the empty wharfs and ruined buildings of Theodford, and the wind veered to the South. Eadward ordered the sail unfurled and smiles lit faces as the spar was sweated aloft and the great sheet billowed. Within the hour they were through the bay, and the prow bucked like a warhorse at the gallop as the water beneath the hull turned from dove grey to slate and the ship made the sea, breasted the first of the waves and ploughed on.

A gaggle of masts came on from the North, the mantle of gulls screeching at the masthead betraying their purpose, and soon they were up on the bæcbord beam. A snake ship like their own, the wave darkened hull lined by grinning faces edged across from its charges, and Eofer watched as Eadward hung from the backstay, his cloak whipping away to the North as he hailed his fellow *scipthegn* at the stern: 'good catch?'

The man made an o with his hands, cupping them to his mouth as he cried above the wind and the squarking of the seabirds. 'The boys are knee deep in herring; little silver darlings!'

Eadward laughed. 'Smoke us a few for our return.'

A grin and a wave and they were past, the tall stern posts drawing apart as the unknown steersman returned to his charge. Eofer looked across at the little fleet as they made their way home with what, he realised suddenly, may very well be their final catch in these waters. A few had already moved to the head of the Sley, ready to begin the overland trek to the River Trene. More would follow as the Sley emptied of snake ships, and Eofer gave a snort as he thought of the reeve at Old Ford and his men, labouring to move a war fleet one way and then back again with a bevy of smaller craft. Eadmund had got his wish, the king had responded to the raids along The Oxen Way the previous year with the greatest ship army ever seen in northern seas, and he recalled with pride that he had played a part in that decision.

His own men were hailing their countrymen and Eofer glanced outboard. The fishermen had taken a break from fish gutting, their bloody knives glinting as they lined the little ships to wave the warriors on their way. Tough men, their weatherbeaten faces almost indistinguishable from the long sealskin smocks and caps which marked them out to other men, even from a hundred paces. Eofer had always marvelled at their skill, harvesters of the trackless wastes. Each and every haul was the result of generations of accumulated experience and knowledge, know-how gained at a heavy cost in silver and lives as the little boats reaped the shoals on the prow-plain.

As the little fleet moved away the *Hwælspere* cleared the shallows, and Eadward's steersman drew the big steering oar to his chest, hauling her head around to the south-west as silvered droplets swept the deck. A hush had descended on the crew, and Eofer saw that they had gathered amidships and were staring aft. Turning to follow their gaze, the thegn looked beyond the stubby grove of masts. The little boats were already hull down as the sea grew choppy, lines of spindrift snaking away to the North, and he watched in silence as the necklace of dunes which lined the shore were swallowed by the gloom. He exchanged a look with Eadward at his side. Their homeland was behind them. Only the gods of war would know whether they would lay their eyes upon it again.

TWO

Draining his cup, the prince slammed it into the ale spills as he firmed his resolve for the thing to come. The king was ailing no less than his kingdom; new blood was needed or Daneland would fall to the wolves which forever snapped at her borders. The action had stilled the room, conversations axed in mid sentence as the men there came to know that the deed was afoot. Hrothulf swept the hall with a look as he pulled himself upright, firming his jaw as wood scraped on wood and benches were forced back. As the other drinkers stared into their cups, each man mulling on thoughts of shame or hope, the huscarls rose to file through the door without a backward glance.

Passing from the gloomy interior to the harsh light of the northern spring, they instinctively cast their eyes towards the place where the royal hall had stood in its glory. The fire ravaged timbers had all been removed now but the blackened earth mocked them still, shameful, a scar on land and honour alike. Hammers rang at the base of the mound as the smith and his apprentice beat the misshapen bronze tiles, warped and twisted by the heat of the inferno, back into shape; a dog moved away, sensing their mood, fearful of a kick.

It was no small thing he had set his mind upon, but the kingdom needed strong leadership and if not from him from whom? Hrethric and Hrothmund were fools, but dangerous fools nonetheless. He would not make the same mistake that his uncle had made when his own father had died.

Caught up in his thoughts, he realised with a start that the hall of the king was before him. The guards flanking the doorway smiled in welcome, and he painted his face with a grin in return as the king's favourite wolfhound crossed to nuzzle his outstretched hand. 'Not joining the hunt today, lord?' the friendly guard asked as the prince began to unfasten his baldric. 'Word has it that those woods shelter a boar as large as a horse.'

Hrothulf tousled the ear of the dog as it wagged its tail happily. 'Not today, Arnkel,' he replied, flicking a meaningful look up at the summit where Heorot had stood in its splendour. 'We have weightier affairs in mind.'

The sentinel nodded knowingly. 'The men who did that will get what's coming to them soon enough.'

A thrall came forward to take the weapons, stacking them with the others as the group moved into the hall. Swords, spears and ale-fuelled bluster were never the easiest of bedfellows; faced with the choice the warriors always chose to forego their weapons, prized heirloom or not.

Inside the hall the long hearth blazed along the centreline, the flames painting posts and men alike with a rosy glow. The young Dane's eyes scanned the space before him, and a small surge of excitement built within as he saw that the plan was working. Skapti's idea had been a masterstroke, beautiful in its simplicity as most good plans were, emptying the hall and removing the majority of the king's own huscarls at the same time. Hrothulf exchanged a look with his leading man and saw the same excitement reflected there, as the other members of his comitatus hailed the few remaining warriors in the hall and ambled across to the benches. As his hearth companions joined the king's men and called for ale, he led Skapti further into the hall. Ahead of them two more spearmen stood before the royal bedchamber, the leaf shaped blades of their weapons glinting with menace in the reflected light of the hearth. Hrothulf threw them a smile as he approached and they nodded in return. 'I wish to see the king. How is he?'

The answering smile faded from the warrior, and he glanced furtively across his shoulder before leaning in close. 'Much the same, lord. Perhaps you can pep him up a bit?'

Hrothulf gave an involuntary snort. 'I will see what I can do.' He glanced up at the great war flag of the Danes, the white hart standing proudly on a field the colour of dried blood, noting the marks and tears of battle with pride as he stepped across the sole-plate and entered the inner room.

The bedchamber was small, itself a reminder that the king of Danes had fallen far from the lofty heights of his youth, despite the great victory over the Heathobeards the previous autumn. Panelled walls of finely planed oak gave the room a degree of splendour, but the few wall hangings which had survived the hunger of the flames still reeked of smoke, a constant reminder of the shame that had visited the Scyldings that fateful morning.

King Hrothgar looked up as his nephew entered and smiled thinly as a thrall woman bent low to mop the sweat from his brow. A small hearth was placed centrally, the heat from the flickering flames adding to the oppressive air, and Hrothulf winced at the smell of disease and decay which permeated the room. 'You are ailing, uncle,' he said sadly as he crossed the floor, 'and we have no time for it.'

The old king clutched at his side and grimaced. 'Who would have thought that something so small could lay a grizzled warrior low? I barely felt it hit, my mail all but kept it out.'

Hrothulf leaned in closer, and his nostrils flared as he shot the slave a look. 'Show me the wound.'

The servant peeled back the dressing as carefully as she was able, but still the king flinched as the rotten flesh tore again. The thrall stepped back smartly, as fearful of a clump as any mangy dog, and the prince winced at the stench which washed over them. A lump the size of a man's fist had risen from the body of the king, its flanks as red as the battle flag which straddled the door head outside. Beneath the surface of the suppurating mound, pus and blood showed clearly in an angry witches broth.

Hrothgar shook his head sadly. 'Wealhtheow says that a spirit has infected the wound. The cunning women agree.' He fumbled at his side and pulled out a slim shaft of ash wood, tossing it across: 'runes.'

Hrothulf rolled the arrow between his fingers, shaking his head in wonder and admiration. The arrangement with the traitor had worked better than he had dared hope. Gods-cursed kings were no use to any nation, especially at such a time as this. Engeln was a low hanging fruit which the kings of Daneland had long coveted; it was ripe for the picking. His mother was right, it had to be now.

King Hrothgar spoke again as his young nephew tossed the rune-hexed shaft aside. 'The guda say that they have not seen the like before, they cannot read them.'

As the thrall ventured forward to bathe the wound, Hrothulf stood and moved to her side. He was close enough to sense her tremble at his presence, and he fed on her fear as he slipped a dagger from its hiding place. Reaching across, Hrothulf spoke softly to the girl as his hand moved to smother her mouth. 'Don't worry little bird. I shall be quick.' His palm stifled her cry of alarm, and a heartbeat later the razor-sharp blade was opening the woman's throat in one fluid movement. A hot jet of blood pulsed from the cleft to shower the face of the king, who recoiled in shock at the unexpected violence. As the thrall struggled and her hands went to her throat in horror Hrothulf pulled her close and stabbed, snuffing out the last flickers of life as he worked the blade up to cleave her heart.

King and nephew locked eyes and an understanding passed between them as the prince cried aloud: 'now!'

Hrothgar quickly regained his composure, firming his mind as the body of the woman slid to the floor and blood pooled at their feet. 'So,' he said with a sigh of resignation, 'this is the day of which all men wonder.'

The younger man nodded sadly as panicked cries and the sound of scuffling carried from the outer hall. Hrothulf held the king with his gaze. 'We cannot wait to see if you will recover any longer, uncle. Besides, who will follow a king who is cursed by the Allfather? First the troll and now Woden-spells. Soon our enemies will get to hear of our weakness and they will fall upon us like wolves in the fold. Your hall lies burnt and still you sit in your bower nursing your body and pride.' The cries of men mingled with the crash of splintering wood as the fighting in the hall reached its bloody climax. Hrothulf gripped the hilt of his dagger and turned the bloody blade towards the king. 'Hrothgar's days as king of Danes have ended. The English will be only the first to feel the wrath of King Hrothulf.'

Hrothgar took a sip of ale and looked back, the heartbreak in his voice obvious. Savouring his last taste of ale on Middle earth, the king slapped his lips and made a final plea. 'What of my sons? They look up to you and they would give you their oath, I am sure of it.'

Shame caused Hrothulf to avert his gaze for a heartbeat, but it was enough for the king to seize his chance. With a burst of energy which belied his years, the old campaigner darted forward as candlelight flashed on steel. For a single moment in time he felt the thrill of combat again, before an explosive wheeze erupted from his lungs as Hrothulf's knife punched into his chest. His own knife hand was knocked aside with almost contemptuous ease, and Hrothgar felt a curious sense of peace as the realisation came that a lifetime of worry and duty was ending. As his successor hugged him close in a final embrace, King Hrothgar, shield of the Spear Danes, fixed his eyes on his kinsman as a final question left his lips: 'Wealhtheow?'

Hrothulf gazed back lovingly at his uncle, the man who had saved his life, raising him as his own when his father, Halga, had died all those years before. 'She will go back to her own people or wherever she wishes, uncle,' he replied with a voice made thick with emotion. 'Likewise our sister, Freawaru, is free to leave or remain here with full honour.'

Hrothgar reached out with the last of his strength, and his nephew moved the handle of the old king's war sword within reach. As Hrothgar Halfdanson closed his fingers around the grip, an image of the doors of Valhall groaning open on their mighty hinges came into his mind. He gave a small nod as the doors gaped before him, and Hrothulf pulled his kinsman closer as he drove the blade up into his heart to send him through.

*

The boy pressed himself back into the undergrowth and listened. The sounds of pursuit were growing ever distant with each passing moment, and he allowed himself a brief smile before the seriousness of his plight threatened to overwhelm him once again. A sob took him by surprise as he took stock of his situation and the boy forced it down, angry at his own weakness as he stifled the shame. He was unharmed and alone but fully armed. In no immediate danger but stranded miles from anywhere without a horse. Every piece of good fortune seemed to be cancelled out by Loki, but he had always prided himself on his ability to overcome all that the gods threw his way, even the trickster god, the slyest of them all. He would survive this and take his revenge.

The day had started out like so many others. Ribald cries, a toast to success, and the hunting party had galloped out from the royal compound as the first lick of pink showed in the sky to the East. Cresting the rise they had laughed for joy as the returning sun warmed their faces, and soon they had moved into a skirmish line as the heath gave way to the woodlands ahead. From the depths of the shadows the first sounds had carried to them as the beaters drove their quarry south, horns and distant shouts hanging in the still air. As the first animals began to show along the tree line their own hunting horns had sounded in the morning, and the riders had dismounted with smiles of anticipation at the killing to come and entered the gloom. Boar hunting was the finest of sports, and the boy gave a snort of irony as he recalled the surprise he had felt that his cousin had not wished to join them that morning. It had, after all, been his idea. The reason had become obvious all too soon, and he fought back tears of anger as the image of the heavy boar spears slicing into his brother's torso flashed into his mind. Outnumbered three to one, his own men and those of his father the king had reacted with speed and vigour. Throwing themselves into a wall of spears, the huscarls had sold their lives dearly to give him a chance to escape the ambush.

Hrothmund looked out into the glade before him and noted the length of the shadows there. They were long, far too long, stretching away to the West as he knew that they would. The whole day lay before him and he grudgingly acknowledged his kinsman's forethought. A dawn start and a hunt on foot would give his men the whole day to track them down if one or other brother had escaped the carefully laid trap.

The soft snicker of a horse dragged his mind back from its meanderings, and he squirmed further into the bush as the long shadow of the animal crept along the clearing.

Within a heartbeat it had been joined by another and Hrothmund's mind raced. Spring was all but on the land, the trees a haze of lush green shoots, but it would be some weeks yet before the foliage was dense enough to hide a man. Flight was out of the question, the slightest movement would be seen by the riders instantly, and the young prince recognised the moment when the calm descended upon him and his mind and body prepared for battle as shadow and hoof finally merged together on the track. This was what he had trained so many hours for, to wield sword and shield, to take the fight to the enemy whatever the odds. Despite the fact that he was certain now that his father must be dead, he was a Scylding, Woden born; he would stay alive to wreak his vengeance.

The closest rider was in view now as he tugged at his reins, halting the mount not twenty paces from Hrothmund's hiding place. The young Dane flashed a lupine smile as his enemies scanned the clearing ahead for signs of movement. Pal and Kari, Hrothulf's men. They had been among the first to thrust their spears into the unsuspecting back of his older brother; it was fitting that they should become the first to pay the price for their lord's treachery.

Hrothmund inched his sword from its scabbard as the riders studied the ground around them for signs of disturbance. A charm of goldfinches took to the air on the far side of the clearing, their tawny bodies flashing scarlet and white as they tail chased through a shaft of sunlight, and the huscarls followed their antics with a smile. Hrothmund slid the blade free, tensing his legs, his body wound up and set to pounce, but froze as a hunter's intuition whipped Kari's head back his way. Hardly daring to breathe, the boy edged his thigh across to cover the blade of his sword lest the growing light catch its edge as his eyes narrowed to slits. The basest woodsman knew that the whites of the eyes shone like torches from the shadows; it was a lesson which his father had taught him, and it may have concealed him now if the sun had not broken through at that moment to paint the forest floor with its light.

Kari's eyes went wide as they picked out their quarry, but Hrothmund was already on his feet, throwing himself forward as Hrothulf's hearth warrior opened his mouth to cry a warning. Bursting from cover he raised his blade high, forcing his opponent to open his body as he brought his spear around in a desperate attempt at fending off the blow. But the move was a feint, and Hrothmund ducked beneath the warrior's wild swing as he pirouetted past, sweeping his own blade down in a powerful arc to bite deep. The prince rolled away, drawing his blade across the tendons of the horse's legs, the threads parting with ease as the animal screamed in pain and collapsed backwards to the floor.

Kari was at his mercy, his unguarded back only feet away as he struggled to throw himself clear of the crippled animal, but Hrothmund ignored the death blow and danced on.

Pal was quickly recovering from his own surprise, hauling at the reins as he dragged the head of his horse around to confront their quarry, but their intended victim was too fast, too wily, and the huscarl sensed in his heart that the predator had become the prey. Even as he dragged his spear around to fend off the blow his face betrayed his fear, and a look of triumph swept Hrothmund's features as he powered his sword blade across to bite deeply into the small of his opponent's back. With an expert roll of his wrist, Hrothmund dragged the blade through muscle and bone and kept moving.

Kari's horse was still down on its hindquarters, baying in its agony, forelegs scrabbling against the turf as it tried to rise again, and Hrothmund vaulted its back as he moved back to finish off its rider. The huscarl had recovered quickly, rolling onto his back in the short time that it had taken for Hrothmund to cripple his companion. The heavy boar spear was swinging around, and Hrothgar's son danced aside as the barbed blade whistled through the air only inches from his belly. A quick glance across the writhing body of the horse told him that Pal was done for, his lifeless legs splayed out behind him as he attempted to drag himself to cover. Lowering himself into a fighting stance Hrothmund circled his opponent as the man watched him warily, desperate for the chance to clamber back to his feet.

The fight had reached a stalemate, neither man could strike without laying himself open to a counterstrike, and Hrothmund's mouth curled into a sneer of contempt as he questioned the man who lay before him. 'So; have we a new king?'

Kari snorted, his expression mocking. '*We* don't have a new king, no.' His mouth drew a cold smile as Hrothmund watched the spear point dance before him. 'Only *I* have a new king. You have a funeral pyre waiting for you back at Hleidre.'

A smattering of burrows littered the ground thereabouts, and the stony spoil lay scattered all about them. Hrothmund worked his foot beneath a pebble as

Kari spoke, snapping a reply which he knew would rile
the man on the forest floor and pin his eyes to his own.
'You have a big mouth for a man dumped on his arse. Call
me lord, and I will make your end as painless as I can,' he
sneered, his lips curling into a contemptuous smile.

Kari gave a savage laugh, and Hrothmund jerked his
foot forward in a flash. The stone spun through the air
between them to strike the warrior on the cheek, and in
the heartbeat it took for Kari's mind to react to the danger
Hrothmund was past the wide spear blade, his sword
darting forward to prick his opponent's throat. The prince
curbed the strike before it became fatal, pinning the man,
wide eyed with fear, to the ground. As Kari choked and
gargled on his own blood, Hrothmund stood over him and
let a ball of spittle fall slowly into the other man's eye.
'You thought to be paid with gold and silver for the
morning's work', he snarled, thrilling to the power of the
moment. 'But I think it more fitting that your treachery is
repaid with steel.'

THREE

The lad dug out another stone with the butt of his spear and aimed a kick, watching with satisfaction as it arced away into the gloom.

'Will you stop that? If the English are out there the first thing that we will know is when we feel cold steel slide across our throat.'

The young Dane threw his companion a sidelong glance, his fresh-faced features made ruddy by the cold air. 'The English won't come this far east, we are wasting our time here. Even if they did,' he boasted, 'we saw off the Heathobeards and we will chase them away too.'

Herulf shook his head and sighed at the youth's innocence, but he could not suppress a tiny smile all the same. Straw blond hair and a complexion as smooth as cream were enough to hush the noisiest girls as he strolled past. That the gods had deemed fit to combine them with a powerful frame and ready smile were a gift worthy of them. Once the youthful bluster had been driven from him by a shield wall or two his brother would have a fine son on his hands, one who would add greatly to the family's standing.

'War Beards are one thing Toki, the English another. Our own raiders have been goading them for a while now, and they are beginning to hit back.' The big Dane spat into the grass and set his face, fixing his young kinsman with a stare. It was the look of a man imparting good advice, words which a wise man would heed. 'You have seen the charred remains of the king's great hall, twenty men did that. I have raided in Engeln and it's not much fun; you go in and get out quickly if you want to live.' Toki dropped his gaze and Herulf chuckled warmly as he tapped the boy's leg with the shaft of his spear. As Toki looked up, Herulf threw him a wink. Perhaps he had gone too far, it wouldn't do to chase the confidence from him, he would need it, and soon. Preparations were under way for the great raid which men said would follow the time when the goddess Eostre rode among them. The new King Hrothulf was a firebrand, a man after his own heart. Every man in the army knew that it had been his leadership and not the old king which had driven the Heathobeards from the land the previous year. It would be good to serve under a young and vigorous leader after the years of drift and shame which had marked the last days of Hrothgar's rule. Danes were not Jutes, King Eomær's rabid dogs would feel the full might of Danish power as payment for the destruction of Heorot. 'You will see the backs of plenty of Englishmen as we drive them before us,' Herulf smiled encouragingly. 'We will smash their spear hedge, burn Eorthdraca and be home in time to sow our crops.'

As the ever-ready smile returned to the youth's face a voice, faint and distant, hailed them from the murk. 'Herulf, we can't find you. Give us a whistle, we can't see anything in this.'

The Dane shook his head in wonder; overconfidence was rife in the army. He gripped his spear a little tighter and stared down the pathway. Cobwebs of mist sat on the land, collecting in the hollows and gullies of the coastal strip like pools of spilt milk. The trees glistened in the light of the moon, silvered pearls festooning the branches as the moisture found a home. Toki appeared at his shoulder, his own spear braced and ready as Herulf challenged the new arrivals. 'Use the password, or the only whistle you will hear is the whistle made by my spear as it cuts the air.'

Shadowy shapes slowly began to harden into the form of their relief as the words floated up: 'Fire Dragon.'

Herulf relaxed as the men laboured up the path and the leader shot him a smile. 'Is that any way to greet the man who carried your breakfast all the way up here? You are too careful Herulf, the English raiders are long gone.' The warrior ran his hand across his beard and flicked the condensation from his fingers as he came up. His smile widened into a grin as he produced two small bundles from his shirt. 'Unless you are about to tell me that we have wasted our time dragging ourselves up to this lonely headland? You've already beaten off a massed English attack and they have rowed for home, licking their wounds.'

Herulf gave a chuckle, shaking his head as he gratefully accepted the package and began to tuck in. 'I wouldn't know if they had arrived Thrain,' he said between mouthfuls, flicking a contemptuous look out to sea, 'not in this. Any more news?'

Thrain shook his head. 'No, I told you. The raiders are snug in their hall now, while we freeze our balls off staring out to sea. It's been two days since we saw the fire over at Skegg Ness, they are long gone.'

With the appetite of a younger man Toki had already wolfed his food, and he asked a question as his uncle took another bite. 'Why would they only send a solitary ship? All they do is land in the dark, burn a few farms near the coast and disappear again. There is no honour or reputation to be gained.'

'They have got the whole of eastern Daneland guarding the coastline every night though,' his uncle replied through a mouthful of food. 'Hundreds of men staring out to sea instead of preparing for the invasion after Eostre. Apparently the new king is gnashing his teeth like a madman, warriors are being sent to bolster the defences on this coast from as far away as Hroar's Kilde.'

'Maybe it's a ruse, uncle,' Toki suggested. 'Draw men away from the West before the main attack arrives there?'

Thrain and his companion shared a look and laughed. 'You see what you have done, Herulf?' He threw Toki a wink. 'Don't listen too closely to the old grey beard, lad,' he chuckled. 'He will have you checking under the bed for Englishmen before you go to sleep!'

Herulf shook his head sadly at the pair, but his nephew's words had struck a chord within him. Maybe the boy had more between his ears than he had given him credit for. Their stint on the coast was over, they were due to travel back to Hleidre at sunup; he would discuss the idea with his jarl and urge him to speak to King Hrothulf. Thrain and his friend were still larking about, but he had seen too much for one night; he needed sleep far more than conversation with these fools. 'Anyhow, English invasions or not' he yawned, 'it's your problem now, we're off. If we are quick we will get the chance of a quick nap before we take our leave of this dump.'

The pair shouldered their shields and took the pathway which led inland as the relief settled in to welcome the dawn. A gully snaked inland from the beach and within moments the Danes had been swallowed in its milky embrace. Tired but rejuvenated by the hot food and the lure of a warm bed, the pair increased the pace as the pathway inclined upwards again. Topping the rise the warm hearth beckoned them on, and uncle and nephew exchanged a smile as the track levelled out and crossed the heath which led to the camp. The mist was thinning as they climbed higher and left the crash of the waves behind them. Gorse and heather, their wind-blown shapes teased into long teardrops by the onshore winds, began to give way to the first birch, the silvered trunks glistening ghost-like in a curtain of white. High above the sky was clear, and a spring moon reigned over the star speckled dome.

Without warning Tofi tensed and plucked at his kinsman's sleeve. Herulf stopped in his tracks and instinctively brought his spear to bear as tired eyes scanned the whiteness. Dropping a shoulder, he had slipped his hand inside the shield grip before he had even realised that he had moved. Herulf questioned the youth as his eyes continued to probe the mist. 'What do you think you saw?'

Tofi shook his head slowly and moved into a crouch as he brought his own shield up. 'I didn't think anything kinsman, I saw the outline of a man moving alongside us.'

Herulf relaxed a little, but stifled a snort. Maybe Thrain's slapdash ways had caused him to overreact. It was good that the lad was alert, and he tried to hide any hint of mockery from his tone as he answered. 'If you saw two warriors carrying spears with shields slung upon their backs, you will find that it was us. I have stood guard in misty weather like this before, the light can play funny tricks.' Calming his breathing, he listened intently as his eyes probed the white wall before them. There was nothing to be seen but the boy was no fool, his comment back there had proven that. They would pick up the pace and keep their wits about them. More than just *manfiend* lurked on the heathlands when the night was calm and the moon shone bright.

They walked on and the older man spoke softly, smiling and gesticulating as if he were telling the lad a tale. 'Keep your eyes to the front and act normally but glance my way every now and again as if we are having a friendly chat. When you do,' he sniffed, 'have a quick look past my shoulder and see if you can spot any movement and I will do the same on your side.'

Tofi glanced across and laughed at an imagined jest as he took another bite of food. The mist had thickened again as the path dipped into a hollow and crossed a small stream. Despite themselves, the men found themselves trotting to the lip to clear its embrace as quickly as possible. Herulf snorted as the path climbed the opposite bank and he chided his young companion. 'You've got me running from trolls now,' he laughed. 'Whatever you do, don't tell anyone when we get back!'

Tofi's head flicked around at the older man, and he was about to reply when he halted mid-word as he saw an expression of horror cross his kinsman's face. A heartbeat later he let out a gasp of pain and surprise and his eyes dropped to stare, horror-stricken, at the bloody head of an arrow protruding from his throat. As the Dane's hands moved up to grasp the shaft and his eyes went wide, he watched as the more experienced man took the next shaft on the broad board of his shield.

Herulf moved between his stricken nephew and the direction from which the arrows had arrived. Covering them both with the shield, he grasped the boy as his legs began to fold and dragged him in the direction of the camp. 'Stay with me lad, I have got you.' Within a yard he felt a searing pain as another arrow found its mark, punching into his knee to shatter the bone. Limping now and slowed down by the weight of his kinsman, the big Dane watched as shadowy shapes moved menacingly about him in the chalky veil. A hoary sycamore emerged from the mist, its gnarled branches and twisted trunk testament to its great age, and the Dane's heart sank. He had remarked on it on the way to the coast and he knew that it lay a good mile or so from safety. His wyrd was upon him, and he turned his face to Tofi and gave the boy a fatalistic smile. 'It seems that the hooded god has us marked for a greater fight, kinsman. I am sorry that I doubted you.'

The boy drew himself upright and attempted to answer, but all that came was a pink froth as the air forced its way out through the shattered remains of his throat. Herulf felt a deep sense of pride at the lad's bravery and they shared a look of understanding, each man determined that they would meet their end like Danes as they moved shoulder to shoulder and faced their attackers.

*

The bow lifted again as the girl brought the bowstring to her cheek and sighted along the shaft. The mist was spoiling her aim, nothing within it seemed to be where it should be. It was, she decided as her face burned with shame and embarrassment, like trying to spear a trout in a stream. She slowed her breathing, calming her beating heart until she felt at one with the stave as the Danes swung around to face her.

A voice sounded at her shoulder, calm and reassuring, and the girl gave a grateful nod of recognition at the confident tone and raised her aim a touch. 'Another to the throat if you can, hawk eye. We don't know how far away their friends are, and we can't afford to let them call a warning.'

The thegn cast a look to the East and grimaced. The fog had thickened again like a living thing but the sky above was still visible. It seemed an age since they had left the ship and the moon was beginning to pale, the dawn must be close. He indicated the Danes with a flick of his head. 'Octa, Osbeorn; finish these two off and catch us up.' The pair exchanged a grin and unsheathed their swords as the others began to move away. As they advanced on the grim faced Danes Eofer spoke to them again. 'Make it quick, lads. We are giving up on this one, we need to get back to sea before the tide turns.'

They had been raiding along the eastern coast of Daneland for the best part of a week now. Following a day coasting northwards under the Danish flag, they had marked their targets before heading across to the opposite shore and landing their supplies on the Wulfing coast. Several camps had been chosen to enable the *Hwælspere* to lay up at a different location each day, each one carefully chosen so that the Danish coastline opposite would be clearly in view from a nearby headland. At first the attacks had succeeded beyond their wildest hopes. Arriving offshore at dusk had given them the hours of darkness to make their depredations and withdraw, but the Danes had countered quickly, flooding the area with warriors. Now, their main task completed, they were beginning to hanker after seeing friendly faces once more. The new moon still held sway and Eofer cast a look to the West. The king's war fleet would be clearing the mouth of the Sley this very morning, unfurling sails and heading east. Before the moon returned, thousands of English warriors would be ashore, and the war of fire and steel would pitch up on Danish strands.

Despite the successes of the past week this evening had been close to a disaster and he wanted away. The fog had risen like spectres from the hollows as soon as they were ashore, and within the hour they had been blundering around the countryside with only the moon and stars to guide them.

Hnæf, Eadward's steersman had been a wonder, carrying them through the murk and depositing the war band in the isolated cove as if it were day. They had found the gully and followed it inland until it had suddenly and unexpectedly petered out to nothing. It had quickly become obvious that they had followed the wrong watercourse but time was short, they simply had to be in position to launch the attack before the sun rose to burn off the mist or risk discovery. Stranded, far from the ship, even a local lad could then shadow them from horseback as others went for help. Cursing the weather, Eofer had just ordered the men back to the *Hwælspere* when they had heard the cry. Following the sound they had stumbled across the track, just as the twin figures of the Danish coast guardians hove into view. The mist had thinned unexpectedly revealing them to the enemy, but it mattered little. The trackway was easy to follow back to the beach, the young Dane's alertness had merely hastened his own end.

Thrush Hemming was waiting at the edge of the mist, and he spoke as Eofer came up. 'Jog or a fast walk, lord?'

'Jog, we have no idea how close their friends are, but it can't be far or they would have been mounted.' Eofer strode to the front and set off back to the East as the men of his war troop filed in behind him. An anxious glance at the sky confirmed that his fears were well founded. The moon still gleamed but the stars were beginning to dull, Shining Mane, the celestial horse, was hauling the sun ever closer to the eastern horizon. The miasma which had obscured the coastal belt began to thicken again as the welcome sound of waves carried to them.

Grimwulf appeared at his side as they jogged on, his nostrils flaring as he sniffed the air like a hound seeking a scent. Eofer could see the lad's concern as he cocked an ear to listen over the jangle of mail and arms. 'Horses, lord,' he said finally, his words thick with worry. 'I can smell horses. Up ahead.'

FOUR

Eofer exchanged a look with Hemming and both men stopped, raising their chins, drawing in the air. Hemming shook his head and Eofer leaned in and lowered his voice to a whisper. 'We can't smell a thing and it can't be Ozzy, he's well downwind. You are sure?'

Grimwulf smiled at his lord's easy humour, nothing seemed to faze him, despite the strain he knew he must be under after the many trials that night. He nodded and replied firmly: 'yes, lord.'

Eofer sniffed again: nothing. He questioned his man once more: 'straight ahead?'

'Slightly off to the right of the path, lord.' The smile drained from Grimwulf's face as he cocked his head and listened. 'I can hear them now, listen. They are moving across to block the path.'

Alert now, Eofer lifted the cheek piece of his helm and concentrated on the sounds of the night. Whatever had made the noise had been quietened, but the trust between members of a hearth troop was absolute. He turned back and placed a finger to his lips, indicating that they leave the path with an arm as he slipped his shield from the carrying strap. A quick glance upwards orientated the direction of the path with the position of the moon and they ghosted into the mist.

Their senses sharpened by the closeness to danger, every bush or stunted tree became a foeman as their shadowy forms hardened from the whiteness which surrounded them. Unable to increase the pace, despite the desperate need, Eofer led them a score paces onto the grassland before swinging back to the East. A shallow dip emerged before them and he held out a hand to halt their progress, turning to beckon Spearhafoc forward. The girl padded up, and he moved his lips to her ear as she listened intently. 'You are the smallest and lightest here. I want you to check the hollow ahead for any signs of opposition.' He squeezed her arm and threw her a wink of encouragement as he drew his head back, and the men stood as still as any stone as the Briton melted away. An anxious glance at the skyline confirmed that the night was almost spent, but he forced himself to remain calm as they waited for the girl's return.

After what seemed an age she reappeared, hurrying along bent double, and they all knew instinctively that they were in serious trouble. Spearhafoc came up and Eofer lowered his head as she whispered into his ear. 'Horsemen lord, mounted warriors. I counted a dozen, but I caught a brief glimpse of others on the far side of the path as the mist thinned for a moment.' He nodded that he understood and went to move away, but the girl tugged his head back. 'I wasn't finished,' she snapped. Eofer stifled a snigger despite the danger of the moment. He had seen men killed for such a show of disrespect towards a thegn, but her self-confidence was an important part of what made her such a valuable addition to his hearth troop and he caught the twinkle in Hemming's eye as he bent his head. 'They are not the local farmers and landowners,' she breathed. 'They are high class warriors, maybe even king's huscarls. They wear only the finest of everything and their arms are heavy with rings. But,' she whispered softly, 'the dip in the land ahead takes a dog-leg to the right between us, we should be able to get past them if the gods are with us and this mist holds a little longer.'

Eofer nodded that he understood. 'You have seen the lie of the land, you lead on. Walk at a steady pace but don't run unless you see me pass you; if you do, run like the wind!' he quipped. 'Mail shirts, buckles and scabbards are not the quietest when you are on the move and we cannot afford to make any noise.' He turned back and splayed both hands, making the universally understood sign for ten before pointing at the waiting girl and scooping his hand to indicate the dip ahead. They nodded that they understood that the girl was leading them through, as the first faint jangle of metal carried from their left. The Danes were close, too close, and the first traces of grey were entering the sky to the East as Shining Mane galloped closer. There was no time to discover an easier route, they would have to take a chance or fight their way back to the ship whether the riders ahead were huscarls or farmer Bjorn and his neighbours.

Satisfied that all were set Eofer nodded at the girl who moved forward, melting into the ground as she stooped to cross the lip of the gully. Eofer was a pace behind her, picking his way carefully down a slope made slick with dew. A small watercourse burbled at the base, and they stole stealthily across the stony bank and began to climb the far slope. A horse snickered softly and Eofer started, gripping the shaft of his spear a little tighter as he realised just how close these Danes must be, but Spearhafoc had already made the lip on the far side and she bent low to disappear from view. Eofer was a heartbeat behind and within moments they were across, the other members of his war band scurrying away from the trap without a backward glance.

Eofer flicked an anxious look at the skyline and was shocked to see that the eastern horizon had been transformed into a splash of pink. The day was upon them, and he increased the pace despite the danger. It was, he estimated, still a good half mile to the beach and the *Hwælspere* must now be in full view of the watchers on the cliff top. As if to confirm his fears a petal of flame flickered on the uplands as the coast guards set the warning beacon, and Eofer cast all thoughts of caution aside as he broke into a run. 'That's far enough lads, we need to get back to the ship before the horse Danes realise what is happening. Get back on the path, quick as you can!'

Within a few paces the trail was before him and Eofer slowed to a jog, moving aside to let the youth through as the duguth clustered protectively about their lord. He recognised the bemusement at his actions writ large on their faces, and Eofer explained as they jogged along in the youngsters' wake. 'I know that it's humiliating running away, but Spearhafoc said that there were more riders at the far side of the path.'

He looked across to Hemming and saw that the explanation had still not done enough to smother his sense of unease, and he listened as his weorthman put their feelings into words. 'We could creep up and take them from the rear, lord. They would be squinting inland into the murk, dead before they even knew we were there.'

Eofer shook his head as he explained. 'She also said that they were dressed like huscarls. Now I don't mind fighting against the king's retainers, the very best men that the Danes can put into the field,' he added, 'but we don't know their actual numbers so there is a good chance that we could be overwhelmed and die to a man.' He threw them a look to emphasise his final words. 'We were not sent here by the king to burn a few farms and kill a few of their fyrdmen, we were sent to draw as many of their best warriors away from the West that we can. It looks as if we are succeeding, so we will have to swallow our pride for now.' He flashed them a grin as their expressions softened. 'Be proud that we have the king's trust,' he added, 'and don't worry. There will be enough Danes left for us when the time comes, even for you Thrush!'

The mist was already visibly dissipating as the first cries carried to them from their rear. It could only mean one thing, and Eofer increased the pace as his duguth cast anxious glances behind. The cry was taken up as the track began to dip, angling off towards the East and safety. The pathway steepened as it neared the beach, hugging the side of the Combe before flattening out as the first welcome sounds of the sea reached their ears. The youth had gained a choke point where several boulders had tumbled down from the cliff face above, halting and forming a loose shield wall as they awaited the arrival of their hearth brothers. It was a sound tactical move, and

Eofer acknowledged it as the sound of hoofbeats began to fill the air.

'Who drew up here?'

They all looked across to Finn who swallowed nervously, but stepped forward all the same. 'I did, lord.'

Eofer pushed harder. 'Why? I told you to run.'

'Horsemen will channel into this space and suddenly be confronted by a rubble-strewn narrow. The gully tapers here to a dozen paces, and half of that is taken up by the stream and its rocky bed, it is ideal for a defensive position.' Finn jerked his head up at the grassy banks which climbed away to each side. 'I thought that Spearhafoc could use the height advantage to pick off those on the end of any shield wall which came against us. A few men could hold them here while the others made the ship and escaped, it's only a short distance across the beach. I sent Grimwulf to tell Eadward what is happening.'

Eofer nodded as the others swung into a defensive line across the narrows and the sound of horses rolled down upon them like an onrushing tide. Thoughts of a disorganised dash across the strand came into his mind and he recognised the value of the lad's thinking. A strategic withdrawal was all very well, but a panic-stricken scramble through the surf was another thing entirely. He could never look the survivors in the eye again if they scattered before the Danes like startled hens. 'You did well,' Eofer said as the youth cast anxious looks across his lord's shoulder for approaching horsemen. Most men running before a foe, whether mounted or not, rarely retained the presence of mind to take in their surroundings, much less curb the headlong flight and throw together a hasty battle plan. It was not the first time that Finn had impressed him on the raid, he was fast becoming an important member of the troop, they would talk again; if they survived.

Eofer handed his spear and shield to Finn as he drew Gleaming with a flourish. 'Here,' he smiled, 'take care of these until I return.' Before the surprised youth could reply, Eofer had pushed through the defences and was trotting back into the mist. A glance across his shoulder told him when the English position began to grow indistinct, and he moved to the side of the gully and paddled into the icy water. A quick look confirmed to him that he was perfectly placed, twenty or so paces inland of the fallen rocks, and he swept the sword back and braced as the sound of onrushing horses filled the air.

A flash of colour and they were upon him, and Eofer swept the blade in a low powerful strike as the first panicked riders saw the obstacles which barred their progress and attempted to rein in the dashing steeds. Gleaming whirred across to take the leading horse at knee level, biting through the joint and emerging in a mist of blood as the animal pitched forward to bury its face in the scree with a sickening crash. Driven on by their riders and the thrill of the chase, the following horses stood little chance of avoiding the mayhem and within a heartbeat the floor of the gully was a tangled mass of screaming horses. Most managed to stay upright, but a few fell to add to the madness of broken riders and thrashing hooves as the Danish charge, an irresistible tide of muscle and bone only moments before, came to a bloody halt.

Eofer leapt among them, his sword striking to left and right as the Danes struggled to their feet. A huge warrior, his arms bright with rings of gold and silver, lay dazed and bloodied before him. Their eyes locked, and the Englishman saw the panic there as the man realised that he would never bring his spear across to ward off the oncoming blow before it arrived. In a last desperate act the man threw up an arm, and Eofer's blade sent the limb spinning to the track in a fountain of blood as he trod on the Dane's chest and launched himself at the scrum. The sea of bodies hardened into a snarling face as another Dane came on, the point of his spear flashing in the light of the returning sun, and Eofer dodged aside as he began to fight his way back to the safety of his own hedge of spears.

Two men, quicker to recover than their hearth mates stood shoulder to shoulder, barring his way, and Eofer saw the look of triumph on one turn to shock and incomprehension as the point of an arrow emerged from his mouth. Shocked his friend faltered, and Eofer lowered his shoulder, barging the warrior aside as a powerful voice began to rally the attackers. The Danes were recovering fast, and Eofer dealt the wounded horse its death blow, stooping to open the belly with a sweep of his blade as he ran the final few yards. Leaving the track awash with blood and the pink-blue ropes of horse guts, the eorle turned back to face his attackers as the English shield wall opened up to gather him in with a roar of defiance. He felt the reassuring press of friendly bodies all around him as his shield and gar were passed through from the rear, and he gripped the handle gratefully, swinging his shield up into position as he couched the stout spear and braced to meet the attack.

Hemming spoke at his side, his voice calm and measured. 'Are we making a break for it while we have the chance, lord?'

Eofer ran his eyes across the men gathering beyond the eviscerated shell of the horse which separated them. He could now see the gruff voiced Dane who he had heard rallying his men as he fought among them, and he watched with interest as he pulled and pushed his men into a wedge. The mist was clearing away by the moment, and the thegn made a quick calculation as he weighed up the rapidly dwindling options which were still open to him. He shook his head as he reached his decision.

'No, I am tired of running, we fight here. We are in a good defensive position and the dead horse will break up any charge.' He exchanged a glance with his weorthman and snorted as he saw the look of joy there. 'If we are to break our fast in Valhall, I will not turn up at the doors with a wound to my back.'

The Danes had assembled in their hog snout and they brought their own shields together with a crash, roaring with battle joy that they finally had the raiders who had evaded them for so long at bay. Eofer took the last opportunity to relay his orders as the men beside him tensed before the onslaught.

'Finn!'

'Yes, lord?'

'This was your idea, come forward and stand on my left hand side.'

'Yes, lord!'

Octa took a pace to the left and the youth stepped smartly into the breach. If anywhere was safe in the front line it was to the left of the leader. Protected by his lord's shield, sword arm and experience in battle it was nevertheless far more dangerous than the rear ranks, and every man there would know that the boy would be judged, not only by the Danes and the gods but by his lord and the more senior members of the hearth troop. Fight well and survive the push of shields and he had taken a giant stride towards becoming a duguth.

Eofer called again. 'Crawa!'

'Yes, lord.'

'Raise my battle flag and stand to my rear. Let's let these Danes know that they are in for a fight.'

A shout filled the gully and Eofer knew that the moment had come. 'Stand firm,' he said, his voice level and calm. 'Youth, wait for an opening and stab, just we like we practised.'

The Danish wedge approached the carcass of the horse and paused as the leading few slid across the animal's great ribcage and waited for those following on to shuffle across to rejoin them.

The English began to beat ash shafts on shields, the age old battle cry of their people rising into the cool dawn air as the *fiend* cast anxious glances their way lest the chant preceded a charge of their own.

'Out!…Out!…Out!'

Thrush Hemming turned his head aside, crying out above the noise. 'We should have rushed forward and used the body as a bulwark, lord,'

Eofer shook his head without taking his eyes from the Danes, hastily reforming their wedge only twenty paces before them. 'The path is too wide Thrush, they would have outflanked us with ease. Besides,' he added with a jerk of his head as the Danes continued to pour across, 'that outcrop would get in Spearhafoc's way, I saw it when I was up there. She would not have been able to rake them from the hillside and I was loathe to lose that advantage.'

The Danes were across and moving forward slowly, the tip of the formation aimed directly at the English leader. Eofer looked above the rim of the ord man's shield and saw the calm stare of a veteran there beneath a helm of chased and polished steel. Twin garnets shone dully from the eye sockets of a silver boar which crowned the warrior's helm, and Eofer dragged his eyes away to watch for the moment he knew was upon them. The instant that the Dane's body swelled as he sucked in air to make the battle cry, the English eorle mirrored the action. With a roar to Woden the Danish leader launched into a run, and a heartbeat later Eofer yelled into the rapidly shrinking space between them. 'Now!'

The English cry to the Allfather resounded from the grassy banks as the shield burh took a pace forward and threw their shoulders behind the big boards. The Danish leader, backed up by his own scrum of warriors, hit Eofer like a thunderbolt, driving him back as the eorle grimaced with effort and pushed back for all his worth. The youth slammed into his back as the thegn scrabbled for a grip on the rocky path, lending their weight to the push, but the line was bowing ominously, ready to break. The Danes sensed victory, braced, dug in and drove again, but Hemming was there and Eofer was pummelled as the big duguth stabbed and stabbed over the shields like a maniac. The desperate counterattack brought down one Dane and then another, and the pressure on the centre eased for a heartbeat as the men fell away. A heartbeat was enough, and Eofer worked his own spear through a gap in the wall, sawing the shaft back and forth as men howled and roared all around him. As the point bit into flesh he worked the blade, worrying the Dane's mail shirt until the links gave up the unequal struggle. Blood ran, and Eofer felt the shaft of his spear go slick as he shoved and pushed: the men reformed around him and the English wall held.

The first rush had failed and the Engles felt the pressure suddenly ease as the Danes too recognised the fact and took a pace back, the rear of the wedge widening as more attackers arrived to bolster the flanks hoping for more luck there.

Eofer risked a glance over the rim of his shield and saw that the boar-helmed man was still in place, upright and apparently unharmed, and he gave a snort of recognition at the man's fighting prowess; he had seen the dancing wolf warrior plate above his left eye and he had expected no less.

With a roar and a crash like thunder the lines came together again as the Danes renewed the assault, but Eofer knew that the huge body of the disemboweled warhorse had saved them for now, robbing the attack of its momentum. Eofer threw his shoulder into his shield, pushing again, driving the Dane back as the place of slaughter ebbed and flowed. A quick glance down told the eorle that Hemming's two Danes lay like bloody wrack at the high tide mark, but no English seemed to have fallen in the opening attack and he grunted with satisfaction and stabbed again. A waft of air kissed his cheek as an arrow flashed by, and Eofer threw a look to his left as the foemen battered the line. A pair of Danes had scaled the bank and were almost upon the Briton. Hunkered down behind their shields the warriors were preparing to skewer the girl as they edged along the shelf, and Eofer saw the moment when she loosed her final shaft and gambolled down the bank out of harms way.

A cry brought his head snapping back as the Danish leader came again and the ash shafts jabbed and probed. The pressure was beginning to tell as more and more Danes crossed the horse barrier to add their weight to the push, and Eofer felt Hemming make a space to draw his sword across his body as the shield wall began to pivot. The English left was beginning to curl back upon itself as the flank there was turned. More and more Danes, free now from the danger of Spearhafoc's arrows, were feeding along the slopes of the gully. In moments they would be outflanked and the killing would begin in earnest. Eofer began to despair as he took a pace to the rear, opening up a small space of his own in which to draw Gleaming. If he could draw them away the Danes would most likely ignore the others, enabling them to escape back to the ship.

Away to his right the bole of a tree lay where it had fallen from the headland above, its shattered branches a spear clad hedge, and Eofer backed towards it as he prepared to make his last stand. With a roar of triumph the Danish warriors finally shattered the English line in two, the duguth backing towards their lord as they clustered into a knot of shields, spears and swords, preparing to fend off their rampant *fiend* for as long as they were able. Hemming and Finn stood shoulder to shoulder before the branches of the tree, taking up position to cover the retreat of their lord as Eofer called across to the now isolated youth and the Danes wheeled to face him. 'Get back to the ship. Tell Eadward to leave now!'

The way now open more Danes were funnelling down onto the beach, and Eofer's small hopes of survival were finally dashed as the clarion call of a war horn sounded and more Danes appeared on the cliff top above. He threw a mournful look at the English youth, now clustered in their own shield burh, ordering them away with an impatient jerk of his head. More than a few of them had shown the potential to grow into useful warriors, men who would be sorely needed if the English were to plant their roots firmly in the new land. If they were to be his final gift to his people it would have to be enough.

The horn sounded again, more distant this time, and Eofer narrowed his eyes in surprise as he saw the Danes begin to back off. Now they were streaming away from the beach, hurrying back up the defile as the war horn's urgent call trailed away.

Eofer and Hemming shared a look of disbelief as the last of the Danes hesitated at the horse barrier. The Danish leader turned back and called across to the bemused knot of Englishmen.

'I am Ubba silk beard.'

Eofer pushed through the tangle of branches and heft his shield.

'I am Eofer king's bane; let Woden choose between us, here on the sand.'

Ubba's eyes widened at the revelation and he took a pace forward. As Eofer watched, the Dane's companion spoke at his side before spitting into the sand. 'The hall burner,' he snarled. 'I hoped that it was you when I saw the war banner.' The horn sounded once again and Ubba grimaced. 'Another time, hall burner,' he snarled as he made the sign to avert evil, turned and hurried away.

Within moments the Danes were gone, leaving behind them clusters of wonderstruck Englishmen who knew that they should be dead. Hemming spoke at his side, and Eofer snorted as they watched the long low shape of the *Hwælspere* begin to harden from the mist as she edged back to shore. 'So, this is Valhall.' He kicked at the trunk, screwing up his face as he looked about them. 'I have to admit that it's a bit of a disappointment, lord.'

FIVE

The lookout in the bow turned back with a look of horror, cupping his hands to his mouth. 'Two sail, bearing up from the South.'

Eadward and Eofer exchanged a look and hurried forward as the *Hwælspere* edged out of the bay.

'How close?'

The lookout glanced southwards before turning back with a grimace, the concern etched upon his features obvious to all. 'Too close, lord.'

The thegns reached the bows and clasped the forestay as they peered around the headland.

Eofer spoke first. 'They are really moving!'

Half a mile away a brace of dragon ships were breasting the waves, their sails sheets of beaten copper as they caught the early morning sun.

Eadward was already striding the length of the ship, bawling out his orders as crewmen scurried to and fro, shaking free the snake ship's own sail and sheeting it home.

Eofer hurried aft as the first wisps of wind rounded the headland to worry the weather vane at the masthead, the long sealskin tassels at its base flicking to the North and safety. The great sail fluttered as the crew hauled at the braces, angling the yard, hunting the wind, but Eofer had seen just how close the enemy were and he harboured no illusions. As he passed amidships he spoke to the upturned faces of his men. 'Clean your weapons and hone the blades. We are not done fighting yet.'

One look at the stern faces of Eadward and his steersman confirmed that they too were of the same opinion. He pulled a face as he came up. 'I am sorry, I should have abandoned the raid as soon as we became lost in the fog. If we had returned earlier none of this would have happened.' Eadward gave a snort of irony, despite the tension. 'From what I could see, you were lucky to return at all, Eofer. We could barely make out the prow from the steering platform last night, I doubt that we could have left the bay much earlier even if you had. Death by weather!' he exclaimed. 'I'll not be the first *scipthegn* it will claim, nor the last.'

The sail began to fill as the ship reached the mouth of the bay and Eadward ordered his men to arm. The headland tapered to the East, the treelined ridge reaching out into the waters which the Danes called Eyrarsund to end in a rocky shelf, as the men of the *Hwælspere* unshipped their oars and lashed them to the crosstrees. Wulfhere, Eadward's own weorthman, came up as the steersman hauled the great paddle blade to his chest and the curving prow swung to the North. 'Are we fighting or running, lord?'

Eadward snorted. 'Both I should think. We will try to put some distance between us, but they are already moving at full speed. If we can keep at least a furlong ahead we may make it out of the bay at least.' He patted the wale affectionately. 'If we can give her enough sea room the old girl might give them the slip yet.' He shrugged. 'We can't hide up on the opposite shore any longer, not now that we are moving about in full daylight. We shall have to clear Eyrarsund and make a break for the open waters of The Cat Gate and home. Let us hope that they are content with seeing us off.'

Wulfhere nodded and instinctively tightened the strap of his helm as he shot his thegn a smile and a suggestion. 'It would be nice to fight under our own war flag if it comes to it, lord.'

Eadward returned the smile. 'You are right, run her up. We are done with skulking in the shadows.'

As the duguth stalked away, the pair returned their gaze to the promontory off the steerbord beam. The *Hwælspere* was heeling to bæcbord as the wind began to fill the sail, silvered pearls shimmering in the air as the big snaca left the calmer waters and headed out to sea.

The cry of a gull drew Eofer's eye away from the headland for an instant and when he looked back they were there, curving to seaward as the Danish steersmen skirted the shoals. He turned back as hope kindled within him, but the smile of deliverance fell from his features as he saw the worried looks on the faces of Eadward and his own steersman. Noticing the look, the ship thegn threw his head to the North. 'The northern arm of the bay is far longer than that on the southern side. We can only hope that we can clear the promontory there before the Danish ships cut us off.'

Eofer looked for'ard, his eyes flicking to left and right as he calculated the speed of the ships and the distance between them. The *Hwælspere* was aimed perfectly at the first patch of calmer water after the wind blown chaos of the shoals. Hnæf, Eadward's steersman, was handling the snaca impeccably, but they were all experienced men of the sea and each of them knew that it would be a close run thing if the Englishmen were to escape the trap.

The ship finally emerged from the lee of the southern headland, the rigging creaking and moaning as the sail finally filled and the ship bounded forward. Eofer turned to Eadward as he began to untie the peace bands from his sword. 'Where do you want me?'

Eadward tore his gaze from the rapidly closing dragon ships. 'Take your men and defend forward of the mast, I will fight aft.' He pulled a wry smile. 'Let us hope that they attack on one side, Eofer, we will only be outnumbered two to one. If they double up…' Eadward let the sentence hang in the air and Eofer nodded that he understood. If they could fight off an attack as Hnæf worked to free the hull and reach the open sea they would have a chance. If the Danish steersmen came at them on either beam the situation would quickly become hopeless. 'If that does happen Eofer,' Eadward continued quietly, 'we will have to split our forces and cover both sides. I will defend Hnæf, he will be our only chance.'

Eofer nodded that he understood, and the thegns gripped forearms as they wished each other gods-luck.

Hopping down from the steering platform, Eofer passed through the length of the ship, flicking a look up at the white dragon flag as he did so. Writhing away to the North, the blood red war banner was aflame as it caught the early morning sun, and Eofer chuckled to himself despite the grimness of the moment as he watched it curl and snap. If there had been any doubt in the minds of the Danish crews as to the identity of this longship in their waters, that would now be quashed. The die was cast, everyman aboard the three ships now knew that it was more likely than not that they would be fighting for their lives before they had broken their fast that day. If it was his wyrd to die this morning, he would go to Valhall in fine company, fighting savagely beneath the flag he loved.

His duguth came to his side as the ship bounded the waves, and he shot them all a smile as he realised just how liberating it felt not to be the one making life or death decisions on behalf of others. 'If the Danes come up, we are to fight before the mast. If they double up on us, Thrush and Ozzy will take the bæcbord and I will fight the steerbord with Octa.' He cast an eye over the youth who were busily arming themselves at the foot of the mast as he worked through the dispositions in his mind. Finn was already set, rolling his shoulders as he stared outboard at the oncoming *fiend*. Eofer gave a short snort. 'I will keep Finn to my left, as before. He did well. The dark twins and Rand are with me, Thrush you get Cæd, Porta, and the wolves. Spearhafoc can do her own thing as soon as they are within range of her bow.' They all pulled a smile at Eofer's description of the youths, Beornwulf and Grimwulf. They had become the best of friends, and their thegn's nickname for the pair always raised a smile.

Eofer peered around the great curve of the prow at the open sea beyond. It was close now, but a look to steerbord confirmed his fears. The dragons were leaping the waves, their bows enveloped in a curtain of spray as their sails billowed, every inch of wool straining as the crew worked the braces to capture the last breath of wind. Above them low clouds the colour of lead were hurrying northwards, their flanks painted pink by the rising sun as gulls began to gather for the feast. The *Hwælspere* would be first to clear the headland and Eadward would have his furlong lead, but little more than that long furrow would separate the longships when Hnæf put the helm about and pointed her bow to the North. That turn would bleed off their momentum and the Danes would be upon them. Eofer looked to Hemming as they finally cleared the headland and the ship began her turn. 'Get them into position, Thrush,' he said with a nod; 'see you on the other side.'

As his weorthman chivvied the men into line, Eofer took up position at the centre. The speed sapped away, and Eofer's heart sank as he cast a look astern, past the crewmen as they belayed the braces and hurried off to fetch their own shields. The Danes were dividing, splitting up as they bore down on their victim, and Eofer watched as Hemming began to split their meagre force to meet the onslaught. Finn appeared at his side, and he shot the lad what he hoped was a smile of encouragement before turning his gaze back to the South.

The stern post of the closest ship was just disappearing beyond the *Hwælspere*'s own wooden tower as it swept inshore. A ship's length behind, the wide curving prow of its companion rose and fell in an explosive shower as it crashed through the waves, the beast head which capped its elegant neck snarling defiance at the interlopers who had caused so much destruction in their land.

Eofer heft his shield as the ships began to draw level and the first spears began to crisscross the air between them. He prepared his own daroth, feeling for the point of balance as he hunkered behind the linden board and prepared to face the dance of spears for the second time that morning.

The crewman grunted as another of the mould covered rocks disappeared overboard and reached back to take another. They could all feel the movement beneath their feet as the ship lightened stone by stone, and Eofer watched as Eadward moved the men about the deck as he desperately sought to float the ship.

A short while earlier a horseman had appeared briefly on the headland, disappearing within moments when he saw the red flag of Engeln flying proudly from the mast top of the stranded ship below. It was obvious to them all that the rider had gone to fetch spearmen, and they were frantically ditching ballast before he returned. Hemming approached his lord, the look of disbelief still etched upon his face from the previous encounters with the Danes that morning. 'Perhaps he has gone to fetch help?' he joked, jerking his head towards the now empty clifftop as another of the great rocks splashed into the waters alongside.

Eofer laughed, but he too was as puzzled by the behaviour of their foe that day. He cast a look to the North, shielding his eyes against the glare as he watched the twin sails of the dragon ships receding. He opened his mouth to reply but could only gasp as he shook his head in disbelief.

The Danish ships, with the English at their mercy, had swept either side of them in a shower of spears before carrying on, beating their way northwards under full sail. Coming hard on the heels of the strange behaviour of Ubba silk beard and his men on the beach, the English raiders could only marvel at their good fortune as they fought to put as many miles between themselves and the coast of Daneland before the spell which seemed to have been cast on the inhabitants was broken. The only dark spot in their fortune so far that day had come with the death of Eadward's steersman, Hnæf. Despite the efforts of his thegn and others to protect the man with their own shields it was obvious that the Danes had targeted the duguth. Raised above the level of the deck, the steersman had attracted the majority of the spear shafts which had been launched against the English ship as the Danes had swept past. Assailed from either side Eadward and his remaining duguth had been simply overwhelmed by the attack, and before they could regain control the ship had pitched up on a rocky outlier. It was highly likely that the experienced seaman had been picked out for special attention in the fleeting attack, and all the men there knew that it could mean only one thing. As soon as the Danes had taken care of the urgent business which was drawing them away, they would be back to settle the score with the raiders who had been plaguing their eastern shore.

A cry from the lookout in the bows drew their attention and the crew paused in their work to peer anxiously northwards. The Danish ships seemed to have reached their goal, the tall prows swinging to the West as they began to enter a bay half a league distant, and the crew of the *Hwælspere* redoubled their efforts as the slimy rocks continued to splash overboard.

Eadward had had the best view of all, watching the dragon ships from the raised steering deck as they made their turn, and the crewmen paused at their work as he called his orders. 'Leave that now, we have shed enough ballast. The ship will be difficult enough to handle as it is. We can't wait for the tide to float us off, they could turn back at any moment.' He unbuckled his belt and began to tug his woollen *serc* over his head as he called down the ship. 'Over the side everyone; we can lighten the ship of our own weight and work her free at the same time.'

Within moments the deck was strewn with clothing as the crew began to lower themselves into the sea alongside. Eofer felt the hull begin to rise as more and more men slipped overboard, and he began to shed his own clothing as he ordered his war band to help. Spearhafoc had settled herself onto a coil of rope to enjoy the spectacle, but the smile fell from her face as Eofer called across. 'And you, princess; nobody in my war band is too precious to get their arse wet. Strip off and over the side.' Leaving the girl to her misery, Eofer lowered himself into the waters of Eyrarsund. To his relief the sea barely lapped at his waist and he worked his shoulder into the curve of the hull, falling into the rhythmic sway of the crewmen as they sweated their ship into deeper water. Spearhafoc dropped into the waters ahead of him, and he slapped the side of the hull to show her where to push. 'Here, put your shoulder into the place where the line of the hull curves down to the keel. It's called the flare,' he smiled, as he sought to distract her mind from the fact that she was the only naked female among scores of men; 'lock it away in your word hoard, I will ask you to name it later.'

They let the first push go as they settled into place, watching as the ship edged forward a foot before settling back onto its keel. Throwing his shoulder into the curve of the hull, Eofer waited until the *Hwælspere's* crew counted down to the heave. On the cry, two score men dug their feet into the gravelly bottom and shoved forwards and upwards. The great hull slid forward several feet as the added muscle told, and Eofer waded forward, readying himself for the next push. The ship was almost free now, but a cry of warning came from the lookout in the bows and they paused as one to look fearfully towards the shore. The rider had returned, watching their efforts from the clifftop as he urged on what could only be another ship, still hidden from the eyes of the anxious English in the bay below him.

Eadward increased the pace as he sought to free his own ship from the grip of the shallows before the unknown craft rounded the headland. It was the worst possible position to be caught in, and Eofer risked a glance aft as he sought to make eye contact with the ship thegn. He could see the indecision in his friend's eyes as he weighed up the conflicting needs to free the ship or prepare for whatever was about to emerge from the shelter of the promontory, but a curt nod and Eofer was already hauling himself back onboard. 'My war band, with me,' he shouted as he slid up and over the wale to slop onto the deck like a landed fish. 'Dress and arm, as quickly as you can!'

One by one a line of familiar faces appeared over the side as Eofer struggled into his trews. Kicking his mail shirt to one side, he squirmed into his undershirt as the sound of his men hurriedly flinging on their own clothing whirled around him. Thrown with desperate haste onto his damp body the padded jerkin stuck fast and, blinded now, he tore desperately at it as Hemming's incredulous voice gasped at his side: 'what now?'

Panicking, Eofer dragged down the neck of his shirt, peeping out to landward just as a small rowboat cleared the headland there. The little boat came on with no attempt to steer clear of the enemy vessel and Eofer exchanged a look of disbelief with his weorthman as the twin oars stroked the little boat closer with every passing moment.

As the craft approached and the incredulous English stood to their arms, Eofer watched as the rower backed oars and slowed the boat a dozen paces from the stern, the steerbord oar stroking the craft broadside on as the man in the stern rose to speak. Casting back his wide hood revealed the visitor to be little more than a youth, but the flaxen hair which fell to his shoulders framed a face the colour of milk, and all those aboard the English ship knew immediately that this was the face of a young man unused to toil in all weathers. He may have been dressed in the muted greens and browns of the lower sort but his demeanour and self-confidence indicated that his upbringing had been anything but. The stranger cupped hands to his mouth and called to them as the Englishmen exchanged looks of puzzlement.

'Have I permission to come aboard?'

Eadward and his crew were hauling themselves back onboard as the big snaca wallowed unsteadily in the swell, and he exchanged a look and a shrug with the eorle as he stood dripping on the deck. The *scipthegn* called out a reply, adding to the bizarreness of the day as he hopped on one foot and struggled into his trews. 'Come across.'

The mysterious passenger turned and waved to the horseman on the headland above as the oarsman worked the tiny craft alongside, and the rider raised his spear in salute before hauling the head of his mount westward and disappearing from view.

The boat bumped alongside and the Engles were no longer surprised to see the boatsman fall to his knees, placing his head onto the outstretched hand of the young man as it did so. The youth raised the oarsman, hugging him close as Hemming formed their feelings into words. 'We really need to leave this place, lord. There is a madness upon it, it may be catching.'

As the Englishmen struggled into damp clothing, the young Dane gripped the wale and vaulted the gap into the ship. Turning back he took a long bundle from the boatsman who, after a final dip of his head, lent his weight to the oar, pushing the rowboat clear of the wooden wall which towered above it. The boat pulled away as the rower arced his back, working the oars, and the youth finally revealed his identity to add his own contribution to the day of wonders.

'My name is Hrothmund Hrothgarson, a prince of Daneland. I request the protection of your lord, King Eomær of the Engle.'

SIX

The *Hwælspere* rolled like a drunk in a gale as the waters of the Eyrarsund sloshed alongside. Eofer gripped the backstay and turned to Eadward. 'Are we going to make it?' The thegn braced as he urged the big snake ship on. Even with the wind blowing directly over the stern and the crewmen sweating at the oars it would be a close run thing. 'Unless we pitch up on a sandbank, we will ease into the river mouth ahead of them,' he answered. 'Then the real fun will begin.'

Eofer cast a look to bæcbord where the prows of the Danish drakkar were carving the waves as their own steersmen drove them on. The reason for the strange behaviour of their enemy that day had become clear the moment that the young ætheling had revealed the reason for his desperate flight, and the Englishmen had been momentarily stunned as the importance of the revelation which had fallen from the young man's lips had sunk in. If King Hrothgar had been murdered the Danish kingdom would be in turmoil, just at the moment when their own king would land his army in the West. The gods were truly smiling on the English, the problem now for the men on the *Hwælspere* was to survive long enough to enjoy what must be a famous victory over their ancient *fiend*.

Eadward jerked his head at the lone figure which stood amidships, nervously fingering the hilt of his sword as he watched the warriors loyal to his kinsman King Hrothulf draw closer. 'We could chuck him over the side,' he suggested with a scowl. 'We saw earlier that he is the only one they are interested in. The bastard will cost me my ship!'

Eofer shook his head. 'The king will replace your ship if we do this thing for the army, and heap treasure and reputation upon you too.' He indicated to the South with a flick of his head and Eadward craned his neck to see. 'Two more!' the ship master exclaimed. 'You are right, Eofer, they really want our friend.'

Just emerging from the lee of a large island in mid channel, twin sails gleamed white in the morning sun as they hurried north to cut them off. 'That's four ships and their crews we are leading away from the fighting in Daneland,' Eofer said with pride. A quick calculation and he smiled at his friend. 'We saw how many bearshirts the two ships to the North carried as they swept past us earlier. Even if the two to the South only carry half that number we should be leading forty or fifty Danish huscarls, their finest warriors, away from the fight. Add to that four dragon ships and their crews and we have a major victory over the enemy before the armies even come together.'

Eadward gave the big paddle blade an affectionate pat. 'You are right of course, Eofer,' he answered with a reluctant sigh. 'If she was still ballasted she could have given them the slip and been away, no ship, Jute or Dane had ever caught her. But like this?'

The coast was coming up quickly, vertical ramparts of yellowish stone capped by thick stands of woodland, oak, elm and beech, and Eofer could see that a low offshore island, little more than a spit, would force the closest pursuers to tack to sea. Soon they were within the line of withies which marked the safe channel, pulling upstream for all they were worth as the Danes entered the estuary and came on. The English crew redoubled their efforts at the oars as the wind spilled from their sail, and Eofer searched the banks for a suitable landing place as Eadward battled the current with the unwieldy craft. Ahead of them the river began to twist and turn as it made its way into the heart of the greenwood and the eorle knew that they would have to abandon the ship soon or be overtaken. The *Hwælspere* made the first turn and the crewmen pulled the ship forward again with great sweeps of the oars, but the instability of the craft had already cost them a ship's length of their lead over the Danish dragons. Eofer threw a look to the West, furrowing his brow as he glimpsed the enemy beast-heads through the thicket; ghosting through the trees like shadow walkers as they chased them down.

Ahead a small settlement hugged the northern bank, and Eadward pushed on the tiller, angling the prow towards the muddy shore as Eofer left the steering platform and walked the centreline. 'Arm yourselves but leave any mail on the ship,' he ordered. 'Leave anything which will slow you down, however valuable. With luck they will stop to plunder our possessions before they come after us. Take a little food and your water skin,' he smiled, 'we are going on a little run.'

The hamlet was almost upon them as Eofer strapped his shield to his back and collected his spear. Cramming his helm upon his head he fastened the strap and cast a last look at his metal armour stowed amidships. It was the byrnie he had worn in battle against the Swedes, the day that he had struck down the king, Ongentheow, in the pale light of dawn; the same mail which had shone red in the reflected flames of Heorot only months before. Soon a Dane would be trying it for size, his face a wonder as he realised the worth of his prize, but he shrugged and kicked it aside. If its loss aided his escape, so be it. There were other mail shirts.

A warning horn sounded from the shore, and Eofer watched as the inhabitants spilled from the huts like frightened mice, snatching up children and valuables as they raced across a water meadow to disappear into the tree line. A moment later the ship lurched as the keel grounded in the shallows and the men were up and moving forward, scrambling over the side and wading for the bank. Eofer cast about to ensure that all were ashore before throwing Eadward a sympathetic look as the thegn took up his own spear and made his way forward. A parting grimace at the body of his friend and steersman lying trussed in the bows and he joined Eofer, the pair vaulting the side to land in the shallows with a splash.

Eofer cast a look at the Englishmen gathered on the bank and snapped an order as he waded ashore. 'Don't stand there looking, get straight through the village. Find the pathway inland and keep going!'

Using the butt of his spear to lever himself up onto the bank, he cast a glance across his shoulder and was horrified to see just how close their pursuers had come. Already prow on to the bank, the first pair of Danish ships raised their oars aloft like the great wings of the fire dragons which had given them their name, the river water raining from the outstretched blades as they glided towards the shore. Bearded faces, the excitement of the chase writ large upon them, were crowding the space either side of the snarling dragon heads, the raking light of early morning sparkling on polished helm and spear point alike like winter sun on broken ice.

Eofer leaned forward, grabbing Eadward by the arm and hauling him ashore. 'Come on, they are already within spear shot!' he grunted as he bundled his friend ashore. The pair took off at a gallop as the first of the Danish darts peppered the ground around them, but the movement of the ships and the closeness of the tightly packed warriors spoiled their aim, and the English thegns were soon within the shadow of the buildings and running hard.

An excited roar behind them told the pair that the Danish ships had grounded, but Eofer's heart leapt as he rounded a bend and saw that the gods were still with them. Dozens of sheep were spilling from a pen which stood hard against the track as Cuthbert, Adda and Wulfhere, Eadward's surviving duguth kicked and jabbed them forward, filling the roadway with wavering cries as they drove them into the heart of the settlement. The fleeces stacked on low wooden paling and the heavy sheers which lay abandoned to one side told the Engles just how benevolent the gods had been, and they forced their way through the bleating scrum and plunged into the shade at the forest edge.

Thrush Hemming slowed to a walk and shot his lord a look: 'here?'

Eofer knuckled his eyes and waited for the flashing stars the action produced to recede before blinking away the tears. It was, he had to admit, an excellent defensive position, as good as they had come across, but his mind struggled to come to a decision, fogged as it was by physical and mental exhaustion. They had all been awake now for getting on for a full day, a period which had seen them blundering around like blind men in the fog of Daneland, fighting against an overwhelming force at the beach before sweating the *Hwælspere* from the rocks and journeying across to Scania. Now they had run for half a day, chased along a winding forest path by a horde of bloodthirsty Danes who would stop at nothing to capture the fugitive prince in their midst.

He looked again as the men sipped from their water skins. Twin oaks, their great trunks rilled with age, stood athwart the path like twin guardians of the forest domain, squeezing the track into little more than two paces in width. The land to either side dropped away into boggy depressions, knee deep in leaf mulch and worm-eaten branches, mute testament to the violence of the autumn storms. It was the perfect place to make a stand but, as desperate as the situation was fast becoming, he knew that he would have to order them on. 'We can't stop Thrush,' he croaked painfully. 'The further we can draw these bastards away from their ships, the longer it will take them to regain Daneland.' Hemming offered his canteen, and Eofer sipped at the lukewarm contents with a grateful nod, working the precious liquid around his mouth as the men clustered around. Somewhere in the stillness of the holt a woodpecker tapped out a staccato beat and the distant call of a cuckoo drifted to them. Eofer ran his eyes around the group, keen to see if the sound would draw a flicker of interest, but there was none. Some of the youth, both within his own hearth troop and Eadward's lads, were little more than boys in men's bodies, thirteen and fourteen winters of age. Normally they would have enough boyishness left within them to claim first-hearing of the elusive herald of spring, bringing fortune upon themselves and their kin for the coming year, but he was unsurprised to find that their faces remained drawn and disinterested if they had even heard it at all.

Hemming spoke again, dropping his voice to an undertone as Wulfhere, Eadward's own weorthman came across. 'I could hold this place for long enough to enable the rest of you to get away, lord,' he said. 'One man could defend this gap until the sun left the sky.' Eofer pursed his lips, conflicting emotions fighting within him as he thought on his duguth's plan. If it was not for Hrothmund he would hold the narrows himself, but he needed to be sure that the boy got away. Having old King Hrothgar's son alive and agitating for a triumphal return would occupy the new king's thoughts night and day. It was a godsend to the English, just when they most needed their old enemy distracted. He had to make the most of that gift, even if it meant running from their *fiend* like *nithings*. He looked up, squinting at the patch of blue which cut the treetops like a wound. The sun was well past the high point, the day was advanced. It was still

Hreth month, Glory month, the goddess Eostre had not yet ridden her wain among the English nor Danes; there were only a few hours of daylight left before night fell and pursuit then would be troublesome at best. Eofer opened his mouth to agree to his friend's proposal when Wulfhere cut in. 'Hemming is right, lord. This is a fine place to defend.' He traced the curve of his spear blade with the pad of a finger and threw them a grim smile. 'I will hold this place, you boys have done enough today already.' Hemming made to argue but Wulfhere cut him short. 'I am fresh and eager to fight.' He cuffed Eofer's man on the sleeve and his lip curled into a smile. 'Look at you two, if you don't mind me saying lord, you both look like shit. Besides,' he added as Eofer and Hemming instinctively took in their pale and drawn features, 'why should you boys have all the fun?'

As Eofer hesitated over his decision, his own youth Finn trotted up from the head of the column. 'Eadward sent word that there is a fast flowing river about half a mile up ahead, lord,' he panted excitedly. 'There is some sort of rope crossing there.'

Wulfhere beamed. 'There you are then, lord. I will hold them here if they reach us in time and you can send word when everyone is safely across. If I cut this rope when I reach it, you can all pull me across the river and they will be left stranded on this side with no way to cross.'

Eofer cast an anxious look to the South. The ridgeway took a dip just beyond their position, but it was still early in the year and the trees were leafless so they could see a fair distance. They had seen the Danes a few times when the wildwood had opened out periodically, and Eofer and Eadward had marvelled at the slow pace their leader was setting as he ran the English down. Still wearing their mail shirts, the enemy were jogging at a steady pace as they sought to conserve their energy for the fighting to come. But, the English leaders had agreed incredulously, with such a large force the Danish leader could easily have stripped his fastest runners of their armour and sent them racing on ahead. Forced to turn and deal with the menace, even if the Engles had prevailed in the fight they would have lost valuable time. A couple of fights and they would have been scooped up like fish in a net. Finally he nodded as he reached his decision. 'It's a good idea. I will leave Spearhafoc here, she can help fend them off with her bow. With any luck that should be enough to give you the edge.'

Finn was still standing beside them, and he cleared his throat to speak. 'She has no arrows, lord,' he murmured apologetically. As Eofer turned to him, the youth explained with a grimace. 'She upended her quiver when we jumped from the bow of the *Hwælspere* and the current just took them away. She has been dreading telling you; she thinks that she has let you down.'

Eofer sighed and pulled a wry smile. He was becoming too weary to think straight, but he shrugged as he turned back to Wulfhere. 'I won't do that then. Sorry, it looks as if you are on your own after all.' He indicated the path ahead to the others as he hefted his spear and clapped the duguth on the arm in a parting gesture of goodwill. 'Let's get going and give this man the best chance that we can.'

Within a hundred yards the ridge line began to dip and arc away to the north-west as they hurried on. Soon they were free of the trees and loping across a water meadow thick with cowslip, the flowers a haze of yellow on a drugget of green. Ahead Eofer could see the crossing place, and he clenched his fist with joy as he saw that a full score or more of the men were already gathered on the far bank.

He called Grimwulf across and the youth came over with a knowing look, despite his obvious state of weariness. 'You have a use for my speed, lord,' he said with a smile. Eofer snorted. 'Go back to the tree line and look for my signal. When I raise my spear shaft, I want you to race back down the path to Wulfhere. Tell him that we are all across and that he is to get himself back here as quickly as possible. Got that?' The lad nodded and took off as Eofer scanned the knot of bodies grouped on the bank.

Eadward looked across from his place at the crossing point as he sought his duguth, and Eofer went across to explain the man's absence. 'Wulfhere has volunteered to cover our retreat if needs be.' He indicated Grimwulf staring intently from the forest edge. 'Don't worry, my lad there will fetch him when we are all across. Grimwulf will be there in no time, I have seen him outrace a horse.'

Eofer looked at the river for the first time, and a feeling of elation came over him as he saw that it was their salvation. Swollen by the spring rains the river was wide and fast flowing; the moment that the rope was cut and hauled away the Danes could do little more than wave them on their way. Twin ropes were attached to stout oak posts, one at head height and the other three or four feet below, and he watched as Octa shuffled the last few feet before throwing himself onto the far bank.

Hrothmund was halfway across, clinging on tightly as the foot-rope sagged and lowered him knee deep into the torrent. There were still a good dozen or so waiting to cross, and Eofer cast an anxious look back the way they had come. Wulfhere could well be fighting for his life at this very moment; they had to speed up the crossing if he was to have any chance of reaching safety.

Eadward had read his thoughts, and the *scipthegn* held his gaze as he turned back. 'Wulfhere knew that he would be feasting in Valhall before sunset when he stepped forward. We can't go any faster Eofer,' he said sadly. 'The rope will never take the weight of more than two men at any one time. With the water level this high, even that many would be up to their chests if we tried it.'

A harsh cawing carried across from the treetops, and the pair exchanged a look as a cloud of rooks rose into the darkening sky. Eadward was the first to speak. 'Wulfhere has already travelled onwards. Call your man back, Eofer. We need to get them all across somehow...*now*!'

Eofer waved his spear frantically and called the youth back as Eadward began to push and pull the remaining warriors into two groups. By the time that Grimwulf had raced back across the meadow the remaining Englishmen had been divided up, and Eadward drew his seax and began to saw at the lower rope. 'The first group,' he cried as the strands began to fray and tease apart. 'Wade into the water and take a firm grip.'

Eofer could see what his friend intended and, cupping his hands to his mouth, cried out above the crash of onrushing water. 'Keep in your groups when you reach the far bank, half for each rope. Pull us across when we are ready.'

The cable was proving tough to cut through, even for Eadward's razor-sharp stabbing sword, and Eofer drew his own as the metallic clatter of mail carried to them from the shadow of the wood. As he began to saw frantically at the higher line the lower finally gave way and Eadward was beside him in an instant. Together the thegns worked to cut the rope as the duguth remaining on the bank made to form a shield wall around them. Eofer could see that the first group were being hauled across the seething waters and he snapped out an order to the hearth men as the rope began to part. 'I won't need you there lads, this is almost through. All you will do is slow us up. Shoulder your shields and start pulling yourself across as soon as this parts!'

A glance to the South, and the tree line spewed forth a tide of Danes who bayed like hounds at the sight of their quarry and tore across the grass towards them. Eofer pulled the rope taut and worked his seax at the final strand as the crash of running men filled the air. The duguth were back at the bank, but hesitating as the Danes tore across the meadow towards their thegns. Eofer frantically snapped out an order. 'I will get this! Get into the water, I am right behind you!'

Eadward leapt aside as the final fibres parted and the rope, the tension released, whipped away. A spear flashed past Eofer's face followed by another, and the eorle turned to face his foe as Eadward shouldered his shield and splashed after the men. The enemy were upon him and Eofer dropped his seax, snatching up his gar with his left hand as he reached across his body and drew Gleaming with his right. A Dane, his features twisted by a snarl of hatred, jabbed at him with a heavy spear but Eofer dodged inside the lunge and speared the man in the thigh. As the Dane fell, Eofer risked a look up and gasped.

The plain was a sea of hate-filled faces, and the eorle knew with certainty that his wyrd was upon him. To seek to join the others now would only leave his back a mishmash of bloody wounds and he resolved that he would go to his ancestors unsullied by such a shameful thing. As he backed against the post a voice cried out above the din:

'*I want him alive!*'

Several Danes reacted to the order, overlapping their linden boards with a clatter, shuffling carefully towards him with stone-hard eyes glowering between helm and shield rim.

Eofer struck out with sword and spear but the space to move was diminishing by the moment as the Danes crowded in, and very soon he was hemmed in from all sides and pressed hard against the great oak beam. A sea of gleeful faces swam before him until they suddenly hardened into one.

'Hello hall burner,' a voice rasped. 'We meet again.'

A heartbeat later his head shot to the side, exploding with pain as silver flashed and the dome of a sword pommel crashed into the side of his skull. As white light sparked in his vision Eofer fell to the floor, his eyes losing their focus as he began to slip into unconsciousness. Darkness crowded in as the noise receded, and he watched as if from afar as the tail-end of rope slipped, snake-like, over the lip of the bank and disappeared from view.

SEVEN

The thegn threw his arm around Hemming and tugged the struggling duguth towards the bank. A spear sliced into the water beside him and then another as more bodies tumbled into the river about them, the Engles throwing their shields around the pair and shepherding them towards safety. As the missiles continued to pepper the water around them, the ship thegn twisted a knot of Hemming's cloak into a ball and hauled him backwards. 'Thrush, come on!' he yelled desperately as the man fought against him. 'There is nothing that we can do.'

Hemming stared at the far bank, his face contorted by a powerful mix of anger, helplessness and shame and, as his body slammed against the muddy riverbank, Eadward watched with relief as the madness began to drain from the big man. He spoke again, seizing the opportunity before the rage could build again. 'Thrush,' he repeated gently but firmly, 'there is nothing that we can do.'

Thrush Hemming's shoulders sagged wearily as he watched the enemy close about his lord with dismay. Eofer was fighting hard, holding his own against the mass of spears and swords until a cry cut the air and the Danes moved in with their shields, hemming him in like a hog on market day. A troll-Dane, huge and menacing in mail and boar helm closed in for the kill, and a horrified moan escaped the mouths of the watching Engles as the warrior's sword flashed and the eorle slipped from view.

As their *fiend* cheered and stabbed the air in triumph another spear arced in towards them, but Octa swept his big shield across and knocked it aside with a look of distain as Hemming's animal-like howl tore the air. Suddenly the big man shook himself free and clambered the bank, tearing across the grassy water meadow towards the place where the first of those to cross the torrent had gathered. Eadward and Osbeorn shared a look as they both realised the duguth's destination, and the thegn desperately snapped out an order. 'Get after him! Don't let any harm come to the Dane, we still need him.'

Osbeorn scrambled onto the bank and tore off after his leader as the other men in the water regained the land, throwing their shields together as they backed away towards the safety of the tree line. Ahead of him he could see the others begin to understand what was about to happen, and he recognised the confusion in their movements as Hemming thundered towards them.

Hrothmund, distracted by the pulsing mass of those who so clearly wanted him dead only a hundred yards away, saw the more immediate danger too late as Hemming closed upon him with a roar. Cuthbert and Adda, Eadward's remaining duguth closed protectively around the Danish prince, but a heartbeat later Hemming crashed through them, bowling them aside before throwing his hand around the throat of the young Dane and slamming him back against the bole of a tree. The breath rasped from the Dane in a violent gasp as the Engle drew his short stabbing seax and raised the wicked blade to Hrothmund's throat.

'I am lordless because of you, you worthless piece of shit,' he spat, their faces almost touching as the Englishman trembled with rage. 'Give me one good reason why I don't just spit you now, like the worthless pig that you are.'

Hrothmund's mouth gaped, and the colour drained from his face as his mind desperately scrambled to form a reply which would stay the madman's blade.

Another voice came as the Dane swallowed loudly, a voice which was clearly doing its best to remain calm and reasoned as violence crackled in the air. 'Thrush,' it said, 'leave him.'

Hemming seemed not to have heard, and the young Dane took a risk, stealing a look towards his hoped-for saviour as his feet hung suspended above the earth. The look was enough, and the faintest spark of recognition cut through Hemming's rage that there was another standing at his side. The voice spoke again. 'Thrush, if you kill this bastard you will be doing the Danes' work for them. Eofer would have given his life for nothing.'

The mention of his lord's name did the trick, and Hemming threw out a sidelong glance. Osbeorn gave a wink and laid the palm of his hand lightly on his hearth companion's forearm. 'Let it go,' he said as he fixed him with a stare. 'Me, Octa, and the youth are looking to get out of this. You are in charge now; time to start acting like it, mate.'

The sight and sound of his friend drained the anger from the big man, and Hemming shoved the Dane aside with a sneer as he slammed his seax into its scabbard. Adda and Cuthbert hustled Hrothmund away as Eadward and Octa finally reached the shelter of the trees.

The thegn cast a quick look at the young Dane and, satisfied that he was still in one piece, indicated that Eofer's weorthman step aside from the throng with a jerk of his head. The two headmen turned to face across the clearing as the Danish host lined the far bank, beating ash shaft on shields as they cried their challenges. The course of the river had taken a wide meander to the South at the point where the locals had chosen to construct the crossing point, eating into the southern water meadow but leaving the northern floodplain a wide grassy swatch of green. With no evidence that the Danes had any bowmen among their number, both men knew that they were as safe as they had been since they had been forced to ditch the ship earlier in the day. Eadward watched as Danes waded into the current, bracing themselves and linking arms as they attempted to force a crossing. He knew that they would not succeed there, he had crossed the swiftly flowing watercourse and knew the waters to be far too deep to ford. Other Danes were already jogging away upstream and down as their leader sought another crossing place from which to renew the chase.

Like fighting men everywhere, the Englishmen of the combined war bands slumped to the ground, grabbing what they knew would be the briefest chance for rest. The day had been a gruelling test of their endurance, more so for the men of Eofer's raiding party, but they would have to move on quickly if they wanted to live. The shadows were lengthening as the sun began to settle in the West, its golden light turning the river to bronze as the body of the first Dane to drown at the crossing attempt spun lazily into view on its way down to the sea.

Eadward gave his companion a gentle shove. 'Are you back with us?' he asked with a weary smile. 'I could do with a little help.'

Hemming stood, staring across at the Danish horde, his chest rising and falling like bellows as he sought to control his emotions. Eadward could see that the duguth's eyes were rimmed red and watery, and he looked away to spare the big man's shame as he spoke of his own losses that day. 'I knew Wulfhere and Hnæf for a score years or more. To lose them both in a day...' He shook his head sadly as the sound of snoring carried to them from the heap of youth, strewn about the floor like clothing on wash day. 'Hnæf saved our lives more times than I like to think, guiding us through Thunor-storms and arrow-storms that left other ships flotsam. Wulfhere is...was,' he corrected himself, 'hand-fasted to my sister. They have a lad, Eadgar and a lass Editha. Both good, strong children, who climb all over their father like he is a great oak tree when he returns to them with armfuls of gifts and a grin as wide and ugly as a horse's arse. What shall I tell them?' he asked in a voice quivering with emotion. 'That I abandoned their father to fight a Danish ship army alone, while I ran off with one of their princes?' He let out a sigh and shouldered his shield. 'Come on,' he said, plucking at Hemming's sleeve. 'Let's get them all up and moving while there is still enough light to see by.'

Octa spooned another dollop of the glutinous mixture, sighing with pleasure as it spread warmth and feeling throughout his body. He had one more scoop from the pot before his share had been taken and he searched the surface of the broth to see if he could spy out an island of meat. A solid peak was breaking the surface on the far side and his arm reached out as he made his play, only for another spoon to dart in and snatch it away.

'Gotcha!'

He raised his eyes and squinted into the gloom as Osbeorn chewed happily on his prize: 'bastard.'

Osbeorn threw him a wink, rolling the hot chunk to one side of his mouth as he made a reply. 'You had your chance Oct'; too slow.'

Octa snorted at his hearth mate's cheek and peered across to the East. Even from within the cover of the woodland it was plain that the sun was approaching Middle-earth as the celestial horse drew it across the dome of the sky. He finished licking the last of the sticky mixture from his spoon and popped it back inside his pouch. 'The old nag's up,' he said with a roll of his eyes, 'time to get moving.'

Eadward whistled softly as he shook the damp from his hair and one of his youth hurried across. 'Lord?'

'Wake the children,' he said. 'And make sure that they are quiet.'

They watched as the lad trotted across to the makeshift shelter and began to nudge the sleeping inhabitants with the butt of his spear. Three spoonfuls each and the broth would be gone, and every man there knew that the meal could very well be their last.

The rain had begun almost the same moment that Spearhafoc had spotted the old wattle hurdle off to one side of the path. It had been an amazing piece of fortune and one which they had eagerly grasped. The pathway had been growing more and more indistinct by the moment, very soon they would have had to squat and take their rest where they were, whatever the danger. Moving single file to limit the evidence of their passage, they had carried the panel to the far side of a gentle rise in the ground. Hidden from the track, the hurdle had been wedged between the trunks of two small beech trees and covered by a layer of the leaf mulch which carpeted the floor. Stacked beneath the makeshift shelter like logs for the hearth, the youth had been asleep even before the more senior members of the troop had set the guards and hunkered down into their cloaks for the night.

The youth came back to his main task as his hearth mates began to pull themselves from the stack. The Danes, even if they had found a way to cross the river, should be a good distance behind them for that night at least. They too, he reasoned, had had a tough day of it the day before, and even if they could see in the dark they would need food and rest before continuing the pursuit.

As the youth gathered to dip their spoons, the fire was smothered with soil and darkness returned to cloak the scene. A quick glance up at the ridge line told Eadward that the guard was alert to any danger from the South, and he indicated that the senior hearth warriors gather in the lee of the back slope. It was the first real opportunity that they had had to converse since they had left the ship, and the thegn was determined to make the most of it. He glanced across to Hrothmund and jerked his head: 'you too.' The Dane's face lit up as he pocketed his own spoon and began to follow on.

The first light of the new day was beginning to touch the sky, anvil grey to match the mood, and Eadward wiped the rain from his face with his hand as he began to address the duguth. 'You have all slept on it. Are we all still agreed?' He looked across to Hrothmund who had attached himself to the end of the line. Eadward could not help noticing that the prince was still giving Thrush Hemming a wide berth and was thankful for it. They were in a bad enough situation as it was, without having to contend with the effects of a man's wounded pride. 'You are sure there is nothing more that you can tell us about this area, Hrothmund?'

The Dane shook his head. 'As I said last night, I have never travelled this path. The River which we crossed used to mark the boundary between our lands and those of the Wulfings, but now,' he shrugged apologetically, 'who can say?'

They all nodded knowingly, everywhere in the North folk were on the move. In the time of their fathers the Wulfing kingdom stretched in an arc from one shore of Scania to the other, hemming the Danes within their coastal pale, even threatening to push them back into the islands in the Belts. But like the Engles themselves the wolf men were now moving away to Britannia, and they were beginning to feel the resurgent power of the Danes pushing upon their borders as the Scylding kingdom spread out into the surrounding lands like a dark stain.

Adda, Eadward's duguth, cut in, sarcasm dripping from every word. 'And we can expect no help from the jarl hereabouts, what with you being a Danish prince and kinsman to boot?'

Hrothmund recognised the scorn contained within the question but replied levelly. Natural enemies of his people or not, he was well aware that his life depended on their goodwill. 'Yes, Heoroweard is my cousin as you say, but equally he is the cousin of the man who now styles himself King Hrothulf. I doubt that he even knows that my father is dead,' the Dane continued. 'But when he does find out he will have to deal with the situation as he finds it, not how he wishes it to be. Hrothulf wears the king helm of Daneland. What is more they are both Woden born like myself, so both men are king-worthy whether I like the fact or not; I could just as likely discover that Heoroweard had designs on the gift-stool himself as find an ally.'

Hemming hawked and spat before throwing his own comment into the discussion. 'That is if he was not in on the murder.' Eadward threw him a look of exasperation as the big man shrugged his shoulders. 'Dodgy lot, the Danes,' he spat again and fixed the prince with a glare: 'untrustworthy.'

The conversation was beginning to drift away from the matter at hand, which was Eadward knew, their survival. He took up the reins of the discussion once again as the youth began to move away to collect their weapons. 'At least we know that there are no settlements in the area. The pathway leads northwards through the backwoods with no access to the coastal belt. That means,' he said, 'that once the Danes are across the river they will have to double back on themselves to regain this path. It could take them a day, who knows? It also means,' he added, 'that they cannot easily detach a ship's crew to sail north and cut us off. It's to be a straightforward chase between us and them and I think,' he said with a weary smile, 'that we have the best reason to win that race.'

Hemming closed his eyes and exhaled as he turned his face to the sky. The rain was still falling, fat droplets percolating lazily through the canopy from the rapidly lightening clouds above. 'So we just run north and hope for the best,' he said, before lowering his face once more with a grin. 'Sounds like a good plan; let's get going.'

Eadward scanned the group and found the smiles echoed there as the effects of a night's rest, warm food and the emergence of a definite plan breathed new life into weary minds and bodies. As the men hefted their shields and prepared to depart the thegn made a parting remark. 'I have lost my two closest friends,' he said forcefully, 'and Hrothmund's father has been murdered.'

'And my brother,' the Dane interjected. They all turned to him as he revealed the death of Hrethric to them for the first time. 'We were invited to a hunt, but it was a just a ruse to remove us and our huscarls from the king's hall. I watched as my brother was spitted like the boar we thought were to be the day's prey. My huscarls stood and died to a man to enable me to escape and continue the fight against the usurper.'

The Englishmen lowered their eyes momentarily as they acknowledged the scale of the young Dane's loss, before Eadward carried on. 'So, as we can all see, Eofer arrived at the great doors of Valhall in good company.' He threw them a watery smile. 'I daresay that they had a more comfortable night than we.'

As they snorted and began to move away Hrothmund spoke again, the tone of his voice betraying his confusion. 'Why would king's bane travel to valhall?'

Thrush Hemming rounded on the youth, his hand moving instinctively to the grip of his sword. 'Perhaps you would like to go and check that he *is* in the Allfather's hall?' he snarled. 'I can send you along right now!'

Hrothmund's eyes moved from one face to another as if attempting to discover if the Englishmen were joking with him, however unlikely that may seem. The faces were stern and he realised with a start that he must be the only one among them to have realised the truth. He quickly began to explain as the first roll of thunder sounded in the distance and the rain began to pummel the group with full force. 'I saw Eofer carried away,' he explained incredulously.

Hemming screwed up his face as he spat a reply: 'so?'

The young Dane looked again at the Engles as if he had said enough, but their expressions made it plain that he had not. Hrothmund carried on. 'What would you do if you killed a warlord?'

They all exchanged a look as the first inkling that he may be right entered their thoughts. Octa formed those thoughts into words. 'Strip the body of its war gear and weaponry.'

Hrothmund raised a brow: 'and then?'

Octa shrugged. 'And then, nothing; leave the body where if fell to feed the wolf and raven.'

Hrothmund nodded in agreement. 'So do we, all civilised folk do so as a tribute to Woden, they are his creatures after all. So,' he said, as they finally began to understand the importance of his words, 'why did my countrymen carry Eofer away, still wearing his battle gear?'

EIGHT

He clenched his teeth tighter as he fought down the overwhelming desire to retch. Moving his hands up to his face, Eofer carefully wiped away the pool of water which was threatening to spill from his swollen eye. His left eye had all but closed from the suppuration there, the swelling tapering slightly before building once more into an egg-shaped mound.

'Hurts, does it?' The warrior raised his foot, pushing the Engle to one side with the sole of his boot. 'You should have stayed at home then.'

His companions, unseen in the glare, laughed at the callous joke. The man crouched beside him and roughly patted Eofer's cheek with the flat of his hand. 'No, maybe not,' he said with a gleam in his eye, 'I wouldn't be wearing this lovely mail shirt then, would I?'

The pockmarked face was only inches from his own, and Eofer fought against the desire to pull his own away. The rank smell of onions and stale ale washed over him as the man spoke, and it was only the thegn's sense of self worth which prevented him from emptying the contents of his own belly there and then.

Starkad's voice carried across from the steering platform of the ship, and Eofer's tormentor backed off with a sneer and a final hard slap to his cheek. As Eofer winced with pain, a pair of boots appeared at his side and the big warrior lowered himself to the deck. Dangling his legs over the lip of the platform, the newcomer sat and placed Gleaming upon his lap as his feet thrummed happily against the upright. 'This is a nice blade,' he said as he slid the weapon from its scabbard. 'It looks old; an heirloom?'

Eofer blinked away a tear as the hammers beating inside his skull redoubled in intensity following the pummelling it had just received from onion breath. Moving his one good eye upwards, he motioned towards the rope which bound him and managed to croak out a request. 'Untie my hands.'

Starkad hesitated for a moment before jerking his head at a crewman nearby. The man hurried over to do his lord's bidding and soon Eofer was carefully rubbing the feeling back into his wrists. 'Thank you,' he said evenly, his words heavily laced with the contempt he felt for the man, despite the seriousness of his situation.

Starkad chuckled happily as he held Gleaming up to the light, twisting the blade this way and that as he admired the ancient sword-smith's mastery of his craft. 'Oh, I know that you don't like me,' he said, before chuckling again. 'Not many people do!' The men nearby laughed dutifully at their lord's quip as Starkad went on. 'It will take us the rest of the day to make Hroar's Kilde, and being a friendly sort I just thought that you might be wondering why I am here, fighting alongside Danes.'

Eofer shrugged, despite the pain. 'Why should I be surprised?' He answered with a snarl. 'You are a man without honour.'

Starkad snorted. Slipping a silver ring from his arm he tossed it across to one of his henchmen who gave it a huff and a shine as he swaggered away to show his friends. 'He is too sharp that one,' the big viking said distantly as he watched the man slip the ring onto his own arm. Eofer could see the old malevolence wash across the warrior's features, the same look he had caught the previous autumn at King Eomær's hunting lodge, back in Engeln. He remembered thinking at the time the man was as trustworthy as a sackful of adders; it seemed that little had changed over the course of the winter months. Despite the pain in his head it was obvious that his captor had settled in to talk, and Eofer decided to use the opportunity to discover what he could about the situation in Daneland. The English army should be ashore by now and moving inland, burning and pillaging as they went as the first riders, their mounts lathered in sweat, arrived at Hleidre to tell the new king the dreadful news. He smirked despite the pain. The Danes which he had led into the wilds of Scania were moving further and further away from the fighting as they chased down the boy who had seemed to be so important only the day before. It had been a good day's work, even if his own future looked grim. 'So, the great Starkad Sorvirkson has outgrown the Heathobeards it seems,' he said as the big man slid Gleaming back into the scabbard.

Starkad snorted with derision. 'The Heathobeards were always a temporary stop on my journey, Eofer,' he replied. 'If you remember, I offered my help to your king but he plainly was not interested.' He shot the Englishman a look of pity. 'You talk of honour, but kings have none. They are the same as everyone else on Middle-earth, only interested in enriching themselves at the expense of others. They send men like us to batter down shield walls on their behalf and supply them with riches. Then they return a few trinkets to us as a reward for watching our friends get hacked to pieces before our eyes and expect our gratitude!' He hawked and spat over the side of the ship as if to reinforce his opinion. 'So no,' he continued, 'I am no longer a Heathobeard, and yes you can now call me a Dane if you wish, but the only oath which I have sworn that I will never break is the one which I made to myself the day that I tricked my best friend into becoming a sacrifice.'

Eofer watched as a small figure rose from her place in the bows, cupping the now familiar yellowy bowl in the hands before her. Despite the pain, he was regaining his old sharpness of mind and Eofer snorted as he recognised the paradox that being knocked senseless might have done him some good. Already exhausted from the fight and flight of the previous day and night, he had not recovered consciousness until they were back on the ship and putting the Wulfing lands behind them.

The volva came down the ship towards them and Eofer's mouth curled into a smile as he watched Starkad's crew of toughened cutthroats quieten, parting before the waif-like woman like barley in a breeze. Hair the colour of pitch framed a face unlike Eofer had ever lain eyes upon, the narrow eyes and high cheekbones of those far to the North shining moonlike above tight fitting sark and trews. The holy woman skipped lightly across to Eofer's place at the stern, and the thegn could sense the amusement in her eyes at the reaction of the crew to her passing as she squatted before him. She raised a finger and pushed his head gently to one side as she examined his wound. 'Not bad,' she said in her strangely accented voice, flashing him a surprisingly warm smile. 'Of course,' she added with a glance at Starkad. 'It would have been even easier if you had not been hit so hard in the first place!'

Starkad chuckled at his side, and the Englishman was surprised again to see that the warlord seemed to share none of the apprehension of his shipmates at the presence of the woman. 'This is Kaija,' he said, as the volva scooped a little of the paste from what had plainly once been the crown of a man's skull, before smoothing the mixture onto the swelling on his own head. As Kaija mumbled an incantation beneath her breath, Starkad explained her presence. 'She was sent by my Foster-father.' He chuckled as he recalled the night. 'We were sat at the benches, plotting the end of King Hrothgar, when the doors opened and in she strode. As the men sat, open mouthed, she came across and said that the Allfather approved of our scheming and that he would ensure that the attempt would meet with success.'

The woman had finished lathering the gunk onto Eofer's head, and she rested her back against the curve of the hull, drawing up her knees as Starkad held up Gleaming once more and admired the workmanship. He shot the Engle a sidelong look. 'It is an eorle's sword Eofer, and I am no hero,' he said with a mischievous smile. 'Heroes keep their word, they have honour.' He offered the weapon to the astonished Englishman who hesitated for a moment, fearing a trick, before taking it gratefully. 'I will get your mail back from that fool too, and anything else that you want returned from the booty. All I ask in return is that you listen to what I have to say, and consider my proposal.'

A stab of pain came but Eofer pushed it down as his curiosity came to fore. In truth the foul smelling paste which the friendly volva had been applying seemed to work almost instantaneously and he was glad of it. He cast a quick look down at the young woman but she appeared to be dozing in the early spring sun, blissfully uncaring as to the nature of Starkad's forthcoming offer.

'I said to you earlier that kings are uncaring, unworthy of the pledges which we make to them, but that is not wholly true,' he began. 'I was taken as a small child in a raid along with Vikar, the son of King Harald of Hordaland. After I grew to manhood we returned together to his father's old lands, killed the usurper Herthjof, and regained his birthright. I was his greatest friend and hearth man, none of the other kings in Noregr could hope to defeat us. One day we became stranded by an ill wind at sea and had to take shelter between two islands. The wind roared and howled, whipping the waves into mountainous rollers and, fearful that we should be dashed ashore, we cast the sacrificial chips to see if the gods would spare us.' Starkad looked downcast as he told his tale, and Eofer could see that there was more to the great viking than his renowned reputation for ferocity and cunning suggested. 'The chips answered that Woden would help us if a man from the ship was hung and dedicated in his name, and we drew lots to discover who the man should be. We did it half a dozen times, Eofer,' he said sadly. 'Each time King

Vikar lost. The men were aghast, adamant to a man that they would not outlive their lord, their ring giver, so we decided among us that we should seek shelter on one of the islands and cast the rune sticks the following morning. That evening the Night Mares hauled a dream into my mind. In it my old Foster-father, Horsehair Grani, came to me and together we rowed across to a neighbouring island in a small boat. In a clearing there were twelve chairs arranged in a circle, eleven of them were taken by gods, but the seat at the head of the circle was empty until Grani left my side and took his place among them. At once the gods hailed him as the Allfather.'

Eofer sat, horrified by the tale which was unfolding before him. Woden was all powerful, but shifty with it. The scheming of the god seemed to be playing an increasing part in his life and he recalled the words of his father as they had ridden the Wolds the previous autumn:

The gods are powerful, but fickle all the same, Woden most of all. Show them respect but place your trust in your sword arm, Eofer. They delight in chaos.

Starkad shrugged. 'I had to choose between loyalty to a god or a man. I chose the god and King Vikar died; who would you have chosen, Eofer?'

Starkad climbed to his feet. 'Join me in a life of raiding, Englishman,' he said as he visibly pushed the melancholic thoughts away. 'A man of your qualities is worth more than a hall and a few acres of land. How many men do you lead?' The viking raised a brow and shot the Engle a look which told the eorle that he already knew that the answer, and that was very few. 'We are both king killers, Eofer,' he added, 'but my name is known throughout the North, my reputation is secure. Don't answer me now,' he said as he began to move away, 'think on it. This ship can deliver you into the hands of your enemies in Daneland or it can sail north; the choice is yours.'

Eofer raised his chin and peered out beyond the curve of the hull as he went. The heights of the island which he knew the Danes called Hven were off to bæcbord, sand coloured cliffs topped by a splash of green, brilliant against a sky of mackerel grey as the lands of the North began to reawaken from their winter slumber.

A voice broke into his thoughts and Eofer looked across to its source. 'It's called Hven,' Kaija said with a trace of a smile as she regarded him with half closed eyes. 'I know,' he replied with a childlike pride which amused him. The volva had never appeared to be keen on conversing with any but Starkad, and his surprise only increased as she continued the conversation. 'But do you know how it came to be called by that name, Engle?' Eofer had to admit that he did not, and the woman continued with a smile of satisfaction. 'There was once a giantess, Hvenhild, who decided that the land in Scania was too flat and boring. So, one day, she took herself over to the island which we now call Daneland and gathered up some of the hills. As she returned with them in her apron, the strings broke and a clod of earth fell into the Eyrarsund.' She smiled again and gave a self-evident shrug: 'the island of Hven.'

As the volva closed her eyes again, Eofer's mind went back to his own future. Once the island was astern, he knew that it was but a short sail along the northern coast of Daneland to the entrance to the great inland sea there and he smiled again, despite his worries, as he recalled his only previous visit to the place; shooting the shoals in the little *Fælcen* as she ploughed onward toward her date with destiny.

Unshackled now the eorle pushed himself to his feet as the pain in his head subsided. The volva was still sitting before him, a smile of contentment painting her features as she basked in the success of her story and the warmth of the sun. He had not felt the fear which seemed to grip most men in the presence of the servants of the gods since he had slain King Ongentheow on the field of battle. Despite Starkad's earlier words, he was sure that his place at the benches in Valhall was secure, and the day when he would greet old friends, past enemies and kinsmen alike held no fear for him. He spoke to her again as he dipped his head, slipping the baldric containing Gleaming back into its rightful place. 'So, you are from the far north?' he began as she opened one eye and glanced his way. The volva smiled and settled back, closing the eye once again and exhaling softly as she luxuriated in the warmth of the sun. He persevered, despite the unpromising start to their conversation. 'You are a Finn?'

Kaija answered in a murmur. 'We call ourselves Sami, but you call me a Finn if that is your wish, Engle.'

'And you were sent by the gods to support Hrothgar's replacement, this Hrothulf?'

She shook her head, snorting with amusement. 'No, I was returning north from Saxland and I had need of a ship.'

It was clear that the woman had exhausted her desire for conversation and he looked down the ship as it crested its way west. Starkad, despite the fact that he had set off to retrieve Eofer's mail byrnie, had fallen into an animated conversation with a gang of his crewmen. Eofer gratefully seized the opportunity to retrieve the item and repay the man for his insult, extricating himself from the awkward conversation at the same time. His eyes scanned the deck, picking Starkad's man out from the herd in an instant. Sat with his back to the stern, the Dane was bellowing with laughter as his hand whipped out to reenact his earlier slap, and Eofer grasped the hilt of his sword as he rose and began to walk for'ard. He stalked the deck as crewmen turned their heads in surprise, the anger building within him as the oaf made another wisecrack at his expense. Conversations were trailing away before him as he walked, an advancing wave of silence and expectation moving along the length of the dragon ship as he went, and Eofer saw the look of surprise turn instantly to delight as Starkad caught on and turned to watch.

The Dane's friends had noticed his approach now and they quietened and exchanged excited glances, shuffling back as steel shone and Gleaming came into view. The man was oblivious to the threat which was rapidly coming down upon him, and he continued with the tale of his one-sided victory over the man they all knew as the king's bane. All other conversations had now trailed away but still the fool gabbled on, and it was only when Eofer lay the silvered blade on his shoulder that he stopped in mid sentence and slowly turned his head. As the Dane paled and his mouth gaped, Eofer fixed him with a stare and spoke in a tone dripping with menace. 'I don't recall gifting you my mail shirt. But I do recall your words to me,' he snarled. 'And the girly slap.'

Eofer took a pace backwards, holding his sword out to one side as he indicated to the Dane that he stand with a jerk of his head. His friends hastily scattered in all directions as the crewman rose slowly to his feet and Eofer watched as the man cast anxious looks amidships, to the place where he knew that Starkad would be watching the unfolding drama. No help would arrive from that direction he knew, and the Engle almost laughed as a picture of the warlord's wolfish delight at the nearness of imminent bloodletting came into his mind.

The Dane's expression darkened, and Eofer saw the indecision in his eyes as they flicked out to either side and he desperately sought a way out of the situation with his life and honour intact.

'There will be no help,' Eofer said. 'Nobody will fight an eorle without good reason.'

Casting a look of contempt at the crewmen around him for abandoning him to his fate, the man began to unbuckle his belt as he prepared to return the byrnie, but Eofer spoke again, his voice a growl. 'Leave it on and draw your sword, or I will cut your head off where you stand.'

As his opponent bowed to the inevitable and slowly drew his own blade, Eofer flexed his knees and dropped into a fighting stance. The ship bucked and surged as it buried its head into the waves, but the Englishman rode the movements with ease, his head and sword arm fixed points in a moving world. Everyman aboard knew that here was a killer of men, and Eofer sensed the anticipation begin to drain from the Danish crewmen as they recognised the hopelessness of their man's cause. His opponent had reached the same conclusion, and he opened his mouth to plead for a forgiveness which was not in the Englishman's heart.

Gleaming jabbed forward, the point of the blade opening a meaty gash along the Dane's cheek before slicing upwards to leave the man's ear hanging macabrely by a flap of flesh. Eofer was back in position before the Dane had reacted and he watched as the man moved his hand, fumbling in disbelief as he slowly came to realise that a good part of that side of his face now rested upon his shoulder. Eofer moved his hand to the weal which marked his own head as the horror-struck Dane attempted to push his face back together. 'Head wounds,' he said, 'not so funny now.' Stepping in, Eofer brought his left hand sweeping across to backhand the bloody mess which had only moments before been the side of his opponent's face. 'Hurts, does it?' he said, repeating the Dane's question from earlier. 'I think,' he said, as a pearl of blood fell from the point of his sword to stain the deck, 'that it was you who should have stayed at home. But then again,' he spat, 'you wouldn't have got to wear that lovely mail shirt, would you? Even for such a short time.'

NINE

'What have you got today?'

Osbeorn's tongue shot forward to reveal a sticky mess before sliding back into his mouth.

'You've got a brown tongue Ozzy,' Octa said with a sparkle of mischief. 'I always suspected.'

Osbeorn laughed as they jogged on. Hemming glanced back at the pair and threw them a fatherly smile.

'I thought that I would have belt,' Osbeorn replied loftily. 'You can't beat a good bit of belt when you are particularly famished, you always get a good chew from belt leather. You?'

Octa spread his lips to reveal a small piece of leather gripped between his teeth, pale and shredded after hours of chewing. 'I am going with baldric,' he said airily. He rubbed his belly with a hand as he glanced down at his friend's midriff. 'I don't know how you do it, I couldn't run on a full stomach.'

The duguth shared a snort at their grim humour. It was not the first time that they had been forced to stave off the pangs of hunger on campaign, and despite the gut gnawing discomfort they sincerely hoped that it would not be the last.

Movement caught Octa's eye, and he glanced back along the column as he spat the ball into the underbrush, exchanging a knowing look with his hearth mate. 'Trouble.'

A youth, gaunt and travel-weary, trotted past them and came alongside the leader. 'There's movement on the track.'

Hemming came to a halt, spitting his own meal into the undergrowth as he attempted to clear his throat. 'Is it him?'

Finn ran his tongue along his cracked and swollen lips as he struggled against thirst. 'I think so,' he croaked with an apologetic wince as his lip split again. 'Whoever it is they are still hidden by the trees, but I thought that you should know as quickly as possible so that you can make your dispositions.' He unstopped his water flask and took a sip, working the life-giving moisture around his mouth with his tongue. Water would not have been a problem if they were travelling at a leisurely pace, it had rained for a full day and night after all, drenching the already tired and hungry Engles and chilling them to the bone. Many tiny rivulets and even fully formed streams cut the path at regular intervals. But they were not moving at ease, it felt like they had been running for weeks and still the Danes came on. Hemming turned his head. Eadward's men had seen Eofer's war band come to a halt and they began to draw up as word was passed along to the front of the column.

They were on the back slope of one of the uncountable number of ridges which seemed to march across this part of Scania like the furrows of a newly ploughed field. It would take them an hour to reach the next crest, and he pursed his lips as he thought. As much as his mind baulked at the thought of retracing even a single step, he knew that it was the right thing to do. 'Go and tell Eadward what is happening,' he said to the waiting youth as he worked the stopper from his own flask. 'Tell him to carry on to the next ridge top as we agreed. We will soon know if this is Grimwulf. If it's not,' he added with a fatalistic smile, 'tell him that I will let Wulfhere and Hnæf know what we have been up to when we pitch up in Valhall.'

The youth nodded grimly and trotted away as Hemming turned back to the others. Most had heard the exchange and those that were too far away had already guessed what was happening. Hemming snorted as he saw that all were ready, shields unslung, heads helmed. Words were unnecessary, and he hefted his own big battle board as he led them back towards the crest of the rise.

It had been three days now since they had left the *Hwælspere*, three days of forced marches, hunger and pain. Most of the men were carrying blisters and sores, their skin rubbed raw by the continual chafing of sodden clothing and boots. Even when they had been forced to stop by the onset of nighttime they had been denied the use of a warming fire and, despite the fierceness of his lord's hearth troop, Hemming knew that spirits were approaching their nadir. A fight with an outlier of their pursuers, he reflected, could actually be just the thing to put some fire back into their bellies. If, on the other hand, the Danes were coming against them with full force, well, he thought, he would go to Valhall light of heart with a bloodied sword. They had led hundreds of the best warriors in Daneland away from the fighting there. King Eomær and the army *must* be in Hleidre, and he gave a snort of amusement as the image of the king's son Icel flashed into his mind, Haystack's blond mop flashing in the sun as he fed another hall to the flames of war and English riders swirled around him in triumph. Even if they fell today it would be more than a week before the huscarls returned to find their land devastated in their absence; the English had won a great victory before they had drawn a sword in anger.

Gaining the top of the shallow rise Hemming planted his feet at the centre of the track and looked to the South. Leg muscles burned after the race to the top, but he pushed the discomfort aside as he peered back along the roadway. Osbeorn and Octa moved to anchor the flanks as Porta slipped into position to his right and Finn returned to take his position on the left. The youth clattered into position to their rear as the duguth caught the first flash of movement among the trees in the vale, but the roadway was now barred by a wall of leather and steel, steadfast and eager to fight. The land fell away to his right and a glance to the West told him that the day was almost done, the sun a balefire as it rested on the treetops and washed the sky the colour of blood. English chests were moving like bellows after the run, breath pluming in the chill evening air like the dragon of their flag. It was, he thought, as fine a way to die as any.

Osbeorn spoke as they all fixed their eyes onto the point in the track where the runner would break free of the tree cover. 'Who's got my back?'

The higher voice of the Briton came back, the pride in her company and disdain for what might very well be impending death obvious to all in the tone; 'Spearhafoc, big man.'

A tortured fart cut the stillness of the moment as the duguth prepared his body for the work to come. 'Look after that for me, lass.'

Even without taking his eyes from the pathway Hemming could picture the youth's face, eyes rolling skyward as she shook her head with disgust. 'Sure; I will let you have it back later,' she gasped. 'If you open your eyes one night and think that you are looking at the biggest moon you have ever seen, brace yourself,' she replied with a curl of her lip. 'Because it won't be the moon you're looking at.'

As laughter rolled along the line Thrush Hemming shook his own head in wonder. Eofer would have prepared them to face the *fiend* with a fine battle speech, putting steel into sword and spear arms, kindling war-fire in bellies, but try as he might the words just would not come. Even as he lamented his lord's absence for the thousandth time Hemming recognised that the pair had lightened the mood, bringing the hearth troop closer into the special bond which English warriors knew as *bindung*.

'Are your arrows all set?' he asked, throwing the girl a look. Spearhafoc flashed him a grin in return and tipped the neck of her quiver forward. 'Four with fletchings and two which are little more than sharpened sticks,' she replied with a shrug. He nodded and threw her a wink of encouragement. 'Make them count.'

Devastated by the loss of her arrows at the riverbank as she had jumped from the tall bow of the *Hwælspere*, the youth had used her forest craft to fashion replacements as they had trudged steadily north. Spearhafoc had managed to gather together half a dozen saplings of the correct width from within the numerous clearings which they had passed, open spaces where trees had been brought down by age or autumn blow. Seeds which fell there grew straight and tall as quickly as they could, seeking to establish themselves before others robbed them of the life giving sunlight and the canopy reestablished itself. They were the perfect place to gather the narrow, straight shafts of wood which were required for arrow making. Stripping the sapling of its bark as she jogged along with the others, the young woman had scooped a small cup into the forest floor at one of the brief rest stops and fire-hardened the sharpened tips. Fletchings had come from the feathers of the hen sparrowhawk which had been fixed in her hair, the same feathers which had given her a new name the previous year, back in Britannia when her Welsh name, Dwynwyn, had proven too much of a mouthful for her new English hearth companions. Now she was ready to face the Danes again, the same men who had stolen her lord from her, and her blood quickened as she retrieved the bowstring from beneath her headpiece. Kept warm and dry, the chord slipped easily into place on the nocks as she forced the bow into shape against her instep before slipping the first arrow into place.

Rand's voice, the relief in the youth's tone obvious to all, drew the duguth's attention back to the pathway. 'It's Grimwulf, Hemming.'

Hemming sensed the shield wall relax as the youth came into view and he snapped a command, his voice a growl. 'Keep your shape. He is not running after us because he is pining for our company.'

As the shields came back up, Hemming walked forward of the line and raised a hand in greeting. Grimwulf saw them at the top of the rise and put on a spurt of speed now that he knew that the end of his chase was in sight. Rising from the gloom of the valley, he managed a smile as he slowed to a walk. 'There are a dozen Danes about half a mile behind me,' he wheezed. Hemming threw him a water skin and the youth pulled the stopper before swilling the welcome liquid around his parched mouth with a grateful nod. He took another swig, gargled and spat onto the path. 'They have split up,' he panted as his chest rose and fell from his exertions. 'Two dozen have come forward from the main pack and they have split into two groups in turn. It seems like a dozen run forward for a certain time and then wait for the other lot to catch them up. Then they switch places,' he explained, 'and the first group jog.'

Hemming nodded as he sought to hide his disappointment, it was the thing that he had most feared. The Danes had finally realised that a small group could chase them down, forcing them to turn and defend themselves until the main force came up to crush them, just like a pack of hounds holding a stag at bay until the horsemen arrived to make the kill.

'There's another thing,' Grimwulf added as he tipped the remainder of the water over his head and shook the droplets from his hair. 'They have torches with them.'

Hemming grimaced, but shrugged his shoulders. It was to be expected after all. 'They can afford to,' he said. 'It doesn't really matter if we see how close they are to us, it might even force us to stop earlier.' He cast his eyes away to the West. The sun was beneath the horizon as the horse galloped on, the first stars appearing overhead as the sky slowly turned from salmon to jet, and he snorted as he saw the look of incomprehension wash across the youth's face as the corners of his own mouth curled into a smile. 'They should be lighting them about now,' he murmured as the plan came together in his mind. He looked at Grimwulf and was once again amazed at the young man's stamina. Calm and settled, he looked as if he could run all night. 'Get yourself along to the next ridge. I want you to tell Eadward and his lads what I am about to do.'

Hemming shifted again as his boot sank into the mud and the dark waters pooled around it. 'Here they come,' he whispered. 'Everybody; as still and quiet as a mouse.' As the men of Eofer's hearth troop settled back into the mulch of the forest floor, the duguth watched as the light from the brand danced and flickered through the latticework of branches which hid the pathway from view. Within moments the blood red point of light flamed as the leading Dane neared the foot of the slope, and Hemming lowered his gaze to preserve his night vision as the war band jogged into view. The daylight was little more than a pale memory in the western sky now, the valley floor as dark as a berry as the Danes skipped across the large rocks which men long since dead had rolled into the watercourse at the crossing place. As the last of the *fiend* gained the northern bank, Hemming rose to his feet and breathed an order. 'They are through. Let's get going.'

As the others hauled themselves gratefully out of the muck, they gripped spears and swords a little tighter and funnelled carefully in his wake. Within moments they had left the cover of the fallen tree which had hidden them from view, scrambling along the bank as fast as they dare as they sought to balance the need for speed and stealth. Gaining the track, Hemming exhaled with relief as he saw that his plan was working as well had he had dared hope. Ahead the Danes were scaling the valley side, moving forward to meet their wyrd within a slowly receding circle of light. The moment had been judged to perfection, and Hemming led his lord's hearth troop onto firmer ground and set off in pursuit. With the comforting knowledge that help would arrive within moments, Eadward would lead his men in a downhill charge as soon as the Danes drew near, abandoning the height advantage afforded by the ridge line in the knowledge that the enemy would be trapped between them. Unable to stand off and await the arrival of their brothers, the Danes would be forced to fight the unequal battle, a fight they were sure to lose.

Spearhafoc moved to his side, bow held low in her left hand while her right closed around the arrows in the quiver as they followed on as silently as ten heavily armed warriors were able. Suddenly a shout went up and Hemming raised his hand to halt the column as it became obvious that Eadward's shield wall had appeared at the crest of the rise, blocking the way ahead for the Danish war party. As the brand was tossed forward onto the roadway by an unseen hand to light the place of slaughter, Hemming placed his hand onto Spearhafoc's shoulder and lowered his head to speak. 'Remember,' he said as the youth selected an arrow from her quiver and tested the fletching with the pad of a thumb. 'Wait until the fighting starts and then pick them off one at a time.' He gave her shoulder a squeeze of encouragement. 'Remember the signal. Once they are in contact with Eadward and his lads, I doubt that they will even notice that you are attacking them from the rear until our own spears are among them.' The shield maiden gave a curt nod that she understood, walking forward up the hillside as she nocked the first arrow and raised the bow before her.

Osbeorn and Octa moved to his side as Hemming followed on and the youth packed the pathway behind them. The trail narrowed as it approached the valley floor but, up ahead, Hemming could see that it widened out a few paces as it approached the crest. 'Finn, Caed,' he spoke over his shoulder. 'Move to the wings as soon as the path widens. We can't be outflanked here.' As their shields swung forward the sound of fighting rolled down to them from above, and Hemming thanked the gods that he had stopped the men from discarding the heavy boards, despite the temptation on the long haul north. He had known all along that this moment had to come, and now they were set. At last surprise and numbers were with the English, they would smash their way through and open up an insurmountable gap between themselves and their pursuers.

A soft grunt came from the shadows and the duguth lifted his gaze, watching as the first of Spearhafoc's shafts sped through the darkness to take a Dane, and he nodded appreciatively as he saw the man clutch at his lower back and spin away from the fight. By aiming low, the youth was ensuring that the Danes would be unaware of the danger stalking them from their rear until the last possible moment. Not only would the sight of a bloody shaft emerging from the mouth of a hearth mate alert even the most heavily pressed warrior to their presence, but any shafts which missed their intended victim would be a danger to their English companions and seen by all as it flashed through the glow from the guttering torch. The next arrow was already speeding on its way, followed quickly by another. Hemming knew that Spearhafoc had a solitary shaft remaining which had any hope of hitting the enemy and he pushed on as the path began to widen and the two youth came forward to take their places at the ends of the line. The final arrow sped away into the gloom, and the woman skipped aside as the heavily armed shield hedge broke into a run.

Four of the Danes had fallen to the shafts, and Hemming watched as a fifth and then a sixth fell to the blades of Eadward's men. The pale oval of a face turned his way, the dark circle which appeared within it marking the moment when the Danes realised that their fate was to die here, and Hemming roared his battle cry to Woden and slammed into the enemy. His sword slashed in the night and the blade bit deeply into the shoulder of a man who fell aside as other blades hacked and chopped around him. Within a very few moments the killing was done, and Hemming's teeth showed white as he exchanged a smile of victory with the *scipthegn* and their men moved among the bodies which littered the path, stabbing down mercilessly at any who still showed signs of life.

Spearhafoc was up and moving among them, tugging each arrow from its victim, wiping the blood and gore from the tip before replacing the arrow into her quiver. Hemming saw Grimwulf among Eadward's men and gave him a hug as the English celebrated their easy victory over the men who had chased them over sea and land for the good part of a week. 'Look around you,' he smiled at the beaming youth. 'This victory belongs to you.'

Eadward came across as the men of the reunited war bands rifled the dead for food and valuables. 'The victory belongs to Grimwulf Harefoot here and his quick thinking duguth,' he said with a smile. They laughed at the description, a nickname which the ætheling, Icel, had bestowed on the youth after he had beaten him in a footrace the previous year. Hemming quietened as he thought back to that day outside Eofer's hall. So much had happened in the few months since that happy day. The war on Juteland and the defeat and capture of King Osea; the raids against the Danes and the loss of his thegn. Only the Dane, Hrothmund, looked ill at ease at the slaughter of his countrymen, and Hemming found to his surprise that he felt the first stab of pity at the young man's plight. Of all the people on the path, he had lost the most during the upheaval of the past few days. His world had been turned upside down by the events in Daneland, as far as they knew his entire family had fallen under the new king's blade. The big duguth had struggled against the growing realisation, but the truth was he wasn't a bad lad for a Dane.

Hemming pursed his lips as the celebrations swirled around him, throwing a look across to the West. Eofer would be in Daneland now, a prisoner with a short and gloomy future as the English army of King Eomær ravaged the land. He had to rescue his lord and soon, he had thought of little else as they had pounded the road north. Turning away with a heavy heart, Hemming stooped to retrieve the brand which lay spluttering in its own death throes on the soggy path. Cupping the embers with a hand he gently blew them back into life as he allowed himself a final smile of self-congratulation at the victory, before forming the men into a line and resuming the trudge north.

TEN

Despite the hart flag which snapped at the mast head, the Danish guard ships arrowed in as Starkad's dragon rounded the final nib of land and approached the entrance to the great sound. Splitting up they moved apart, their sails taut and full in the following wind, sweeping out to either side as they doubled up on the incoming vessel.

Starkad threw Eofer a look of pity. 'You did get your chance, it's too late to change your mind now.'

The Englishman shrugged as a passage from a long forgotten verse came into his mind, and he spoke as the Danish shipmaster hailed them across the swell:

'Wyrd often spares the man unmarked by death if his courage holds.'

Starkad looked downcast, and Eofer was surprised to hear the sadness in his words as he replied with a verse of his own:

'As the eagle who comes to the ocean shore,
sniffs and hangs her head,
dumbfounded is he who finds at the thing
no supporters to plead his case.'

The big man laid a hand on Eofer's shoulder as he paced the steering platform, cupping his hands to his mouth as his reply to the challenge carried the gap. To his surprise the mysterious volva sidled across, smearing the last of the unction onto his wound. 'Stay strong, Engle,' she said, before adding gleefully as excitement sparkled in her eyes. 'The day is not so far off when you will dance with the wolf.' He blinked as his mind tried to make sense of the prediction as she moved away, throwing him a look of amusement as she went. A cry brought him back, and Eofer watched the guard ships as crewmen rushed forward to pull the belaying pins, spilling the wind from the sails as oars slid proud of thole-pins to bite the waves. As the big woollen sheets were brailed up, the dragon ships pirouetted on their keels and took up station on their charge. Aware now that the new arrival carried none other than the man who had so recently burned the king's hall, Eofer gave a fatalistic snort as the rowers snatched every chance to look his way. It was, he reflected proudly, a measure of his reputation, and he leaned back and smiled as he recalled a saying of the High One:

Cattle die, kinsmen die,
the self must also die;
I know one thing which never dies:
the reputation of each dead man.

Unable to tack now, Starkad's crew had shortened their own sail, the long pinewood oars sliding proud of the hull as the steersman pointed her prow towards the sound. Soon they had shot the gap, and as the sentinels sheared away to resume their watch on the beleaguered kingdom, the shipmaster of one caught the Englishman's eye, grinning gleefully as he drew a forefinger across his throat.

Eofer took advantage of his final moments of freedom as the longship entered the bay and the full power of the Danish kingdom spread out before them. It was the same bay which they had entered the previous winter, and he smiled as he recalled the little *Fælcen* running down the darkened fjord, her knife-sharp bows carving the waters as she raced down to keep her appointment with fate.

Starkad was right, he would find no supporters to plead his case at any *Thing* here. Maybe, he snorted ironically, he should have taken up the man's offer and become a raider, just another sword for hire; maybe he should have sailed north after all.

'Well, well, well, what have we here?' A great smile of joy spread across the Dane's face as the warrior shoved Eofer forward.

'Another Engle for your motley crew, Ulf. This one is a lord.'

Ulf's grin widened. 'So I see!'

Stripped of his armour, weaponry and arm rings it was still plain to any that the person who stood before them was a man of some importance. Taller than most and with the build to match, Eofer's shoulder length hair and neatly trimmed beard would mark him out as an elite warrior in any company.

'That's not all,' the escort added with an unmistakable hint of glee. 'This is the bastard who led the attack on Heorot last Yule.'

Ulf's eyes widened and Eofer watched with a sinking heart as he saw a look of malicious joy come into them.

'And sent men to burn my lord's barn, here in Hroar's Kilde,' he spat in reply. Fumbling inside his shirt the man whipped out his hammer amulet and gave it a kiss. 'Thank you Thunor,' he said, 'for answering our prayers.'

Ulf walked across to a table, taking up a cudgel as Eofer braced for the strike. To his surprise the first guard stepped between them, clasping the man by the wrist as he prepared to swing. 'The guda want them all unharmed, you know that Ulf. If you must be a fool, you can wait until I have left. I want no part of upsetting gods or priests.'

Ulf indicated a nearby stockade with a jerk of his head. 'Over there if you don't mind lord,' he said with a mocking smile. 'There's plenty of room for you.' Eofer winced as the club was rammed into his lower back, but he kept his posture upright as he made his way towards the wooden pen. 'Don't worry, Swain,' Ulf called a parting remark over his shoulder as they walked, 'I know just where to hit them to cause the maximum pain without leaving any marks.' A pair of grinning spearmen flanked the entrance to the compound, and one reached out to push the gate wide as Ulf returned the smile; 'isn't that right lads?' Eofer stumbled through the gate as the guards aimed a kick. One of the pair flicked out the butt of his spear in an effort to upend the Engle, but Eofer was half expecting it and he managed to kick the shaft aside as he stumbled through into the compound.

As the gate clattered shut behind him a group of men came forward, shamefaced and hesitant. 'It saddens me to see you in such a place, lord,' the leader said sorrowfully.

Eofer looked around him. There were half a dozen men in the compound, ceorls, warriors for the working day.

The man who had spoken however was obviously more of a fighter, broad and muscular, the telltale scars which crisscrossed his forearms telling the tale of a lifetime of spear work. Eofer snorted in reply. 'It would seem that we have both fallen a long way.'

Eofer pinned the men with a look as he judged his new companions' worth. Most were unable to meet his gaze, but a few were made of sterner stuff and he memorised their faces and noted their response as he spoke. His father had once told him that you never discovered a man's real worth until you have seen how he responded to a setback or crisis. Their current situation certainly qualified as that, he thought with a snort of amusement. 'We are all in the shit, it would seem. We will talk later; perhaps we can work together to find our way out again.'

As the men moved away, Eofer's head continued to take in his surroundings. The corral was isolated from the nearby buildings of the town, wide open spaces, dust strewn, the deep ruts which cut the surface testament to the heavy wagons which constantly passed by. He looked back and was unsurprised to see the amusement writ large on his new companion's face. It was obvious that Eofer was already planning his escape, and the Englishman's chin stabbed out to left and right as he described their surroundings to the newcomer. 'It is twenty paces from here to the nearest cover, lord. That hall,' he pointed out one of the larger buildings with a jerk of his head, 'is the hall of a man called Ubba silk beard, although from what I can gather, he seems to have gone missing along with most of his war band.

Eofer laughed for the first time in days at the revelation and the man raised a brow in question. 'I have met this

Ubba and I know where he is,' he explained with a look of triumph. He pumped a fist, sure now that Hemming and Eadward must have got away at the river and were still leading the Danish huscarls away from the scene of the fighting in Daneland; his heart soared as he knew now with certainty that his own sacrifice had been worthwhile. With any luck it would be some time before they returned, time he could use to affect his own escape.

'There are still a good number of warriors left in the town though,' the warrior continued when it became plain that it was all the information that Eofer was about to divulge, 'and not only the old or injured.' He shot Eofer a grin. 'It seems that the town and anchorage were attacked last year, lord. They don't want it to happen again. There are two guards on the gate, as you know, but also two pairs which walk the perimeter of the clearing night and day. It used to be only a single guard but they upped the numbers this morning. Seeing you here, I now know why. They are relieved every hour so they are always nice and alert, but that's not the worst of it.' The man spat in the direction of a small crate which stood beside the stairs to Ubba's hall. 'That prick Ulf has got a pet which makes him look like a fluffy bunny.' Eofer looked across and saw for the first time that a heavy chain led from the dark interior of the box to a thick oak stake. 'Its name is Freki. It is the name of one of Woden's wolves, the one which we call Greedy. All head and teeth he is.' He spat again; 'a proper bastard.'

Eofer nodded as he listened. The warrior, despite the fact that he had allowed his honour to be sullied by being taken alive by the Danes, had obviously been planning an escape and had been astute enough to recognise the same thoughts in the new arrival. Besides, Eofer knew, it was unfair to judge the man until he learned the story of his capture. He was after all in the same position himself. He looked the man in the face and was pleased to see that his gaze held firm. 'You seem to know me?'

'Yes, lord,' the man replied. 'I was at the *symbel* when you gave your speech before the Allfather.'

Eofer raised his brow in question, and he was pleased to see that his new companion was sharp witted enough to supply the answer he sought. 'I am Swinna lord, a duguth. Æmma of Hereford was my own lord.' He cleared his throat before he was able to continue as his emotions got the better of him for the first time. 'Unfortunately the gods decided that it would be a great joke to play that I should survive while my hearth companions travelled on without me.'

A whistle from beyond the paling drew their gaze in time to see several loaves come sailing over the top of the fence. Eofer looked across as a movement caught his eye and Ulf's dog emerged from the shadows. He had seen the dogs which were called mastiffs before, down in the South, but he never ceased to be amazed at the ferocious mien of the breed. He had heard a tale told by a trader in Britannia that the Franks released such dogs as they charged home against Saxon shield walls, and he grimaced as he imagined the carnage a dozen or more of the beasts like the one now before him could achieve before they were cut down. With the head and neck of a bull, the dog was covered by a coat of coarse dark hair from the tip of its tail to the end of a fight scarred muzzle. Within it twin points, as dark as berries and hard as any stone, stared at the Englishmen with all the malicious intent of the goddess Hel herself.

The guard tossed the final loaf over the fence and shot them a look of distaste as he bent to retrieve a bowl of meaty stew. 'Meat for Freki, mangy old bread for Engles.' he spat into the dust as the dog wagged its tail and trotted across. 'Even bread is too good for cowards who allow themselves to be taken.'

Both Englishmen's hands went instinctively to the place where their sword hilt would usually be in response to the insult, and the guard looked back with a frown as their laughter cut the air. Eofer sighed. 'Come on,' he said, 'I will be *hlaford*.' The ceorls had gathered up the bread and Eofer shared the loaves equally among them as a good loaf lord should. Despite the Dane's words, Eofer was surprised to discover that the loaves were still warm from the oven, and he eagerly broke the crust apart to get at the soft inner bread as the delicious smell made him realise just how hungry he was. The Englishmen rested their backs against the fencing as they ate, and Eofer noticed for the first time that Swinna was carrying a leg wound as the duguth lowered himself gingerly to the earth: 'sword work?'

'A spear thrust, lord. High up too,' he added with a look. 'Nearly cost me my bollocks!'

Swinna carefully peeled a torn flap from the inside of his trews aside to expose the wound, wincing as strips of skin came away with the wool. The men exchanged a look as the smell of rotting flesh escaped the suppurating gash. Swinna shrugged. 'I was thinking of escape when I first got here, just like you lord. Then this started getting worse.' He gave a fatalistic shrug. 'All I want now is the chance to die with my hand on a sword hilt so that I can rejoin Æmma and the lads. They should have finished me off with my hearth mates, but they kept me alive for some reason.'

Eofer looked along the fence. The others were eating heartily, without any of the misgivings which the duo were experiencing at their situation. He broke another piece from the loaf as he thought. 'Well, whatever they have in mind,' he said finally, 'I think that it will happen soon. With that leg, you are not going to last long.'

Swinna dropped the legging back into place, and Eofer's lips tightened in sympathy as he heard the short gasp of pain escape his new friend's lips. Across the clearing Freki had bolted his food and stood staring at the English prisoners, the great pink expanse of his tongue sweeping back and forth as it removed every morsel from its fleshy jowls. 'Do you think that it wants to eat us?' Eofer asked as the dog sniffed the air. Swinna let out a short laugh. 'I am bloody sure that it does. When we arrived, Ulf took a piece of clothing from each man and gave it to the dog.' He shook his head. 'They didn't last long, tore them all to pieces he did. He knows our scent, if he could get close enough we would all go the same way as our shirts, make no mistake.' He shifted as he sought to take the weight off of his injured thigh, settling back with a frown. 'Do you mind if I ask how you came to be here, lord?'

Eofer sensed the hesitation in Swinna's voice and he moved to allay his fears. Ubba silk beard's weeklong absence meant that Thrush and Eadward must have managed to get the Danish prince to safety. His personal sacrifice at the river crossing had played a large part in that success and he was proud of the ongoing disruption and uncertainty that it was causing the new king and his subjects. He had handed his own king and folk a bloodless but significant victory at the very moment of greatest need. Eofer cast a glance across his shoulder to ensure that there were no Danes within hearing distance and leaned in closer. 'I was knocked unconscious at a river crossing in Scania.' Swinna's brow creased in shock that an English war band could have been operating so far from home, especially given the fact that the invasion they were calling the war of fire and steel had just been launched. Eofer saw his surprise and he chuckled happily. 'We are the reason that Ubba silk beard and his men are missing.' His brow crinkled as a thought came to him. 'Does the army know that King Hrothgar is dead?' Swinna nodded. 'We found out the first day that we landed. The Danes which we have taken have all been cocky buggers who seem to have a lot of faith in this new king, Hrothulf. They say that he was the one responsible for the defeat of the Heathobeard attack last year, leading the fightback after old Hrothgar was injured.'

Eofer pulled at his beard as he listened before continuing with his own story. 'Hrothulf murdered his uncle the king and one of his cousins, but the other one got away. We managed to rescue him, but the new king's men, led by this Ubba silk beard, were hot on his heels. Luckily for us we just managed to make the coast of Scania before we were overtaken, and we led four shiploads of Danish huscarls off into the forest. I was overpowered defending a river crossing but all the others must have got away.' He sat back again with a self-satisfied smirk. 'It's the reason why the Danes are reluctant to attack our army. A good number of their best troops are chasing shadows in the backwoods, huscarls, the best of the best. Men who don't even know of our invasion and are in no great hurry to return empty handed.'

'No wonder Ulf is such a foul tempered arse,' Swinna laughed. 'His lord is off gods know where while he babysits prisoners and feeds the dog.' They shared a laugh as it became obvious that Eofer and his men were largely responsible for Ulf's bad temper. Eofer dug Swinna in the ribs as the laughter trailed away. 'You said that you wished to travel on to Valhall,' he said as the smile left his face. 'How do you feel about taking that journey tonight?'

ELEVEN

'Suit yourself, although I tend to find that most people prefer to eat them. Mind you, you can always go and join them if you like *that* sort of thing.' Hemming laughed along with the rest and took another gulp from his ale cup as Ena bustled off with the empties. Imma Gold leaned in and cried into his hearth mate's ear as another of the warriors, hairless, earless, noseless, his features scorched and blackened by the heat of the flames, bent forward, spreading his arse cheeks with a maniacal expression as he prepared to receive another pickled egg. 'The Danes are here.'

Hemming choked on his ale, showering the table as the burnt man, a Jute by the looks of his smoke sooted brooch, grimaced with pain. Imma shook his shoulder to gain his attention; 'Thrush, the Danes are here.' He looked back, screwing his face up in confusion as he realised that something was not quite right; his best friend was dead, how could he be in the Barley Mow? Come to that, how could *he* be in the Barley Mow? Imma Gold was standing over him, his blond hair falling forward as he threw his old friend a warm smile and spoke again. 'The Danes are here, mate. Come on, drag your arse up off the floor.'

Another shake, harder this time, and a face swam into Hemming's view as he attempted to focus. 'All right Goldy, I am coming,' he murmured. 'This is funny. Just one more egg.'

The hand patted his shoulder and Hemming recognised the sadness in his voice as Octa replied. 'If only Goldy were here, and Eofer; Eadward sent one of his lads down from the hall to tell you that the Danes have reached the town.'

As his consciousness came back with a rush, the duguth sat bolt upright and instinctively checked that his sword was to hand. He nodded at his hearth companion, wincing as he dug out a sharp stalk of hay from the neck of his shirt. 'I will be there. Get the others up.' As Octa moved away, Hemming hauled himself to his feet and attached his sword scabbard to his baldric. A quick splash of water from the pail by the door and he was ready to face the foe who had chased them clear across Scania.

Osbeorn was already waiting and he threw him a look: 'helms?'

Hemming nodded as the dark twins moved around them, brushing the last of the hay from backs and trews. The boys had already spent the last part of the night polishing the duguth's silver and steel: helms, buckles, arm rings. Now they shone like ice, and Hemming indicated that they finally grab some well deserved rest as the others dragged themselves wearily to their feet and saw to their own weapons.

The pair exchanged a nod and a look. 'Let's go.'

Hauling the big door inwards Hemming screwed up his face as the full light of morning hit him but he squared his shoulders and raised his chin, aware that unseen eyes would be apprising him every step of the way. The hall of the local thegn lay at the highest point of Skansen, and the English pair fixed their gaze upon the boar heads which decorated its gable end as they navigated their way towards it.

Like most towns in the North, the Geat settlement had no enclosing defensive works and no watch towers studded its perimeter, but it was far from indefensible. Hemming studied the layout of the town as they walked on with the practised eye of an attacker. What at first looked little more than a haphazard collection of huts, halls and barns, to the experienced eye resolved itself into a maze of blind alleyways, dead ends and killing grounds. Any hostile army would quickly be forced to split apart as it moved towards the centre of the town to avoid bunching, dissipating the energy of its attack and making an organised assault on the heart of the settlement almost impossible.

Hemming allowed himself a small smile of satisfaction as he walked. The crushing victory over the Danish outlier had transformed the English situation. Bolstered by the bloodletting the war band had picked up the pace, jogging into the night behind the flames of the dead men's torch. With the bodies of their attackers carefully hidden the Engles had reasoned that, even if the chasing Danes came within view of the flickering light, they would assume that none but their own men would risk travelling beneath the revealing glow.

As the darkness of full night had moved in to envelop the little band the first signs of the hand of man began to appear. First a side path snaked away into the gloom, followed a little later by the distant lights of a farm as the greenwood began to pull back to reveal gently undulating meadows and well tended fields. Spurred on by the realisation that the end to their weeklong journey was in sight, they had somehow found the energy to raise a small cheer as the lights of the town glimmered into view.

Once they had revealed themselves as Engles to the startled old veteran charged with guarding the entrance to the settlement, the welcome had been warm. A longstanding friendship existed between the two nations. Eofer was kin to the Geat ruling family, and the fact that the very men who had rescued King Heardred and his warriors from a Frankish war fleet the previous summer had pitched up unexpectedly among them had swept the town like wildfire. That the local thegn, Gudmund, and his levy had fought alongside the men of Eofer's war band in the battles outside Skovde and at Ravenswood a couple of summers previously, had only served to heighten their welcome. Prince Hrothmund had requested that he be taken under the protection of King Heardred of the Geats, and, his uncle's men hot on their heels, he had been quickly supplied with a horse and escort and despatched to the king's fortress at distant Miklaborg.

A loud hiss came from his right and Hemming glanced across as a sword smith's tongs withdrew a tongue of twisted iron rods from a large tub. Stripped to the waist despite the chill of the spring morning, the craftsman moved the piece this way and that as he judged his handiwork, the muscled body which was a prerequisite of his trade glistening from the heat of the forge. Sensing their eyes upon him the smith looked up, throwing the English pair a gap-toothed smile and a friendly nod, before turning and disappearing back into the shadows.

'Friendly lot,' Osbeorn sniffed.

Hemming snorted. 'Smiths always are; warriors are good customers.'

They shared a chuckle as women and children began to gather at the doorways, eager to weigh-up these foreign warriors, comparing them to their own men in size and splendour.

Geatish warriors began to appear in groups of twos and threes as they scaled the rise. The welcome here was less enthusiastic despite the long standing alliance. If the talks which were about to take place within the hall failed fighting was sure to follow, and they harboured no illusions as to who the victors would be. A powerful force of Danish huscarls, some of the best men that the kingdom possessed, had unexpectedly appeared in their midsts. Although riders had been roused from their slumber and dispatched immediately to summon the levy, it would be some time yet until reinforcements arrived in any numbers. Hemming noted the stands of throwing spears which were being stacked at choke points within the town as he walked and felt an awkward tug at his conscience. He hoped that Gudmund was a skilled negotiator, otherwise the English could very well have brought death and destruction down upon the friendly people here.

With a final switchback the path opened out before the hall, depositing the Englishmen within a circular courtyard. Irregular stones had been set into the floor here to lay the dust of summer and keep the cloying mud which plagued all settlements, large and small, at other times of the year at least manageable. Hemming ran his eyes along the hall of the thegn of Skansen as the pair approached the doorway. It was, he decided a little to his surprise, a handsome hall. A stout frame of oak, the posts and beams weathered a silvery grey, carried a recently thatched roof of honey-coloured reed. Washed panels of lime plaster filled the framework, flushed pink in the slanting light of the early morning sun.

Geat spearmen flanked the entrance, their size and bearing a match for the Engles who now paced towards them. A steward came forward to usher them inside and Hemming removed his helm, cradling it in the crook of his arm as a thrall took their swords into safekeeping. The Geat led the pair into the hall with a smile, and Hemming risked a quick look to either side, instinctively probing the shadows despite his trust in their host. The entrance lay midway along the long wall of the hall and sturdy beams of oak, chased and carved with tales of the gods, marched away to left and right. Benches lined the walls, with several fire-pits smouldering dully between them, the brume drifting up to the smoke hole high above in the light airs which the heat of the flames sucked in through the open doorway.

Thegn Gudmund sat on his gift-stool facing the entrance flanked by further spearmen, and Hemming blinked in surprise that the young Geat would act in such a high-handed manner to greet men, some of which would likely consider themselves his social equals. Eadward, the English thegn stood to one side, and he dipped his head in recognition as Hemming and Osbeorn moved to his side.

Three Danes, huscarls dressed for battle in mail and war shirt, their arms heavy with rings of gold and silver, glared at the Engles across the rush strewn floor as they took their place, and Hemming could not resist throwing their leader who he now recognised to be the same Ubba silk beard who had trapped them at the beach in Daneland, a sly wink. To his credit the big Dane lowered his gaze as he sought to suppress a smile, and Hemming gave a soft snort as Gudmund began to speak.

'Welcome to Geatland,' he began brightly. 'We seem to have become unwilling hosts to a small disagreement.' He turned his smile on Ubba. 'May I ask why there are armed Danish huscarls tramping across my lord's lands?'

Hemming watched with interest as Ubba pursed his lip and formed his reply. It was obvious to all who the Geats regarded as the hostile force. It was equally clear that the Danes, at least until the men in the country thereabouts flocked to the war banner, had numbers on their side. Plainly their quarry had escaped them, but the desire to raze the town, if only to assuage their sense of frustration, must have been overwhelming.

Ubba shifted the grim helm which he held at his side, his hand straying across to stroke the boar which crowned it as he made to reply. The action had carried a clear threat, betraying his anger as he cleared his throat and spoke. 'We were unaware that we had entered the lands of King Heardred, please accept our apologies,' he answered diplomatically. Nodding his head towards the English he continued. 'We were in pursuit of a shipload of vikings who had been raiding our coastal districts for a week or more. The pirates helped a fugitive escape, a pretender to the king helm of Daneland. King Hrothulf would act very favourably towards any nation which returned this man to his homeland and, I am sure,' he added with a look, 'be open handed in his generosity towards any man who unlocked his own store of wisdom to enable that happy situation to come about.'

Gudmund's shoulders slumped and his face took on the pained expression of a man who had been denied a fortune by fate. It was clear to the Englishmen that the negotiations were little more than a farce, a false display for the sake of the accepted code of behaviour in such situations. The deadpan look which crossed Ubba's features and the anger which flared in the huscarl's eyes, told them all that the Danes now realised this too as the Geat replied. 'Alas, the man you seek is no longer here. He rode north several hours ago and should be past Geatwic, well on his way to the hall of King Heardred at Miklaborg by now.' Gudmund raised his brow with such a sense of innocence that Hemming winced, hoping that the man had the sense not to push the Danes too far. 'You will have to forgive we country folk, we are often left in the dark,' he smiled. 'But who is this King Hrothulf you speak of? The only man by that name known to us is a gangly nephew of your king, Hrothgar.'

As Ubba's expression darkened, Hemming was relieved to see that Eadward shared his misgivings at the turn the conversation was taking. If they could send the Danes on their way without bloodshed they would, quite literally, be out of the woods. Dishonour proud men and this day could still turn very nasty, very quickly. As Ubba's eyes widened and his nostrils flared, the *scipthegn* pulled a gold ring from his arm and took a pace forward. 'Unfortunately we met a handful of men on the path. It was dark,' he offered, 'and we took them for wolf heads. It was only after we had fought that we knew them to be Danish huscarls.' He held the ring towards Ubba. 'I offer this as wergild for the killings in good faith, and I hope that he will remember that we paid handsome compensation the next time that he sees my good friend Eofer king's bane.'

Hemming watched Ubba for the slightest sign that Eofer yet lived, and his heart leapt as the Dane considered the offer without any hint that his lord had fallen at the crossing.

The Danish leader hesitated, but Hemming caught the man's eye and was relieved to see the realisation there that he was being offered a way out of the situation with honour. As he watched he recognised the moment when Ubba buried his anger, and the desire to leave this place overcame the temptation to visit the home of the upstart Geatish thegn with fire and sword. Ubba stepped forward, took the arm ring from Eadward and slipped it on his own arm with a nod of recognition. Turning to Gudmund the Dane spoke with the voice of a man clearly suppressing his emotions, and Hemming fought down a smile at the thinly hidden barb the Dane's reply contained. 'We thank you for your hospitality, even the rustic ways of countryfolk are welcome after a week in the wildwood, but we must away to the South as soon as we can buy horses to carry us.'

Gudmund held out his hands apologetically. 'Alas, all of our horses went with the riders who accompanied your countryman north or are scouring the countryside raising the levy.'

Ubba frowned. 'A ship then, from the coast? We carry enough silver to pay handsomely.'

'Again, we have only fishing boats nearby. I am sure that the fishermen would take your silver but it would hardly be fitting for the king's huscarls to return to Daneland smelling like a week old herring.'

Ubba lowered his voice to a growl. 'It is a chance that I am willing to take, lord. I lead violent men,' he added with menace. 'We could sit at a wedding feast smelling like ox shit and everyone would laugh at our jokes and ask us to dance.'

Gudmund shrugged. 'I am sorry. At another time of the year if may have been possible, but springtime? The winter supplies are all but exhausted; the meats are long since eaten in many households and the barley bins a scoop or two from the bottom. I am sure that you understand a thegn's duty to his people. They need the fish those boats bring in to survive until the first harvest is gathered safely in. Besides,' he replied, as his voice took on a steel-edged tone and he added a menacing glare of his own. 'The men who accompanied your prince to Miklaborg should by now have explained to King Heardred that the very same Danes who assaulted his kinsman and took him prisoner have had the misfortune to fall into his lap, so to speak.'

Ubba glared as his patience finally snapped. He made to move but the spearmen lowered their weapons and a low growl came from the foot of the dais as a wolfhound, its shaggy grey fur bristling like the crest on a boar helm raised itself, its lips drawn back into a warning scowl. The big Dane snorted and the corners of his lips turned up into a mocking smile. 'Congratulations Geat,' he snarled. 'You have made a powerful enemy.' He flicked a look at the Engles. 'Yes, your eorle lives, he was taken to Daneland where he will pay a heavy price for the burning of Heorot.' As Hemming and Osbeorn exchanged a smile at the confirmation that Eofer was alive, Ubba threw the Geatish thegn a look of contempt. 'We have unfinished business in the West, after which I am sure that my king will wish to repay you for your generous and helpful actions here today.'

Ubba dipped his head briefly and swept from the hall closely followed by his companions, snatching his weapons up as he went. The dog had sensed the difference in his master's attitude between the opposing groups and he loped across to nuzzle Hemming's outstretched hand.

Gudmund gave a shrug of indifference as the Danes disappeared from view. 'It would seem that I have made enemies of violent men,' he smiled. 'And all before breakfast.'

TWELVE

Battle horns wailed and Hemming and Eadward turned their faces to the North, grins parting beards as the first of the outriders cantered into view. Taking the ford in an arc of silvered spray, the pair watched with glee as the riders put back their heels and galloped towards the town. As the defenders clashed spears against shield rims and called their acclamations the scouts divided, sweeping to both sides of Skansen in thunderous columns of muscle, leather and steel.

Moments later the war horn sounded again, and the people of the town tumbled excitedly from their halls to peer northwards as the head of a mighty war host emerged from the tree line and came on.

Free of the tree cover, Eadward gave his companion a dig in the ribs as the white boar war flag of Geatland was teased out in a cats paw of wind. 'That's a sight I would have liked to have seen a few days ago!' They shared a laugh as Hemming picked out the figure of King Heardred, his steel clad figure gleaming like the Morning Star at the head of the riders. The scouts had completed their encirclement, and the English pair watched as the horsemen rode this way and that, scenting for danger like wolfhounds at the hunt.

The roadway led directly through Skansen and Hemming spoke excitedly as the king approached. 'Come on, let's get down there.'

The town had been steadily filling with armed men all morning as the men of the Geat levy rushed in to bolster the defences, and they crowded the vantage points, yelling themselves hoarse at the sight. The path dog-legged down to the road, and the Engles jogged down as the ground shook and the sound of hoofbeats resounded. As they emerged at the roadside Gudmund came from the southern end of town, the thegn throwing the pair a happy smile which mixed pride with relief. Even if Ubba's force had been outnumbered, they all knew that several shiploads of huscarls would have made short work of an army composed mainly of a rag-tag collection of farmers, fishermen and shepherds if the Danes had chosen attack over ignominious retreat.

The standards were close now as the king approached, the gaudy banners, red, green and blue glimpsed as a flash of colour among the muted browns of the settlement as they flashed past. Suddenly, the tall figure of the king was before them and the trio bent the knee as Heardred curbed his mount and guided the great war horse across. A pair of boots appeared on the ground before him and Hemming felt strong hands grip his shoulders and haul him to his feet. 'Thrush Hemming!' the king exclaimed, as the warriors clustered about their king beamed happily. 'You have brought us new enemies!' He glanced back across his shoulder, and a ripple of laughter swept Heardred's bodyguard as he added a comment with a smirk. 'Just what we needed.'

A far smaller figure threw himself from the back of his horse, and Hemming blinked with surprise as the boy, magnificent in scale armour and boar helm, shot him a question. 'Hemming, your lord is taken, yet you stand before me.' Weohstan fixed him with an accusing stare. 'Explain how that can be?'

King Heardred held out a hand to still his charge, before turning to Eadward and Gudmund. 'On your feet, it's unbecoming for men of worth to grovel in the dirt.' The pair rose and Hemming watched as the warm smile on the king's face fell away to be replaced by the fearful countenance of a king. 'Gudmund, how long have these Danes been gone?'

The thegn pulled himself erect as he replied. 'Three hours, lord.'

'You let them go, despite the fact that they had attacked and taken a kinsman of mine?'

Gudmund cleared his throat before he replied, but the reply was steady when it came nonetheless. 'With the situation in Swedeland and the arrival of our new guests from there, I thought it best to rid your kingdom of them as soon as possible, lord.'

Hemming watched with interest as the king raised his brow in surprise. After sweeping the trio with his gaze, Heardred turned back to the men of his hearth troop: 'Ranulph!'

The big warrior raised his chin. 'Yes, lord?'

'Take two hundred riders and the men from Geatwic. Ensure that these Danes have left my lands.'

'And if they haven't, lord?'

'Kill them.'

As wicked grins spread across the faces of the mounted men and they hauled at the reins and clattered away, Heardred indicated that the trio follow him up to the hall with a jerk of his head. The king strode up the path as they filed in his wake, the look on his face enough to wipe the smiles from any onlookers as they scrambled aside. Weohstan was a pace behind the king, and Hemming's spirits sank a little lower each time that Eofer's son shot him an accusing look over his shoulder. The little group reached the small paved compound, and Heardred pointed to the spearmen flanking the doorway as he approached and snapped out an order. 'You two; clear the hall and then get back to your posts. Nobody is to enter, for any reason.'

The guards blanched and scurried inside as Heardred led them in. Gudmund's own wolfhounds rose in greeting but quickly sensed the mood, slinking away as the king indicated that they all sit. As the thralls and kitchen hands were ushered out by the guards Heardred paced the floor, chewing his lip with impatience until the big doors thudded closed and the unfortunate trio awaited the storm which was so obviously about to break upon them.

The king turned back, the intensity of his gaze pinning them like a fox beneath a hound. 'Gudmund,' he spat. 'Before we look for a rope and a stout bough, let me make sure that I understand what happened here today. You had the men who took my foster-brother within my grasp, but you decided to let them go.'

The mention of the possibility of a hanging had clearly shocked the thegn and the Engles shifted uncomfortably as Gudmund swallowed before replying with less steadiness than before. 'Yes, lord, I did.'

'Prince Hrothmund has told me of the circumstances of Eofer's capture. It is his opinion, one which I share, there was nothing that the men who were there could possibly have done to save him.' Heardred's gaze swept from Weohstan to Hemming and Eadward, and the English pair felt a sense of relief that the young Dane had spoken in their support as the king turned his face back to Eofer's son. 'So, we are in agreement Weohstan, that your countrymen have not forsaken their honour?' The boy's lips tightened into a line, and he gave a curt nod as he was forced to accept his uncle's judgement. 'Good, that's one problem solved then, but that doesn't help you,' he said, returning his gaze to his unfortunate thegn. 'Did it not occur to you that I could have arranged for these men to be exchanged for Eofer?'

Gudmund straightened, and Hemming watched with admiration as the young Geat composed himself. Clearly confident that his decision had been the right one, the man had decided that if he was to fall, he would do so with dignity. 'I felt that it was the best course of action to take to safeguard your kingdom, lord,' he explained as Heardred raised his brow in surprise.

'Oh, you did,' the king gasped. 'Perhaps you could explain a little more fully, so that we could all understand your reasoning?'

Gudmund was clearly warming to the task, and the air of confidence which he had displayed that morning faced by a Danish war band was returning to his voice as he saw that his king was willing to hear him out. 'I reasoned that, although there is a very strong possibility that war with

Daneland will come sooner than we would like, it was to our advantage to delay that clash for as long as possible. When I spoke to this Ubba silk beard and his men, it quickly became apparent that they had no inkling that their homeland had been attacked by the English. If they *had* known, they would not have been asking me if they could hire boats to take them home, they would have taken them and gone, killing the Englishmen here and any Geats who stood in their way.'

Heardred was clearly calming as his thegn continued with his explanation.

'It would only have taken one word out of place, some fool to goad a Dane with this knowledge, for the secret to be out. The whole population here knows about the fighting in Daneland,' Gudmund said as he risked a smile. 'The fishermen down by the sound are out every day, lord. They meet other ships, traders and the like, all the time. There's not much that happens in The Cat Gate that we don't get to hear about down here. By packing them off, back the way they had come as quickly as I could, I reasoned that I could help the English king in his war on our common foe by depriving the Danes of some of their finest warriors for another week or so before they discovered the truth.' Gudmund looked apologetic as he continued. 'We have yet to recover from the losses we incurred in Frisland last summer, lord, and what with the recent developments in Swedeland...' His voice trailed away and Heardred flicked a questioning look at Hemming and Eadward. 'You have been told?'

Gudmund interjected and risked a nervy smile. 'I didn't know how much to tell them, lord. We did have rather a lot to be getting on with.'

King Heardred exhaled and nodded as he began to understand the thegn's line of thought. 'You were right, you acted in the best interests of my kingdom.' He pulled a weary smile as the anger began to drain away. 'I will forego the lynching.'

As the tension lessened and they all began to relax, Heardred rubbed his face wearily before explaining Gudmund's reference to Swedeland to the mystified Englishmen. 'The Danish prince that you have so generously gifted me is not the first to reach my hall looking for protection, I have already extended that help to the Swedish princes Eanmund and Eadgils, the sons of King Ohthere. You are obviously unaware,' he said looking at the Engles, 'that King Ohthere of the Swedes has been assassinated by Danes, apparently acting on behalf of Ohthere's brother Onela who has seized the kingship.

Hemming and Eadward exchanged a look of shock. 'Why would the Danes kill their own king and the king of Swedes at the same time?'

'The machinations of a woman,' Heardred explained. 'Yrse, the wife of Onela and therefore the new queen of Swedes is not only a Dane by birth but the mother of Hrothulf, Daneland's shiny new king. Believe me,' Heardred snorted, 'I know her well. I spent the winter as a guest of the pair a few years ago when I was an exile. Nothing is beyond her.' The young king looked downcast as he exchanged a look with Gudmund. 'It seems that we are becoming ringed by powerful enemies just as our friends move away. I fear dark days await Geatish folk.'

Hemming shaded his eyes from the brilliance of the setting sun, as the little ship was rowed steadily towards them across a sea as smooth as milk. A swirl of gannets plummeted to spear the waters of the sound, rising with their catch in a silvered spout as the raucous calls of their flock filled the air.

It was good to see the little scegth again after so many months, despite the absence of his lord. He looked about as the emotion of the moment threatened to overwhelm him again, inhaling deeply as he fought back the tears. Despite the judgement of the others, it was his responsibility that they were lordless men; he should never have taken to the river before his lord. *Eardwræcca*, a lordless exile, to be wrecked. It was not without reason that men thought it the bitterest word in the English tongue.

'So,' Osbeorn said, 'his cousin is his mother?'

'No,' Hemming sighed with a look of frustration, 'this Queen Yrsa is King Hrothulf's sister.'

'So not his mother, then?'

'Yes, she is, that's the point. King Halga, Hrothulf's father, married her not knowing that she was his daughter.'

'Because of the ravaging of the shepherdess when he was raiding in Saxland?'

'Right. So when the Saxon queen told her the truth out of spite, Yrse left Halga and got herself married off to Onela the Swede, leaving behind her son...' Hemming let the question hang in the air and raised a brow at his friend who was still clearly struggling with the complexities of royal bed hopping.

Osbeorn gave a hesitant reply, obviously still far from certain: 'Hroth...ulf?'

Hemming's face lit up and he stabbed out a finger. 'Yes! So she sits brooding in Swedeland, biding her time, scheming and plotting until her son comes of age, and then, *bang!* Strikes back like an adder.'

Osbeorn beamed. 'Like an adder.'

Hemming settled back with a sigh of relief, but his shoulders began to slump as he recognised the now familiar look of incomprehension cloud his friend's features.

'So, who was the shepherdess?'

The big duguth could sense Sæward's amusement at his side and, desperately seeking an excuse to escape this explanation without end, he raised his head and looked down the ship. 'Edwin and Bassa are at the ham again,' he said with his best false frown. 'It will all be gone soon if they don't leave it alone.' The remark had the desired effect, and Osbeorn was jumping the thwarts before he knew that he had moved. 'Oi, you two; leave that alone and get back to your ropes.'

Hemming turned to the steersman and they exchanged a grin. Sæward was the first to speak, the happiness at the reunion with his hearth mates shining in his eyes. 'The gods know, I have missed you boys. You have to say though,' he added with a frown of his own, 'none of these king-worthy families make it easy for normal folk to follow what's going on. It's all Hroth this and Hroth that, they all sound the same.'

Hemming snorted his agreement, thankful that he was finally free of the subject; he had enough on his mind as it was. Hauling himself to his feet he crossed the steering platform, gripping the wale as he stared out across the wind shredded waves. The shadows were lengthening as the sun dipped, and Hemming allowed his gaze to wander, out past the spear-like outline of the little *Skua's* own mast to the Geat warship which was accompanying them south. It was a furlong off to bæcbord, its monster capped prow rising and falling as it breasted the swell. Eadward grinned and waved from his place at the stern, as the ship's own steersman hauled the steering oar and guided her inshore. Soon they would part company, King Heardred's hand-picked war band adding steel to the English *scipthegn* and his crew as they stormed ashore to recover the *Hwælspere* from Danish captivity. Hemming snorted as he pictured the faces of Ubba and his men when they finally reemerged, travel worn and empty handed from the forest path, and saw their ships burned, the ship guard slaughtered. They would know then, if they had not yet already realised the truth; they had been deceived. The flames of war had come to the land of the Scyldings. Daneland bestrode the sea lanes, both lock and key to the Beltic Sea and the rich trade route to Byzantium and beyond, growing rich on traders' taxes and the tributes collected from lesser folk. Maybe the king's life itself was in danger while they had been chasing shadows in Scania, the kingdom shredded, torn apart like smoke on the wind?

He idly fingered the unfamiliar brooch at his shoulder as he teased apart the weft and weave of his plan, such as it was. Circular like those of the Danes, the central hole and shallow engraving marked it out as distinctively Jutish in origin. The ploy was, he had to admit to himself, a desperate gamble, but these were desperate times.

Sæward was leaning outboard as he wrestled the paddle blade, peering around the billowing sail as the sandy cliffs of Daneland drew a line on the horizon. 'Not long now,' he said as he fixed Hemming with a look. 'Going over the plan?' He threw him a sympathetic smile and Hemming had to laugh, despite the seriousness of the situation. 'So,' Sæward continued, with a mischievous glint in his eye. 'Let me see if I have misunderstood any part of this loki cunning scheme. I drop you and the boys on a remote beach. You then go and find horses and search Daneland,' he said, raising a brow, 'a country undergoing the torments of a rampaging ship army...our ship army... hoping to stumble upon Eofer. Once you do, you spring him from captivity and set off, evading the armed might of the Danish *leding* who are all running around like their arses are on fire because, well,' he shrugged, 'there is a ship army of Engles torching their farms in the South. That done, you head off to meet up with our lads... er...somewhere.' As Hemming pulled a pained expression, Sæward gave him a hearty clap on the shoulder. 'Yeah,' he nodded, 'what could go wrong?'

THIRTEEN

The moon peeked from the clouds, bathing the clearing in its steely light. Eofer shifted, rolling his neck to make it appear to any onlookers that he was waking from sleep. At his side Swinna raised his chin to the sky, speaking softly as the cloud, its edges rimmed silver, moved back to extinguish the glow. 'That should be it for a while,' he breathed, 'there is a big bank of cloud moving across from the West.'

Eofer tensed as the dog shifted in its sleep, the chain which held it grating as it stretched its legs and yet another squeak of wind escaped. Within moments the foul smelling air had wafted across to the pair and Eofer squeezed his eyes together, blenching as he waited for the fug to clear. He risked a murmured question to the man at his side, despite the danger of waking the dog. 'Is that sharp enough yet? Some things deserve a grisly death.'

Swinna's smile flashed as the last sliver of the moon was swallowed by the brume. Raising the shard he flicked the pad of his thumb over the wicked point with a wink and a smile of satisfaction.

Back within the welcome embrace of the shadows, Eofer began to work the paling gently back and forth, loosening the nail a little more with each and every tug. Within a few more twists the wide head of the pin stood proud of the surface, and the thegn worked his fingernails beneath it to wriggle it free. Sure that it was loose enough to remove in a moment, he pushed the nail back a touch to hold the plank in place for now.

A gentle nudge was all that was required for Swinna to shuffle up, his shoulder supporting the beam as Eofer hauled himself to his feet and walked across the compound. One of the patrolling Danes pulled up, lowering his spear, but Eofer ignored the young lad as he loosened his trews, pulled himself free and began to piss. Eofer caught the Dane's eye and raised a brow as he splashed into the dust, and the boy pulled a face, looking away in embarrassment as he resumed his beat.

The plan was working far better than they could ever have hoped. It was obvious that Freki's gut was akin to a brewer's barrel, the dog little more than a fur covered fermentation tank, quickly converting the rich meat and gravy of its earlier meal into a throat gripping miasma. As the sun had left the sky and the population of Hroar's Kilde had drifted away to the halls and ale houses in the town the guards, tiring of the never-ending farts, had moved the dog to the far side of the clearing, staking it out as far away from Ubba's hall as they could. It had also meant that, with the dog chained only feet away from the English prisoners, they had felt able to cut back on patrolling and cluster near the shelter of the hall and its outbuildings. As soon as the dog had drifted off to sleep, Eofer and Swinna had set about loosening the nails which held the lower planking in place on the corral. Now that the first nail was free, Eofer had used the excuse of needing to take a piss to cover up the need to exchange places with his companion.

Eofer settled back against the fence as another soft *phut* broke the air behind them and he stifled a giggle as, despite the seriousness of their situation, Swinna caught his eye and jabbed upward with the sharpened stick. To his delight the nail had already worked loose from the earlier movement of the planking, and Eofer placed a hand on Swinna's shoulder to let him know that all was set. A quick glance at the sky told the thegn that the clouds were still a broiling mass of grey as a steady wind carried them away to the East. He looked back at the ceorls and was met by a line of sullen faces. They had been given the opportunity to join the escape of course, but had elected to stay and trust their fate to the gods. Eofer could hardly find it in his heart to blame them; he had suckled the flames of war from his mother's teat, but he had seen enough of the world to know that the gods rarely troubled themselves with the fate of men.

Swinna had moved into position and the pair exchanged a look. Together the nails were worked free, and the stave was lowered carefully to the floor and slid to one side. A look over his shoulder told him that the guards were still at the hall, firelight reflecting orange from spearpoints and faces as the men there endured the boredom of their watch. Swinna slipped the stake into his hand, and Eofer lowered himself to the ground with a parting smile as he wriggled under the paling.

A deep growl, and a shadow hardened into the shape of powerful shoulders and an ox-like head; a flash of white at the edge of his vision as the dog lunged. Eofer pulled his head aside as the chain snapped taut, the dagger-like teeth brushing his cheek. He could feel Swinna tugging him back but his cloak was snagged, and he felt a rising sense of panic as the dog's fetid breath washed over him. The sound of running feet and the snarling dog was hauled back and replaced by a familiar face: 'going somewhere, lord?'

Strips of light cut the floor like the furrows on a field, motes of dust gliding lazily in the musty air as they drifted down from above. Eofer shifted onto his right side, grimacing in the dark as the blood flow returned to prickle the left. The days had come and gone with agonising slowness, and he chastened himself again for not counting them off. Was it three or four? He thought that it must be more like four now, but in truth time had lost it's meaning. Arching his back he pushed into the corner of the cell and straightened his legs, working his knees until the pain there subsided.

He was in a space not more than two paces by one. By hanging his head or dropping a shoulder he could sit upright, but only just. Wood lined, the musky smell of damp earth was all around, coffin-like, and the thegn gave thanks that so far the spring had been unseasonably dry in the northlands.

Footfalls crossed the floor above, and he looked towards the trapdoor in hope. Even if it was to be the final journey, he would be glad to out in the air one last time. A powerful snort came, and Eofer watched as the blast of air sent a new shroud of dust swirling into the void. He tensed his body as he prepared to move towards the sound but fell back with a sigh. In the early days it had amused him to entice the big mastiff to press his nose against the floor as it sought his scent, waiting patiently for the right moment to thump the wood to draw a growl, but those days were past; he just couldn't be bothered to make the effort anymore. The bolt snapped back, and Eofer squinted into the light as the hatch was levered upright. 'Steady now boy,' came the voice he had grown to hate. 'Not long now and you will be chewing on his innards.'

Despite his thirst, Eofer raised his face and attempted a weak smile. 'Deer flesh today, Ulf?'

The blur hardened into the form of a man as Eofer's eyes grew accustomed to the light, and the thegn recognised the familiar look of contempt twist the Dane's features. 'You think you're funny don't you,' Ulf spat. 'Let's see how hard you laugh when the priests get their hands on you.'

Despite himself, Eofer let the fear which he felt flicker momentarily into his expression and the Dane gave an evil chuckle. 'Oh!' he exclaimed in triumph. 'Found your weak spot at last.' Ulf lowered himself down onto the edge of the opening, drumming his feet against the wooden wall. It was unusual for Eofer's jailer to allow himself to come within reach of his prisoner, but the Engle's brief surge of hope was quickly extinguished as he saw that a ring of spear points hovered menacingly in the background. Ulf had recognised the look for what it was and he laughed. 'Eofer; boar by name, boar by nature eh?' he snorted. Eofer gave him a look of surprise. 'What? You didn't know that I could speak your tongue? Yes, I know that Eofer is the English name for a boar, all of the guards here speak other languages. You would be surprised what prisoners can let slip once they become delirious or,' he mused as he fondled the dog's ears, 'what they will reveal when Frecki here is sinking his fangs into a tender part of their body. Come on,' he said gleefully, 'out you get. I will tell you what's going to happen to you on our way to the wagon.'

Eofer slid across to the hatch and eased himself upright. Frecki let out a low growl as the Engle came into view, straining forward as a thrall tugged him back by a heavy chain and the dog's spittle-flecked lips drew back in a snarl. A dozen spearmen eased away as Eofer hauled himself out onto the floor of the hall and stretched his weary body. Amused at the number of guards the reeve had sent to move him a few feet, Eofer threw them a smile. 'Don't worry lads,' he said. 'I won't give you any trouble.'

To their credit, those Danes who didn't return the smile looked away in embarrassment as Ulf snapped an order to the dog handler. 'Once we have got rid of our guests, feed Frecki and tie him up. Then get down there and clean up,' he added with a nod towards the underground cell, 'it smells like someone's been living in it.'

To Eofer's amusement none of the Danes showed any emotion at the warder's weak joke, and Ulf was sour faced as he led them away. Several warriors were at their ale, and Eofer noticed the sadness in their expressions as he was led towards the big double doors. An enemy of their folk or not, the Englishman suspected that the respect in which the leading warriors of all nations held their foemen was behind it. It did not bode well for his immediate future, and the suspicion was confirmed as the guard turned back with a glint of malice. 'Oh,' he said, as they neared the doorway, 'I almost forgot. I was going to tell you what they intend doing with you, wasn't I? It seems that you are to be honoured. King Hrothulf has got your army pinned down in the south of the country, they never even got close to Hleidre.' The Dane had been looking sidelong for a reaction from Eofer, but the thegn had quickly recovered his senses now that he was back among men and he stifled any show of interest. Struggling to hide his disappointment, the Dane frowned again and went on. 'So much for your great invasion,' he spat. 'All it has done is hasten the fall of Engeln itself. King Hrothulf has gathered his host and is preparing to move against Eomær and his rabble of an army. When he does he will chase them back over the Belts, clear across the Wolds and into the German Sea. Which makes it a shame,' he added with a murderous glint, 'that you won't be there to see it; after depriving the gods of the company of your brother last yule and burning old Hrothgar's hall, the king has decided on a suitable end for you.'

Eofer fought to keep his expression deadpan, but he could see from the glint in the jailer's eyes that the end in question was to be far from pleasant. Sure that he had got his charge's full attention now, Ulf continued in a matter-of-fact voice. 'It's to be a blood-winding for you, king's bane,' he said with glee. Ulf reached across and flicked an imaginary blade the length of Eofer's belly. 'The priests will cut you here and nail your guts to the trunk of a big old ash. Some say that it is the same tree which Woden himself hung upon when he learned the mysteries of *runecræft*, you might have seen the compound in the barrow field outside Hleidre the night you burned the king's hall. From there it all gets a bit grim,' he added

149

with a malicious wink. 'I will let you imagine what that could be.'

They had passed the fire-pits and the doorway loomed ahead. Eofer was close enough now to see that a large crowd had gathered before the hall, the hubbub building as the mob realised that he was on his way. Eofer allowed himself a snort of irony as he realised that the number of guards which had been sent to escort him from the building were for his protection, not to prevent his escape. To his surprise the hall steward handed Gleaming across to one of the guards as they passed, and, despite the fact that his ancestral sword was in the hands of a foeman, the glimmer from the gold backed garnets which decorated the hilt caused his heart to flutter with pride.

Several of the guards pushed their way to the front as they exited the hall, moving out to the sides as the crowd vent their fury. As the harassed spearmen bundled the people back with the shafts of their spears, Ulf chivvied him on. 'Come on,' he said as he snatched at Eofer's sleeve, 'on the back of the cart. The guda demand a sacrifice, and if the crowd kill you first that poor sod might be me.'

Stones began to rain on their heads as the warriors forced a path through to the place where the carter was growing visibly paler by the moment and the crowd, whipped up into a frenzy by the sight of the man who had ordered their town burned surged forward. Unarmed, Eofer bunched his fists, ready to strike out as individuals dodged the cordon and rushed forward to try to land a blow of their own. It would be an easy thing for a man, woman or even child to slip through and plunge a dagger into his side and earn reputation for themselves. The guards were beginning to cast anxious glances across their shoulders as they struggled to contain the mob and Eofer prepared to go down fighting.

He looked ahead and saw the fear etched faces of the other captives lining the cart as a bevy of Danish spearmen clustered about them. He was glad to see that Swinna had survived the last few days, despite the infection in his thigh, and they exchanged a fatalistic look as Eofer drew nearer to the cart. A scrawny Dane found himself thrust in front of the Englishman as the crowd surged forward, and Eofer almost laughed as the curses and hate-filled cries drained away from him as he came face to face with the object of his ire. Before he could retreat back into the anonymity of the mob, Eofer's hand shot forward to grasp the man by the hair. A twist and a tug, and the Dane's face was falling to meet the eorle's upcoming knee with a crack of shattered cartilage and a spurt of blood. As the Dane fell away with a howl of pain the crowd drew back, some of the venom drawn from their sting as they saw that the object of their hate still packed a punch.

The respite was all that the guards needed and Eofer was manhandled onto the lip of the cart and pushed onboard. Immediately the wagon set off, the iron rimmed wheels rolling across the uneven ground like a ship in a swell. A pair of Danish spearmen leapt aboard as the goad flashed overhead, dangling their legs outboard as they swung their weapons to point at the crowd.

Eofer felt helping hands slip beneath his arms, dragging him upright until he rested against the side of the cart. He exchanged a look with Swinna, and the big duguth shook his head and laughed despite the obvious finality of their journey as Eofer grinned and cried above the noise: 'how's your leg?'

FOURTEEN

'Woah!'

The carter guided the horse to one side of the track as it slowed to a halt. Glancing back his mouth drew a line as he shot his charges a look of sympathy. 'This is as far as I take you, boys.' He fingered the pendent at his neck and lowered his voice: 'stay brave.'

As the outriders dismounted, Eofer glanced across to the royal compound one last time. The blackened remains of Heorot had been removed and the beginnings of a new hall, the stout oak posts buttery yellow in their newness, were reaching skywards in their place. Swinna sniffed at his side as the ceorls began to disembark. 'Is that the place, lord?'

A ravening smile came to Eofer then as he recalled one of his greatest victories, old Hrothgar's hall a balefire in the night. The staircase up which he had ridden the horse during the attack was still there, the wooden steps a dark line on a rampart of green, and his mind's eye saw the flash of steel as he once again fought the shield wall single-handedly at its summit.

'Yes,' he answered, the pride obvious in his tone. 'That is the place.'

Slipping from the tailgate his hands were bound tightly behind him as he noticed the group across the brook for the first time. A wicker sided cart had pulled up at the ford, the white oxen yoked to it gleaming in the morning sun as a line of silent figures lined the bank. One look was enough to make even the battle hardened thegn falter in his steps as they stood, stock still, watching the prisoners approach. The guda were dressed completely in black beneath a crow head helm, the long polished beaks lending the men an unspeakable air of malevolence as they glinted in the sun. Guards waited at the exit to the ford, their own dress unremarkable apart from a wolfskin cloak, the snarling head of which encased their own as the great grey pelt hung down to cover their backs.

Swinna was struggling to the end of the wagon, and Eofer was surprised to see the care with which the Danish guards lowered his new friend to the ground. One of the warriors moved forward with a length of rope, and Eofer furrowed his brow as he threw the man a sarcastic look. 'He's not going to run far, is he?'

The Dane glanced at his leader who shook his head, and the man lowered his gaze as he stepped away.

'Here,' Eofer said. 'Rest your hand on my shoulder.'

The ceorls were already being shepherded towards the crossing place by spear wielding Danes, the shambling gait betraying the fear they felt for the men awaiting them across the brook, and Eofer followed on at Swinna's best speed. Soon they had managed to stumble across the narrow waterway, and the pair hauled themselves aboard the wain as the whip cracked overhead. The royal compound was soon lost from view as the wagon entered the barrow field, the grassy domes which guarded the remains of the kings of Daneland awash with the blooms of spring. Butterflies flicked to and fro in the breeze, and the air resounded to the rasp of crickets as each man sat lost in his own thoughts. The kingly mounds gave way to a stand of woodland, the trees, ash, oak, gnarled and twisted by their great age.

And then, with startling suddenness, Eofer realised that they had arrived. As the woodland opened out into a sun filled grove the wagon halted before twin pillars of great height, rune carved, each mighty timber capped by the figure of a raven. Craning his neck to see beyond the wattle fencing, Eofer could make out the telltale glint of sunlight reflecting from water through a screen of alder. One of the ceorls was simpering with fear at his side, the distinctive tang of piss filling the air, and Eofer moved aside with a look of distaste. He cast a look about him, waiting until they were all aware that he wanted their attention before speaking. 'A great man, one of the last of the Romans, once said to me that how we face death is important. It is the final act in our life story.' He looked from one man to the next, fixing each man with his gaze as he drove the message home. 'The gods move in this place, they are watching you now. Brave men are guided to the place of their ancestors, the rest are sent down to Hel's bone hall beneath the earth. Look to your courage lads,' he said with a smile of encouragement. 'Choose your destination carefully, you will be there a long time.' One or two watery smiles greeted his speech, but most of the men still looked too fear struck to comprehend what was about to happen to them. Eofer was about to speak again when wolf snouts appeared at their side and the spearmen ordered them to disembark. The crow priests had gathered at the entrance pillars to the grove, and Eofer once again waited for Swinna to join him as the ceorls moved fearfully away.

Once through the entrance the air felt oppressive, pressing down upon the men as they made their way forwards. At the heart of the grove an ancient ash had been chased into a giant figure, its single eye glowering balefully as the sacrifices were led before it. A wolf, a real one this time, it's once muscular body now hoary and withered with age watched from cover, the amber beads of its eyes flicking over them before it slunk away and was lost from sight.

A bell chimed close by, concentrating his thoughts, and Eofer watched dispassionately as the first of the ceorls were taken to the nearby trees and hauled aloft. As the macabre fruit kicked out the last of their lives in the canopy a priest, tall and wiry, his face whitened by ash, approached the pair. Eofer knew that this must be the chief guda of the grove but, despite the weirdness of the place, he was taken aback as the priest greeted them warmly and an acolyte moved forward to cut Eofer's bindings. 'Welcome to our grove, king's bane,' he chirped happily. His eyes moved from Eofer to Swinna and back again. 'We reserve a special treat for proven warriors, it gives them a chance to enter Woden's hall.' He threw them a wink.'We try to be helpful like that, considerate you might say. Now,' he said with a clap of his hands, 'who would like to go first?'

Eofer and Swinna exchanged a look of incredulity as the ceorls choked out their lives only yards away.

Æmma's duguth was the first to recover his wits, and Eofer gasped in disbelief as the guda threw back his head and laughed at the big man's retort: 'after you.'

'Oh, indeed I envy you,' the priest replied as they stood and gaped, 'I really do. But it is not my wyrd to go to the Allfather quite yet.'

Guttural cries carried to them from the outer compound, shouts and the familiar sound of steel clashing on steel as the wolf warriors celebrated the sacrifices. To Eofer's surprise the noise drew the guda's attention from them, his eyes narrowing as a look of puzzlement briefly flashed across his features. As the guards around them clutched their spears a little tighter and started to drift towards the sounds, the priest pressed on with a shrug. 'Has anyone explained what is expected of you?'

Eofer attempted to remember what Ulf had called the death which awaited him but the surreality of the moment fogged his mind. It was, he decided, like talking to a kindly uncle rather than the man who was about to oversee his killing, a death that was almost certain to prove slow and painful. Finally it came, and the priest beamed with pleasure as he gave the hesitant reply. 'A blood-winding?'

'Yes! Yes, it is!' he exclaimed. 'Come across and we will get things started.'

The Englishmen exchanged a look which confirmed to each other that they had both already grown weary of the priest's joviality. They were about to die in a gruesome fashion; it was not a laughing matter. Swinna turned to Eofer. 'I will go first, my thigh is half eaten away and there is something which I plan to do before I travel on. The three sisters are already poised to cut my life thread.'

He pulled a tight smile. 'Remember though lord. Until the moment some bastard spills your guts, *your* wyrd is not yet set.'

As Eofer narrowed his eyes, puzzled at his friend's words, the priest reached a line of wooden stakes and turned back. 'Here we are, the blood-winding. I will use this knife to slit you up the middle, and then nail your gizzard to the Allfather. All you have to do,' he beamed, 'is weave your way between those posts, feeding your guts out as you go. I shall wait for you at the end with your sword. Touch the hilt and...' he made a slashing move across his throat with his thumb, 'I will finish you off and you are on the way to Valhall.' He grinned again: 'got that?'

Swinna shook his head. 'No,' he said, 'that's not how it is going to happen at all.'

The guda blinked in surprise, but quickly recovered. 'Oh, I assure you,' he replied as the mask of geniality fell away and he regarded the Engle with eyes as hard and cold as ice. 'That is how it always happens.'

Swinna leaned in as his hand dropped to his belt. 'Oh,' he said as he held the priest's stare, 'that might have been how it always happened before. But this time it's going to be different. Have *you* got *that?*'

As the priest's face began to register surprise at his words, the Englishman's hand shot up between them. Taken unawares, Eofer jumped back as Swinna's fist punched into the man's throat. As his head shot back and shouts of alarm filled the air around them Eofer recognised the end of the wooden shaft, reddened now by the blood which gushed from the wound, as the one from the compound back in Hroar's Kilde. They had intended to use it on Ulf's dog, Freki, but Eofer's lips curled into a smile despite the mayhem which surrounded them as he saw that Swinna had found a use for the crude weapon on a very different mad dog. Staggering under the blow the priest looked back at the pair, and Eofer saw the bloody shaft of the weapon filling the void as the man's mouth gaped in horror. A brief look of incomprehension came into his eyes before a red mist of blood veiled them and he began to collapse to the ground. As the guda clasped at Eofer's leg and choked out the last few breaths of his life the sounds of running men came to them, and the eorle bent to snatch the ceremonial dagger from the dying man's belt as he prepared to sell his life dearly. The avenging wolf warriors were almost upon them, and Eofer and Swinna went back-to-back, lowering themselves into a fighting crouch as they prepared to go down fighting under the dispassionate gaze of the Allfather.

The first warrior reached them, the big man an unnerving sight with a body the size of a bear and the snarling head of a wolf, and Eofer felt a brief kick of pride and gratitude that Woden had sent such a man to take his life.

Swinna had retrieved the gore soaked splinter from the corpse of his victim, and the pair snarled their defiance as more wolf-men came up and clustered around their leader.

The thegn tensed his muscles as he awaited the stabbing spears, *get inside their reach*, a voice told him, *show Woden your worth one last time*, but at the moment he prepared to launch himself forward he hesitated as he began to realise that the wolf-men were laughing. As he hung back, the bear-wolf gripped the snout of his mask, pulling it up and clear of his head, and it was the turn of

Eofer's jaw to gape in surprise as the familiar face before him creased into a grin and spoke: 'woof.'

Hemming sniffed the air, shooting Eofer a look as the men of his hearth troop grinned in their wake; 'smelling like a week old turd and as tatty as a thræl.' He shook his head sadly. 'And to think of all the trouble we went through to get you back.' They shared a laugh as they rode south, a group of men with spirits as high as the gull grey clouds which drifted away to the North.

Eofer twisted in the saddle, shooting Grimwulf a question as the riders trotted on. 'Where to now?'

The youth indicated up ahead with a nod. 'The road forks about a mile ahead, lord. The pathway which leads away to the South branches off there.'

Eofer smiled his thanks. The young Engle's time spent as a slave in Daneland was providing them with an invaluable stock of information.

The track made a curve as it neared the crest of the ridge, swinging back to the East, and Eofer caught his breath as the others gathered at his rear. The wide valley below them was awash with Danes, sword Danes, spear Danes as the *leding*, the great levy of Daneland moved south to strike back at the men who had burned their farms and razed their villages. Bright spots showed within the dun coloured mass as sunlight reflected from mail and spearpoint, each glittering star a huscarl or a jarl, gathered beneath their banners of gold and red. Hemming had moved to his side and the duguth spoke as the others watched the host in silence. 'We had best get a move on, lord. The king will need to know they are on their way as soon as possible.'

He nodded and guided his mount on without a word, some of the humour of the moment drawn from the others, but not from him, not today. He really should be dead, lying gutless at the end of the blood-winding, tossed into the lake or hanging from Woden's oak but his men had appeared from nowhere and saved him. The same men he now knew, who had recovered from his loss at the river crossing, leading some of the finest warriors in Daneland on a weeklong trek through the wilderness as their homeland burned. Hemming, Octa and Osbeorn had remained resolute in the face of adversity, carrying out his last orders with intelligence and guile as he knew that they would. Finn, Spearhafoc and Grimwulf had outshone the other youth in the victory and he would need to think on their position in the hearth troop once they were back on the ships and safely away. He turned to Hemming as the road switched back to the West. 'Tell me about Weohstan again, Thrush,' he said with a proud smile.

Hemming chuckled as the tongue-lashing from the boy came back into his mind. 'Your son appeared from the tree line at the side of his uncle, lord,' he started, 'shining like a star beneath the white boar *herebeacn* of Geatland. King Heardred greeted me as a brother, but Weohstan pinned me with a terrible stare,' he said as Eofer chuckled with a mixture of pride and amusement at his side. 'Hemming, says he. Your lord is taken, yet you stand before me. Explain how that can be?'

They shared a laugh as Grimwulf called out from the side of the track. 'This is the place, lord.' He pointed away to the West as they craned their necks to see. 'You see that hedgerow a mile yonder, heading away to the South? That flanks a sunken lane, it leads directly to the coast.'

Eofer unstopped a water skin as he followed the line of the track. 'We will stop for a drink and a piss before we head down there. With any luck we will back among friends by nightfall.'

As they dismounted he noticed that Spearhafoc was already working on her charge. 'How is our boy?'

The Briton looked up from Swinna's groin with a look of distaste. 'He will live. The maggots I put in have eaten away most of the dead meat. Once they have finished their work I can soak it with willow pulp and pack it with honey. It would be nice though,' she added with a curl of her lip. 'If one of you boys could manage to catch a wound which wasn't a couple of inches from his bollocks, you know, just for a change.' As laughter rolled around the group she continued with a wicked smile and a sharp flick which made Swinna yelp with surprise. 'I have seen more cocks since I joined you lot than a fowler, although,' she said with a look of mischief, 'not too many that look like a baby's arm.'

As the laughter redoubled, Eofer felt his mood lighten as he marvelled that he was once again back where he belonged. The thegn shook his head as the men laughed at another quip and turned his head back to the South. From the top of the hill the woods, lakes and carefully tended fields of Daneland stretched away before them, and the men of his troop crossed to his side as they too regarded the land of their bitterest enemy. Hemming spoke as he offered his lord a pull from his canteen. 'It's a good land, lord,' he said before throwing Eofer a look. 'It makes you wonder why they covet ours so much.'

A brawl of clouds, as thick and dark as a meaty stew was coming up from the south-west, its shadow sweeping across the land in a tidal rush. Spots of light flashed and flickered against the grey wall as swifts and martins twisted this way and that, cutting the air as they fed in the updraft. Away to the South the light still played upon the distant waters of the Beltic Sea, but Eofer's gaze was nearer. Hauling himself back into the saddle he clicked his tongue. As the others hastened to follow he put back his heels as he picked the thing out from the fields and woodlands; wending his way down the back slope he led them into the vale.

FIFTEEN

The stench hit them first. As thick as honey in winter, it wormed its way in despite the cloaks which covered their mouths, sank its claws into their throats and refused to budge; made each breath, each reluctant sip of air a conscious effort. Finn had been scouting ahead and the war band reined in and waited as the youth cantered back towards them, his long hair teased out in a comet tail as the horse came on. He drew up in a shower of spinning turf, sliding his hand forward to calm the mount with a heavy pat of its neck. 'Battlefield,' he gasped out as the horse, as spooked by the miasma as any, flared its great nostrils and stamped the earth; 'through the trees.'

Eofer nodded as he slipped the woollen screen from his mouth with a grimace. 'How many bodies?'

Finn looked nonplussed but answered his lord as accurately as possible. 'Twenty-five or thirty in the open, lord. There is also the remains of a small balefire on the far side of the field.'

Eofer fixed him with a stare. 'Finn you have seen battle before, and you know the difference between a battlefield and the site of a skirmish. You are not a scop and this is not a mead hall. I want hard facts, not histrionics in future.'

He glanced across to the members of his hearth troop as the closeness to danger caused them to shift nervously in the saddle, their heads in constant motion as their eyes scanned the vale: 'Grimwulf!'

The youth raised his chin. 'Yes, lord?'

'Take Spearhafoc,' he barked. 'Ask those people if they know anything.'

He indicated an isolated farmstead with a flick of his head, and the youth kicked back their heels, the horses cantering across the hillside before he could speak again. Eofer turned back to the scout. 'Any sign of the living?'

Already admonished, Finn shook his head and answered firmly. 'No, lord. Just hoof prints leading away to the South, about fifty horsemen I would say.'

Eofer nodded. 'Spread out, let's go and see if we can learn anything from the bodies there.'

The troop moved into a skirmish line and trotted towards the trees. Soon they were there, and Eofer ducked beneath the low hanging branches as he led the men through. The stand of trees was only a few yards deep, sparse, the dappled light from above freckling the floor as they rode through the shadows and emerged onto a sunlit plain.

The bodies which lay before them were clearly Danes. To the unpracticed eye very little could distinguish them from his own people, but Eofer knew the telltale signs which distinguished the warriors of one nation from another. Small differences, things which would go unnoticed to those unaccustomed to the idiosyncrasies which separated the sons of Ing, differences in hair style, brooch design, even the weave of the clothing, all these things added together told the experienced northern warrior that each and every body which lay sprawled on the meadow before them was from the Danish folk.

'Well, it's not recent at least,' he murmured. 'Thrush?'

'Yes, lord?'

'How long do you think that they have been here?'

'Three days,' the big man answered confidently, as he watched a rat slip out from a distended belly and scamper away with its prize. He cast a glance at the sky. 'In this weather a body will swell to that size in three days; if it was hotter more like two.' The cloying smell of death was almost overpowering and Eofer halted again before they reached the scene of slaughter. A scattering of pale humps covered the greensward, bloated and swollen in the weak spring sun like seedpods sown by a monstrous yeoman. Long since plundered by the local population, the pathetic remains of brave men looked macabre in their nakedness beneath a haze of crows, the dark sheen retreating like a shadow before light as they hopped away from the riders with a bad tempered *craaak*.

Hemming spoke again. 'There are our boys.'

They looked across to see the charred timbers which were all that remained of the balefire of the Engles who had fallen in the fight. The pyre was ringed by a ridge of smoke blackened bosses and heat twisted edging, the metallic remains the only evidence remaining of the enemy shields which had been stacked against its sides.

The sound of hooves made them reach for their weapons, but Grimwulf and Spearhafoc emerged into the sunlight and the men exchanged weak smiles, embarrassed at their nervousness. The pair guided their mounts through the body field and slipped their cloaks from their mouths.

'It happened three days ago, lord,' Grimwulf reported as Hemming allowed himself a smile of self-satisfaction at his side. 'A strong party of our lads out foraging ran into a smaller group of Danes.' He smiled. 'We won.'

Eofer nodded. 'Then we are getting close.'

There was a tall elm hard on to the skirmish site and Eofer guided his horse across, unfastening his baldric and handing Gleaming to his weorthman as he went. Hemming followed, grasping the reins to steady the mount as Eofer hauled himself into the lower branches and began to climb. Within a short while he was in the canopy, and he settled himself onto a stout bough and peered away to the South.

He picked out the trail of the king's *sciphere* straight away, a long dark scar which cut across the patchwork of greens mottling this fertile land. To the eye of an experienced warrior, the movements which the English ship army had undertaken were as detailed as any campaign report. Storming ashore on the western beaches, thousands of men and horses had formed up and struck out for distant Hleidre, singing their war songs as gaudy banners rippled overhead. At the same time that Ubba silk beard and his huscarls had chased the *Hwælspere* across Eyrarsund to Scania, the army had moved across the rich undefended lands of southern Daneland, crushing what little opposition there was and burning as it went. From his elevated position it looked as if a *fyrdraca* had visited the land, the great swathe marking the passage of the belly, the outliers of burned and ransacked farmsteads where the fire dragon had turned its head, spewing death and destruction as it passed. Following the scar to the East he had them, a dark mass moving away under a cloud of banners five or six miles distant. Eofer turned his head, searching out the fields to the north-east, and was gratified to see that the Danish host was not yet in sight. He would be there by nightfall, reunited with his king and folk, and they could prepare to greet Danish steel with English.

Shimmying down the bole he was soon back in the saddle, and he turned to his troop as he slipped Gleaming back into place at his side. 'Come on,' he said, as he raised the cloak back up to cover his mouth. 'Let's get going, before the Danes come to claim their own dead.'

Within the hour they had picked up the trail, an unmistakable track beaten into the earth by thousands of feet, hooves and wheels. Soon they were in sight of the mighty host, and the little group shared smiles of homecoming after the trials and near-misses of the previous month. As the mounted rearguard turned their way, galloping down to identify this war troop which had appeared to the army's rear, Eofer ordered the spears to be reversed and held upright in plain sight lest they be taken for Danes by a nervy rider.

Finn spoke as the horsemen thundered down upon them, great clods spinning in their wake from the chewed up ground. 'Shall I raise your banner, lord?'

Eofer shook his head. 'No, keep it lowered but in plain view. Even the most excitable horse guard should recognise that as a sign of peaceful intent, whether the design is familiar to him or not' He reined in then, waiting patiently for his countrymen to come up. As the riders on the wings swept around to envelop the little group, the leading warrior drew up and growled a challenge. 'Who are you?'

Eofer laughed at the man's bluff demand. It contained none of the flowery prose, the veiled threats, of a reeve or coast guardian trained in such matters and was all the more welcome for it. In an instant he felt back at home. 'I am Eofer Wonreding, king's bane, and this is my troop. We have been away doing the king's work.' He paused as he glanced at those around him with a smile. 'And now we would like beef, ale and a place to rest our heads.'

The rider prised the helm from his head, and a grin came as he replied. 'Welcome back, lord, the whole army has been thrilled by your exploits. I am Eadric of Theodford. We have warm ale and a damp sod to rest your head each night,' he laughed, 'but I am afraid that the food might be a disappointment. If you follow us I will escort you in. The Danes have started to sniff around us at last, I wouldn't want any doubts as to your allegiance. Some of the lads are beginning to get a little jumpy.'

As the two parties began to mingle, swapping tales and sharing news, Hemming gave Eofer a look of wonder as the events of the previous month ran through his mind.

'It seems like an age ago that we left the Sley,' he began. 'Do you remember the fishing fleet?' Eofer nodded as he recalled the little boats, awash with herrings as they reaped the shoals off Engeln for the last time. 'I wonder if they all got away?'

'They will be long gone, I daresay that they are wetting their nets in the waters off Anglia as we speak.'

'And the fight on the beach, when Ubba silk beard and his men had us hiding behind a fallen tree. I thought that was it.'

They shared a laugh.

'So did I!'

'Stuck on a sandbank, chased the length of Scania, and you carted off to live in a hole.' Hemming sniggered. 'You stank like a pig when we caught up with you. And that bastard guda! I thought that we were too late when I saw the knife come out, and then Horsa sticks him with a shard of wood!'

They laughed again, before Eofer turned and raised his brow in question. 'Horsa? The horse?'

Hemming chuckled. 'It's what the lads have started calling Swinna, ever since Spearhafoc's comment about the baby's arm.'

Eofer glanced back and saw that the big man was happily emptying the contents of a rider's ale skin, the smile draining from the face of Eadric's man at the same rate as the ale from the container.

'He seems happy enough. What does he think of his new name?'

Hemming smirked. 'Hates it.'

'That's settled then, Horsa it is.'

The king saw them first and Eofer was overjoyed to see a smile spread across his features, despite his lord's careworn appearance. As the warriors surrounding King Eomær parted and looked his way, the thegn slid from the back of his horse and knelt before him. Eomær gripped Eofer's shoulders, hauling him back to his feet as wide grins illuminated the faces of the surrounding gesith.

'Your boys managed to get you back then!' the king exclaimed.

Noticing Eofer's look of surprise, King Eomær gave a warm chuckle. Despite the king's obvious fatigue following the rigours and worries of the sea journey and campaign, the eorle was pleased to see the twinkle of mischief which he knew so well remained in the king's eyes as he explained. 'The ship thegn, Eadward arrived back last week. He described the events surrounding your capture and Hemming's harebrained plan to free you. I have to say,' he added with a shake of his head, 'that we all had our doubts that they would be successful.' He looked back across his shoulder and Eofer saw for the first time that his brother was among the warriors there, shaking his head slowly as his mouth curled into a smile. 'Apart from Wulf, of course,' the king chuckled. 'Who I had to place under guard, to stop him racing off northwards to help. You will be pleased to know that King Heardred's men burned the Danish ships after they helped Eadward to retrieve his own. Eadward cruised off the coast to ensure that this Ubba couldn't return to Daneland in a gaggle of fishing boats, but they must have got word to the Danish mainland somehow because a fleet of dragon ships put in an appearance and the *Hwælspere* was forced to flee.'

Eofer nodded. 'The Danes are on the march, lord. We watched their army moving south this morning. They are looking to pin us here against the coast.'

The king frowned. 'That is a problem.' He plucked at Eofer's sleeve and guided him towards the summit of a grassy knoll. The day was all but spent, but the pair emerged into blinding sunlight as they reached the summit. King Eomær turned his back on the orb and pointed away to the East with his chin. 'They appeared before us, just as we started to make camp here for the night. The light had just started to go, it was perfect timing on their part. Too late for us to mount an attack, but just light enough for them to form a battle line. Now, with the information which you have just provided about the whereabouts of the main Danish host I can understand why.' The king turned to Eofer and pursed his lips. 'You now know these lands better than most, Eofer. When would you expect King Hrothulf to arrive?'

Eofer scratched at his beard as he thought. 'Armies move at a slower pace than either mounted war bands or flying columns,' he replied. 'Their levy, the leding, will have to tramp along behind the mounted warriors so…' He sucked his teeth as the journey which the Danes would need to take to cut them off unfolded in his mind's eye. 'They cannot be here in full force before tomorrow evening, lord,' he finally decided. 'Of course that does not stop them from reinforcing the men straddling the road before us long before then. Once Hrothulf discovers that we are being held here he will move with speed and vigour.'

The king nodded, the worry etched upon his features plain to see. 'I thank the gods that you have returned, Eofer,' he replied. 'Eadward told me what knowledge he had gained from Prince Hrothmund of his cousin, Hrothulf. I know him by reputation, what impression did you gain of the new king during your time as a captive?'

'All men speak highly of him, lord, his accession to the king helm has reinvigorated the kingdom. The overthrow of old King Hrothgar was well planned and executed. Hrothmund's huscarls died to a man to allow the boy to escape, his brother was not so lucky. Starkad told me that

172

most Danes attributed the victory over the Heathobeards last year to his leadership after Hrothgar was wounded by an arrow.'

The king interrupted with obvious surprise. 'You saw Starkad Storvirkson?'

'Yes, lord, he has hired out his sword arm to the Danes. I got the impression,' he added with a look, 'that this arrangement predated the Heathobeard invasion.'

Eomær snorted. 'Well, at least we didn't invite that wolf into our own fold last year. King Ingeld did and paid the ultimate price.' The king glanced Eofer's way. 'You know that the Swedes also have a new king and that the old king's sons are with your kinsman in Geatland?'

Eofer nodded. 'Hemming told me, lord.'

Both men looked back, their shadows stretching before them as the wolf chased the sun down in the West. The land dipped before the English camp, bottoming out in a wide valley before it rose sharply to the crest of a ridge. The Danish holding force was a line of silver as the last rays of the sun picked them out from a carpet of green. The woodland pinched the roadway there as it trailed away to the East, and king and thegn both recognised the strength of the enemy position. The shield wall was already long enough to anchor itself against the trees to north and south; reinforced it could prove insurmountable.

'Another day and we would have been away,' the king lamented.

Eofer looked at him in surprise, and the king explained.

'You will have to forgive me. I never intended there to be a great battle during this campaign Eofer, despite my words back in Sleyswic. We had to guard against news of our planned attack reaching the Danes before we arrived.'

The king shrugged apologetically. 'We had to set a false trail to encourage them to hold their armies back to defend Hleidre, but the fact is there is simply no need for it on our part. This war was never meant as a war of conquest; to take and hold land or capture the king's hall.' He gave an ironic chuckle. 'I will leave the hall burning to younger men like yourself. No,' he continued, 'if I could have kept the Danes occupied while the people got away to Anglia without losing a man I would have counted that a great victory. I daresay that there will be plenty of fighting for us in the new land, we will need every warrior we can muster to ensure that we have a future there.'

Eofer had been racking his memory as the king had spoken. There was something familiar about the landscape before him. Suddenly he had it, and he clenched a fist with glee. 'I know this place, lord!' he exclaimed. He rounded on the king, and Eomær saw the excitement shining in the thegn's eyes as he spoke. 'Lend me fifty of your best warriors, lord,' he said. 'Make your dispositions; plan to attack the ridge at dawn and I will hand you the victory.'

SIXTEEN

He had come awake the moment that the tent flap had been tugged aside, but Eofer remained where he was, eyes tightly shut in the hope that the time had still not arrived. A moment later a hand was shaking him gently on the shoulder and he tried not to smile, despite his exhaustion, as he sensed it was Hemming who towered over him. 'Come on open your eyes, I know that you are awake.'

Hemming shook Eofer again, and the thegn fought down a grin as his duguth tutted in frustration. 'Eofer, wake up. The lads are ready.'

One eye flicked open, and he finally let out a chuckle at the sight of his weorthman standing over him, hands on hips, shaking his head slowly from side to side like a long suffering mother. Eofer rubbed his face, levering himself up onto one elbow as his mind came back to the matter at hand. 'What's the moon like, Thrush?'

'Well, it's big and round and hangs in the sky. Some people say that it's made of cheese, but then some people think that women are just like men without cocks. Those folk have either not met many women, or they are one.'

Eofer snorted. 'I did ask for that. Is it going to be a help tonight?'

Hemming threw him a smile. 'Why don't you come and see for yourself?'

As the big man left the tent, Eofer swung his legs to the floor and crabbed across with his toes to hook the lip of his boots. Forcing his feet inside he laced them up, dragging himself from the comfort of the king's cot as he reached for Gleaming. Eofer took a last look around the interior of King Eomær's campaign lodging as he attached the baldric and tightened the straps. In the corner the king's own battle gear rested proudly on an iron stand, the mail shirt and full faced grim helm gleaming in the wan light of a lantern. *Stedefæst*, the king's ancestral sword was already on his person, but Eomær's stabbing spear with the distinctive gold and blue bands rested against the weapon stand alongside his battle board. The oversized war shield, blood red, sparkled as the light danced on the golden dragons and ravens which decorated the leather, while the eye of Woden stared balefully at the eorle.

The king had eagerly grasped at Eofer's plan earlier that evening, a scheme which would hopefully go a long way towards removing the men who had rushed to block their eastwards progress. The thegn had quickly surveyed the nearby coast from the adjacent spur of land before the onset of full darkness had hidden the features from view, but what had been revealed had been enough to confirm that it was the place which they had visited during the coastal attacks from the *Hwælspere*. On his return, the king had insisted that he rest from his exertions in his own tent while he discussed the plans for the dawn assault with his ealdormen and war thegns. Eofer had gratefully accepted as the rigours of the past week caught up with him, and now he was fully alert and ready to go.

The men's smiles flashed red in the sawing light of a brand as he exited the tent, and they came together as he returned the smile. 'All set?' Nods and a chorus of mumbled comments answered his question as Eofer ran his eyes over the group for the first time. Aside from his own duguth, Hemming, Osbeorn and Octa he had allowed the king to choose the men who would mount the attack, men who had already distinguished themselves during the campaign in fighting spirit and valour; by the looks of the men before him the king had chosen well. Many of them he already knew from past campaigns or the king's mead hall, and he hailed them now, picking them out from the crowd, recalling past deeds and showing them honour. Eofer was surprised to see that Hemming had added the youth, Finn, to the numbers but he found that he approved and he caught his weorthman's eye and gave him a small nod of endorsement as the youth looked proudly on.

A quick glance upwards told him that the weather had taken a turn for the worse while he had slept. Slate grey clouds broiled and tumbled in the skies above the English camp and the air fairly crackled as a strengthening wind gusted in from the sea. 'It looks as if we are going to get wet,' he said as the men followed his gaze, screwing up their faces to peer southwards. 'Let us hope that it keeps the Danes huddled around their campfires.' He looked across to Octa and threw him a sympathetic smile. 'Oct'; get yourself over to the corral and fetch a bucket of horse shit. Make sure that it is fresh, nice and moist.' As the men swapped questioning looks, Eofer ran his eyes across their weapons and armour. 'Has everyone brought a spear, and is the blade covered by cloth as I ordered?' They all nodded. 'Everything metallic wrapped in a bundle?' Again the warriors mumbled the reply: 'yes, lord.'

As Octa bustled off with the pail, Eofer ran through the final instructions. 'It will not be easy tonight, but if we can pull this off we can sweep these Danes aside in the morning and the army can be on its way once again. I am sure that you have all learned by now that the Danish king is coming against us with full force. I myself saw the army of King Hrothulf earlier today.' He paused to add emphasis to his words as the men looked on, stern faced. 'It is a mighty host, one which the king is eager to avoid meeting on the field of battle if that is at all possible. Remember,' he said, repeating the king's words from their earlier meeting in an effort to expand on the reasons for the lack of aggression, 'this is not a war of conquest. Even if we swept the Danes aside and crushed them utterly we would still be sailing away forever. And it would be a costly victory, make no mistake. Other folk, Heathobeards, Wulfings, Jutes or Swedes would gather the harvest which our bodies would have sown on that battlefield.' He fixed each man with a stare as he moved down the line and was gratified to see the acceptance there. The king had chosen well. Eofer could sense that the men's fighting ability was matched in the keenness of their intelligence. 'Our own people should be safely away by now, sowing the first crops in the new country across the German Sea and harvesting the shoals. But remember, it is only a new country to us. To the Britons it is already an ancient land, the land of their forefathers back to the days when Woden walked the earth. Despite what you may have heard they are a tough and vigorous people, we

178

will need every spear that we can muster if we are to survive and flourish there.'

The first rumble of thunder sounded out to sea and the men instinctively touched hammer pendants for luck. Eofer did likewise and threw them a smile. 'Old red beard,' he said, 'come to watch the fun. Let's give Thunor a worthy tale to tell our ancestors at their mead benches in Valhall when he returns over the rainbow bridge to Asgard.'

Octa had returned as the first spots of rain arrived and Eofer reached inside the pail, scooping out a handful of the fibrous dung before rubbing it into his hands and face. 'Come on lads,' he smiled, his teeth flashing unnaturally white against his darkened features, 'get stuck in.' As the men wrinkled their noses and came forward Octa spoke. 'We could have used earth and ash, lord. It's a bit smelly.' Eofer glanced upwards again as the storm crept nearer. 'Not in this, it would soon be washed away. Shit is greasy Oct', it stays where it is put.'

A last look around the group and they were set. 'Remember, the going will get tougher after we reach the cliff face. Use the heel of your spear to feel your way forward. If it comes to a choice between going into the sea and losing your bundle, let it go or you *will* die. It's the reason that we are carrying our armour after all.' He shot them all a parting smile as spears clattered together in the binding. 'We will be moving slowly and steadily. It is not so far, and we have until dawn to be in position, so take things easy.'

A gully sloped away down towards the nearby coast, and Eofer shouldered his pack, melting into it as the men filed in behind him. It was a purposely inconspicuous start to their night, disappearing into the gloom as the king, lit by great fires which glinted from the armour and spear points of his army, rallied his troops in full sight of the Danes opposite. Away to the South the first spot of light flickered in the dark as lightning arced, and Eofer pulled his head into his shoulders as the rainfall increased to a steady patter.

The first part of the descent was the easiest. The rock strewn Combe snaked downhill, its wide banks making it good going for the war party, but soon the cutting took a turn to the East, steepening, its sides drawing together as it approached the place where it joined the main valley. Soon they were there, and Eofer waited until all the men were up with him before he slid into the watercourse below. The rain increased in tempo again as they hugged the valley side, each man feeling his way through the boulder field which littered the floor with the butt of his spear. The storm was almost overhead now, the occasional lightning flash causing the men to turn to stone but also lighting the way ahead for a heartbeat, the chalky valley aglow. Eofer could already hear the waves, driven ashore by the force of the winds, and he grimaced as he thought on the trial to come. It was bad enough, he reflected, that the passage had to be made when the tides were at their peak. Now it would appear that the weather had turned against them, and he fingered the silver hammer which hung at his neck as he sent a plea to the god of storms that he quickly move on.

The distant rumble of the sea slowly became a roar as the war band reached the beach and Eofer raised his head to spy out the clifftops for any signs of life. As he had expected the Danish force were still too small in number to guard against attack from all directions and, satisfied that they were in the clear, he indicated that the men follow him across the stony beach to the foot of the cliff. The crash of the surf filled the air as the sea grasped hungrily at the steeply sloping strand to their right, wave following wave as they were driven ashore by the power of tide and wind. Satisfied that all were set, Eofer waited until a bolt of lightning illuminated the scene, the blue-white frond fizzing through the sky turning night to day. A heartbeat later thunder boomed and they knew that the storm was directly overhead, the thunder god hurling his hammer all about them as they waited to move forward. Hemming placed a hand on his shoulder and Eofer turned to see the weorthman's grinning face inches from his own. The big duguth pointed at the sky and gave the thumbs up, as pleased as his lord that the storm must be moving away soon.

Eofer had picked out the path as the fire-bolts flickered overhead, and placing the heel of his spear shaft deliberately he hauled himself up onto the narrow platform. Within a few steps the curve of his shield had caught on an outcrop of rock and he cursed as he slipped it from one shoulder to the other. For a moment he considered letting it drop to the beach below but he knew that he would quickly come to regret the decision in the morning's fighting. It would be hard enough with the protection, he knew, without it they would be unlikely to prevail. Only seasoned warriors, the best of the best, could hope to hold an army at bay for the best part of a day until help arrived. To face such men shieldless was to invite a quick trip across the rainbow bridge.

Hemming gripped the rear of his belt and he waited for a few moments to enable the chain to form behind him before moving carefully forward. As the path wend its way northwards the beach below petered out until they were passing only feet above the spray as the storm driven waves pummelled the rock face below their feet. By tapping the butt of his spear along the edge of the path and groping the cliff face opposite, Eofer could just about navigate his way forward despite the near absence of light, a darkness made almost solid by the overhanging wall of rock which towered above them. Hemming still gripped the rear of his belt as they shuffled closer to the point of greatest danger, the few yards which he feared more than the Danes, the *fiend* which could well decide whether the English nation had a future or not. Surmount it and he felt confident that his attack would overcome Danish resistance. Fail here and the army could very well become trapped against a ragged coastline with no hope of rescue from the sea. With the full might of King Hrothulf's army bearing down upon them the ramifications could be dire. Shorn of its warriors, the new kingdom of Anglia would wither and die.

He could hear it now, and Eofer recalled the familiar howl with a rising sense of dread. The last time that he had come close the *Hwælspere* had been all but sucked into its maw, as the tidal rush gripped the big snake ship and dragged it towards its doom. They had spoken to fishermen from the lands of the Wulfings opposite and knew that the Danes called the horror which lay before them 'Skerkir', 'Rowdy', the name of a particularly boisterous giant from a gods-tale. It was only the experience gained by a lifetime at sea which had saved them then, and Eofer had hoped that his shadow would never fall across the blowhole again. Hnæf, Eadward's duguth, the man who had worked so hard to save them that day was himself gone now, his body no doubt mouldering on a midden in Scania, and Eofer sent an invocation for the peace of the steersman's soul as he led the men forward the final few yards.

If the sea god Wade appeared to have sided with the Danes, the tidal rush seething back and forth in the space ahead, Thunor the thunderer had clearly thrown in his lot with the Engles. Above them the base of the clouds, a dark boiling mass hastening away to the north-east became a torch, illuminating the way ahead as fingers of light snaked to-and-fro between them.

The great wall of rock became a lantern, the whiteness of the chalk turning night to day as Eofer led the war band around the final outcrop to come face-to-face with the monster. It was the moment which he had been dreading, ever since the plan had come to him on the hillock with the king. Before him Skerkir was a boiling maelstrom of water and spume as Wade pushed the waves in, the water rising and rising until it seemed that it must overwhelm the little pathway before falling rapidly away to become swallowed by the darkness.

He paused then as he stared at the thing, heaving like the sweat covered flank of a war horse run hard.

Hemming clasped his shoulder, leaning forward to shout above the din: 'nice.'

It was enough to break the spell, and Eofer forced a foot forward as he recognised the need to keep moving. If he showed even the merest hint of doubt here, the fear would quickly spread down the line and the attack could stall. The thought of retracing his steps and explaining to the king and ealdormen that their courage had deserted them was unthinkable, there was no choice. They had to move forward.

A flash revealed the size of the beast, and Eofer spied out the path as the water fell away once more. The sea had cut a notch in the chalk here, twenty yards wide, fifty deep, widening a cleft in the rock face in its unending quest to level the land. Ahead of him the narrow path swung back around to the South for twenty or thirty feet, hugging the chasm, before rounding a knob of rock and moving away. It was only a short distance, a moment's stroll elsewhere, but he caught his breath, watching with mounting dread as the sea surged up again. Before it reached his level the light from above lessened like a guttering brand, finally extinguishing itself completely to leave them smothered by an inky blackness. Sightless, Eofer froze in terror as the water pushed the air up before it, setting up the mournful howl which he had heard before. A recollection from his childhood flashed into his mind as he waited for the wave to pluck him from his perch, and he snorted despite his fear as he pushed it down deep. Old Mother Holle snatched the souls of wayward children, the grey haired hag gathering them in to keep her company as she travelled the northern lands. The little waifs wailed in their misery and he shook the thought from his mind with difficulty as he grasped the rock.

Slowly the rush of air subsided and, as the yowl died away he realised that the water must be retreating. Pushing himself on as fast as he dared he had cleared the back wall and was nearing the turning point before the howl started to build again. Lightning arced, and Eofer stole a look back the way he had come. The men were strung out around the gaping maw, each man gripping the belt of the man ahead as bone white faces stared into the abyss. The water was returning, swelling to fill the blowhole in a mighty rush as the men clutched at the wall and, just as the water slowed and stilled and they thought that the danger would pass, it seemed to gather itself and surge again. Eofer looked on in horror as the dark mass advanced, the air rushing on ahead with an unearthly cry just as the thunderbolts fled the sky, plunging them all back into darkness.

Eofer threw his arm around an outcrop, bracing his body as he waited for the savage jerk on his belt which would tell him that the men had been swallowed down by the giant as the air screamed around him.

SEVENTEEN

Hemming hawked and spat a gobbet of bloody phlegm as he wiped more blood from his face. 'Could have been worse; could have been a lot worse.'

Eofer chewed his lip as his eyes searched the swell. 'They might turn up further along. If I remember rightly the beach shelves once we are past this point. If they ditched their gear like I said, they would stand a chance.'

'If they didn't?'

'Well, if they didn't they are fucking idiots,' he snapped as the tension of the night threatened to overwhelm him. 'Dead fucking idiots!'

Hemming gave his shoulder a shove and, as the thegn glared his way, puckered his lips and blew him a kiss. 'It's all right, you can throw churlish language my way. I know that you love me really.'

Eofer shook his head and exhaled softly. 'Do something for me Thrush,'

'What's that, lord?'

'Never change.'

A wide smile lit Hemming's face at the praise from his lord as the last of the men rounded the beak of rock and threw themselves down onto the path. To a man they were soaked, from rain and seawater, and it was obvious to Eofer that more than a few had lost shields and spears as Skerkir had done its utmost to prise them from the rock. He clapped his weorthman on the arm as his self discipline reasserted itself. 'Come on, lets go and see what we have left.'

Safely above the reach of the waves now he slipped the shield from his back, propping the great board against the cliff face as he dropped the bundle containing his heavier items to the ground. The last of the lightning was flickering overhead as the distant sound of thunder told them all that the storm was moving on. Thunor had done his best to guide them past Rowdy, and he reached inside his shirt to move the hammer of the thunder god to his lips in silent thanks as his eyes moved along the line of dishevelled warriors before him. They met his gaze as he approached and Eofer was gratified to see that the fighting spirit still burned within, despite the blow they had just received.

'How many?'

'The two in front of me went,' a warrior replied. 'I tried to hold the belt of the lad in front but the water just seemed to uncurl my fingers and carry him away.' He blinked the water from his eyes and wiped his face on a sleeve. 'It's lucky that it did, lord,' he said with a grimace. 'If I had gone too, like as not the boys behind me would have followed. You would have been facing the Danes at dawn with a dozen spears.'

Eofer nodded as he recognised the truth in the man's words. Two or three men were a setback, many more would have dealt his plans a fateful blow. 'Any others?'

'Eadgar went,' a voice replied from the gloom. 'I saw him in the water though when the lightning flashed again, so he must have ditched his gear.'

'Well,' Eofer replied as he wiped the salty water from his own eyes. 'Thunor has had our backs so far tonight, maybe he can watch over our friend and guide him to shore.'

Grunts of agreement filled the air and hands went to pendants as they made their own pleas and promises to the red bearded one. Of all the gods, Thunor had always had a wide following among the Engle, his plain speaking, bloody minded traits matching their own.

'So that's it then?' he said with relief. 'Just those three?'

'Me too lord,' a man answered with a frown, pointing to his leg. Laid out carefully before him the leg looked fine, and Eofer raised a brow in question. 'Broken,' he replied with a scowl. 'I was thrown about like a rag doll by that wave and bashed against the rocks. I heard it snap, even above the roar of the wind and sea.'

'We will carry you down to the beach,' he replied in a sympathetic tone, 'we are almost there now. If we squirrel you away somewhere we can send help when we have seen to these Danes.' The warrior pursed his lips in frustration. To come so far only to be left almost at the moment that the attack went in was a heavy blow, but they all knew that it could not be helped. He had been fortunate to survive his meeting with Skerkir at all. Eofer turned away as his thoughts turned back to the dawn assault, and he pitched his voice to carry over the sound of the wind. 'Let's get down there, then I want everyone to dress in their war gear. Mail shirts, arm rings, the lot, everything but helms. Carry them and keep them covered for now.' He shot them a predatory grin as he spoke. 'We have already overcome our greatest trial tonight. Now it is time to reap our reward in glory and renown.'

A horse snickered and the men sank down as one, merging with the forest floor as best they could. Despite the near total absence of light, Eofer's insistence that they forego their helms until the commencement of the attack was repaid handsomely as a Danish guard sauntered across and peered into the tree line. One of the horses, a big chestnut stallion, was clearly agitated; he knew that they were there and he showed his displeasure by snorting and pawing at the ground with a hoof. As the Dane turned away to speak calming words to the animal, one of Eofer's men sidled across and pressed his mouth to the thegn's ear. 'It's the horse shit, lord.' Eofer gave him a look of incomprehension and tilted his head in a clear indication that he wanted to know more. 'The horse shit which we smeared onto our hands and faces. The big lad in front is the leader of the herd. He can smell it and thinks that there are rival stallions nearby.'

Eofer cursed inwardly and nodded that he understood as the man regained his place in the underbrush. His mind raced. A quick glance to the East told him that the small patch of sky that he could see remained resolutely dark. With the thickness of cloud cover that night it had been impossible to judge the passage of time, but he knew that the dawn must be approaching and he hoped that it would come soon, before the horse gave the game away. Eofer rose to his haunches and gave the Danish camp a last look over as he reached his decision. Turning back he ushered the war band to the rear, back into the depths of the wood. He knew the place that he was heading for, a small clearing where an oak had succumbed to age and windstorm a few years back, tearing a rent in the canopy which would enable them to catch the first signs of the dawn. Within a hundred paces they were there, and Eofer snatched up a handful of sodden leaf mulch from the forest floor and gave his face a scrub. 'I forgot about this,' he said as the men gratefully copied his actions. 'And we didn't even need it!'

'We don't know that for sure, lord.' Hemming answered, backing up the initial decision. 'It could have got us to the cliff face unseen, who knows whether the Danes had men posted on the high ground.' As the men nodded their agreement one of them added his own voice. 'Imagine if they had spotted us, lord. We might have found ourselves facing Danish spears the moment we got past the blowhole.' Eofer was gratified that the men mumbled in agreement. It had been no small thing to ask proud men, men chosen by their king to spearhead the English attack to smell like stable boys, and he thanked them as he tossed away the foul smelling leaves and unfastened the battle helm from his belt. 'Time to get ourselves ready, lads,' he said as he tossed the covering aside and lowered the helm onto his head. 'We know the layout of the Danish camp now, when we go in, we go in hard. I saw half a dozen men guarding the horse lines, a couple of men preparing hot food and a dozen tents.' He raised a brow. 'Do we all agree? Is that what we all saw?' A mumbled chorus told him that they did. 'When we leave here we will drift to the right and come out on the road behind them, form up and straight in. I will kill anyone in my path, and then wait on the far side for you all to mop up. Clear the camp and then reform on me. Be quick,' he said with emphasis. 'It doesn't matter too much if we miss one or two, they can't harm us. The main battle line will be distracted by the king's attack, with any luck we will be among them before they are even aware that we are there.'

They all acknowledged his instruction with a nod of their head as Octa pointed away to the East. 'Is it me, or can I see a smidgeon of grey there?' They all looked, and hearts leapt as the speck widened into a strap of iron.

The men slipped their shields from their shoulders and tore off the drab covering to reveal the beauty within. Reds and silver, blues and gold, each great board carried the owner's personal design or that of his lord. Silver domes shone in the weak light, the bosses polished to a high gloss to match the edging, hawks and ravens which surrounded them. Gripping his own shield, Eofer hefted his gar, holding the stout spear out as the men came forward to clash their own in the binding.

As if in response, the first sounds of ash shaft on lime-wood board carried to them from the West as King Eomær formed his army into battle array. In his mind's eye Eofer saw the silvered line filling the valley side, a roistering mass of *hild-thegns* and warriors as gaudy banners snapped in the wind. Men calling their war cries, moving down into the valley to challenge the *fiend* who had the gall to bar their path. As the army's spears clacked and the voices of champions drifted to them in their hidden glade, Eofer, his own blood quickening, shot his war troop a grin and a wish that Thunor's protection hold sway a little longer.

A fold in the ground, its lip edged by oak and hornbeam ran away towards the road, and Eofer jogged ahead of the men as the returning light made pearls of the raindrops from the night's downpour. Soon they were within earshot of the enemy camp, and the eorle slowed to a walk as his eyes picked out the track ahead. The familiar smells of camp life, woodsmoke and roasting meat, drifted across to torment the hungry men as they emerged onto the roadway and took up position, and Eofer took a moment to pick out Osbeorn, throwing his duguth a mischievous sniff and a wink as the smell of the breakfast bacon enveloped them. Despite the tension of the moment Osbeorn's face creased into a smile as the war band fanned out to either side, couching spears and hunkering into shields as they fixed the camp with a ravening glare.

The sun had broken free of the horizon now and their shadows stretched away before them, filling the roadway as Eofer flicked a last look to left and right. The warriors filled the road, ten men wide, five ranks deep, leaning forward like hounds at the slip, and the battle fire began to course through his veins as he raised his gar aloft. All eyes were turned to him, and Eofer thrilled with the power of the moment as the blade flamed in the sun's rays.

Chopping the spear down he surged forward and accelerated into a run. Their long shadows raced towards the tents which straddled the track, climbing the pale woollen walls to plunge them back into darkness as the troop approached. Eofer's breathing was loud in his ears as he reached the tent line and raced between them. Emerging on the far side he got the momentary glimpse of a face turned his way, the boy's mouth falling open in shock as freshly split wood tumbled from his hands.

Eofer's spear shot forward to take the Dane in the throat, the shock of the strike forcing his own shoulder back as the wide bladed stabbing spear stuck fast and the boy fell away. Ahead of him a Dane stared at this death dealing apparition which had suddenly appeared in their midst, a steaming ladle held comically before him as he puckered his lips for a taste. He was a dozen paces away and Eofer recognised the moment when the shock left the cook and his mouth widened to shout a warning. The Englishman's arm was already drawn back as he shifted the grip on his throwing spear, the slender daroth flying forward as he released with an explosive grunt. The dart was still airborne as Eofer reached across his body, drawing Gleaming from its scabbard with a nerve tingling swish. As the spear punched the Dane backwards Eofer was on him, kicking the pot aside in a torrent of steaming gruel as he brought his blade down to take the man in the neck. The cook's cry was stillborn as Gleaming bit deep, a jet of arterial blood pulsing from the wound to darken the ground at his feet. Eofer twisted his wrist, sawing the blade through muscle and tendon as he jumped the dying man and turned back.

The others were emerging from the tent line in a wave of flashing steel, and Eofer twisted this way and that as he sought out another opponent. Hemming was finishing off the wood carrier, and he watched dispassionately as his weorthman's own spear stabbed down into the boy's unprotected chest as he writhed like an eel beneath him.

A face appeared at a tent flap, the eyes like moons as they took in the carnage unfolding around him, but a warrior was there and a spear stabbed forward to pierce his head and hook him free of the shelter. Hemming had reached his side and the duguth gave a chuckle at the sight. 'Like winkling mussels from their shell.'

Men were moving around the tents, cutting guy ropes before stabbing down at anything that moved within. As the muffled screams began to subside and the telltale crimson stains began to blossom, Eofer quickly scanned the clearing. His men were already beginning to cluster together as any opposition faded. Stern faced and grim in the grey light of the dawn, they looked away to the Danish battle line at the top of the field and steadied themselves for the main fight to come. Eofer followed their gaze and was elated to see that their small victory appeared to have gone unnoticed by the men there. Away to the left the last of the Danish horse guards was being brought low by a well aimed spear throw and the Engle there was moving forward to finish the job. It seemed as if none had escaped the blades to warn their brothers at the danger which had appeared in their rear, and Eofer felt a rush of excitement as he realised the opportunity which the gods were handing his little group.

Eofer walked the few paces back to the wood carrier, grasping his spear and giving it a tug. The gar was stuck tight, wedged between two of the boy's neck bones, and he was about to place the sole of his boot onto the Dane's face when he hesitated. The first rush of battle fury had left him now, and his eyes lingered on the face of his victim as he lay in the mud. He had lived, Eofer estimated, no more than seven winters before the English had come to his land, not many more than his own son. A blond fringe, the gossamer strands of childhood now thick crimson ropes from the lifeblood which covered them and an upturned nose covered in blotchy freckles. Eofer wondered if the nose was replicated on a woman nearby, whether it was true that she would feel a stab to her heart at the very moment her man or son was cut down on a battlefield somewhere.

Hemming's voice came at his side as the duguth read his thoughts. 'Tough shit,' he shrugged, 'you might have just saved Weohstan from his blade on another battlefield.' Eofer narrowed his eyes and Hemming explained. 'There are no innocents here, lord, everyone is a warrior or wants to be one. We all made that choice and we knew the risks. Just think how many men this boy would have killed if he had grown and got his wish.' It was true, ceorls and thræls were rarely killed on raids, there was no honour or advantage to be gained. Without them there would be no food grown or fish harvested from the deep, and without the food they supplied there could be no warriors to protect them from enemies. It was a circle of interdependence which had existed ever since the sons of Mannus, the first man, had walked Middle-earth.

He pushed the thoughts aside as the Danes at the top of the field roared and clashed their shields. It could only mean that King Eomær was leading his thegns against them, and his mind snapped back to the duty which had been entrusted to him by his lord. A quick look told him that his own battle troop were set, shields raised, bloodied spears held before them as they waited for him to lead them to death or glory. Wiping the cook's blood from Gleaming he sheathed the blade, glancing back at the Danish shield wall to be met by the amazing realisation that the warriors there were still unaware of the danger to their rear. He had to grasp this opportunity while it lasted, and he stamped his foot down as he twisted his own gar free of the young lad's throat and strode across. 'Form a boar head,' he called as he reached them. 'I am ord man with my duguth tucked in behind me. The rest of you sort yourselves out quickly, we must move now. If we can hit them before they see us, we can turn the fight.'

As the men rushed to follow his instructions, Hemming gripped Eofer's sleeve and spoke in a voice filled with wonder and excitement. 'Look!'

Eofer peered at the Danish shield hedge and frowned. 'Yes, I know. They still don't realise that we are here.'

Hemming gave him a shove. 'No, Eofer! Look!'

Eofer narrowed his eyes as he sought the reason for his duguth's excitement but could see nothing but a line of backs, spear blades winking in the light as they cheered and stabbed the sky. Osbeorn, Octa and Finn came up and the trio clapped each other on arms and shoulders, grinning like madmen as Octa added his own thoughts to the mix. 'There they are! The bastards!'

A breath of wind teased out the war banner of the Danish leader, and Eofer finally shared the look of glee as he too saw the image of the bearded man.

EIGHTEEN

Fifty paces to go, forty, and still the Danish spear wall showed their backs to Eofer's charge as they prepared to defend the ridge line against King Eomær's desperate onslaught. Eofer's eyes flicked from side to side as he ran, and he felt a kick of excitement in his gut as he saw that Ubba's battle line was disposed in the way he had expected. Ubba himself stood proudly at the centre of the line, his boar helm gleaming in the pale dawn light beneath the bearded man. A knot of men surrounded the huscarl, men of similar worth and ability, anchoring the centre where the fight would be keenest. Similar groups tied the shield wall to the woodland at either side of the roadway, bolstering the wings, guarding against the flanking attack which would turn the wall back on itself in a tumble of bodies, spreading chaos and death among them in the blink of an eye. Between the three groups Eofer could see that the line thinned considerably as Ubba awaited the reinforcements which must be hurrying his way.

They were almost upon them as Eofer changed direction, angling his approach to the right to hit the weaker spot in the Danish defence. Only twenty paces to go and the first Dane glanced back towards them, his face a mask of joy as he mistook the attackers for the longed-for relief coming up in the nick of time.

Ahead, Eofer just had time to recognise the moment when Danish spears and swords began to rise and fall, the length of the wall sparkling like shattered glass as the armies came together with a crash, and he threw his shoulder into his shield and braced against the impact. The roar that went up as the armies met fled his mind as his own world narrowed down to encompass nothing more than the pair of warriors before him. A heartbeat later the air was driven from his lungs as he crashed into the back of the Dane, driving the man forward despite the weight of bodies which were packed tightly together on the hilltop. Eofer's right hand shot forward at the same moment, his gar skewering the man's neighbour in the small of the back, passing clear through the Dane's midriff to impale the warrior to his front.

Eofer let go of the spear, snatching fang tooth from its scabbard, angling the seax forward as Osbeorn smashed into his back. The man before him had fallen to his knees despite the crush, opening a small gap but threatening to topple the eorle at the same time. Eofer desperately tried to place his feet on firmer ground as the men of his war troop continued to throw their weight into the breach. As the momentum built, Eofer's breath caught in his throat as he realised that his feet were trapped beneath the fallen Dane. He let out an involuntary cry as he started to tip forward and fall to his death. It was almost unknown for a warrior to survive once he had lost his footing in the chaos of the fight. All warriors knew that it was with good reason that a man killed in battle was said to have fallen; but an unknown hand reached out to grab the neck of his battle shirt, tugging him upright until he managed to throw a leg forward and plant a foot astride the body beneath him. Stabbing downwards, he threw his weight behind his shield and drove forward again.

The Danes before him were attempting to turn as they became aware of the new threat which had appeared in their rear, but the crush of bodies and the overlapping shields which had meant to be their salvation now worked against them.

Hemming and Osbeorn shoved forward, and Eofer worked his seax back and forth, the wicked blade sinking into undefended backs as he stabbed and stabbed again. Slowly the pressure at his back began to ease as the English boar snout began to widen, the warriors hacking into the Danish flanks, widening the breach as the rearmost Englishmen arrived to roll up the line.

Eofer attacked again as the men before him squirmed and turned, desperate to escape the thrusting blade. Stab, twist, withdraw, stab, twist, withdraw to stab again, his sword arm working methodically as hot blood sheeted his tunic, soaking it to the elbow.

A flash of steel, and he dipped a shoulder as the point of a sword blade scythed down to glance off the crest of his helm with a bone shattering screech. The tip of the blade had been pointing his way, towards him, and Eofer realised with a kick of joy that he had reached the front ranks of the Danish hedge. Sword blades were rising and falling the length of the line as they reaped a grim harvest, hacking at the remaining defenders, driving the hapless Danes back onto the seax and gar of Eofer's attackers.

Ahead of him he could hear the cry from the warriors in the valley roaring the name of their nation:

Engeln! Engeln!

Sword and spear blades were hacking into the last few remaining Danes who twisted and turned this way and that in their desperation. As the last defenders fell Eofer lowered his shield, echoing the war cry as a line of grim and blood spattered faces crashed their shields together and stepped towards him with a roar.

Engeln! Engeln!

A spear blade darted in and the thegn threw his shield across to deflect it aside as he continued to cry above the din of battle.

Engeln! Engeln!

Eofer flicked his eyes up for a heartbeat, away from the point of the sword blade which hovered before him, and he forced a step back as he recognised the fighter and cried his name.

Coelwulf!

Still his friend's eyes remained fixed on the bloody point of Eofer's blade and he took a chance, lowering the seax, moving it out wide as he cried again.

Coelwulf!

At last, Eofer saw a veil of incomprehension come over his friend's features as he realised that his intended victim was not only calling his name but laying himself open to a killing stroke. Eofer seized the moment, raising his own head above the boards of his shield as he yelled again into the din. Coelwulf! Finally the cry cut through the fog of war and Eofer laughed aloud as his friend's lips curled into a bloody grin. 'Eofer!' he cried, the light of victory shining in his eyes; 'you made it!'

Eofer roared with delight, moving forward to embrace his old friend and neighbour as both sets of duguth roared their acclamation and clustered protectively about their lords. The danger was moving away as the combined might of the two English war troops drove the Danes apart, widening the gap which Eofer's attack had punched through the shield wall.

Coelwulf grasped Eofer's wrist, forcing his arm skyward as the cluster of men cheered.

'*Eorle!*'

The cry rolled along the ridge as men saw the breach and pushed forward with renewed vigour, the English word for hero their new battle cry.

'*Eorle! Eorle!*'

A flash of colour caught his eye and he looked across, watching with pride as his own burning hart *herebeacn* was rushed to his side. As more men poured into the breach and curved away to attack the rear of the Danish line, Coelwulf attempted to speak but the words came out as a mumble of gibberish. Eofer smiled as he saw that the thegn's lip was swelling visibly before his eyes and he raised a brow in question: 'shield rim?'

Coelwulf nodded and Eofer's knife flashed. The cut was barely a nick, but blood gushed to soak his friend's beard as he winced at the unexpected pain. 'Do me a favour,' he said as he spat bloody spittle onto the grass at their feet. 'Warn me next time that you are about to do something like that.'

Eofer's youth clustered around them beneath his war banner, and he raked them with a look of pride. Eofer's brother, Wulf, had taken them under his wing while their lord and the senior members of their hearth troop had been away skirting the cliffs, outflanking the Danes to deliver the hammer blow which had crushed their hopes of pinning the English army against the sea. A gesith, Wulf had stood alongside the other members of King Eomær's bodyguard, watching with pride as his brother's detachment had prised the enemy apart and opened the way ahead before releasing his youth to rejoin the victorious eorle.

Hemming and Osbeorn were peering away to the South, their eyes fixed upon Ubba silk beard and his knot of huscarls, eager to take revenge for the long chase through Scania. 'Come on, lord,' Hemming said. 'We have dues to collect.'

Coelwulf handed Eofer a water skin and the thegn eagerly gulped down the warm liquid as he looked about him. The majority of the fighting lay to the south of them where Ubba was skilfully drawing the remnants of his shattered position into the formation which Eofer knew the Danes called a *scyldborg*, the English a shield burh. Edging backwards towards the nearby tree line, the big Dane was fighting at the front of his men as more and more Engles flooded up from the valley to engulf them. Hundreds of warriors now stood between the men of Eofer's hearth troop and the object of their ire, and Eofer shook his head as he replied. 'You will have to take your vengeance another time, Thrush.' He handed the skin across and wiped his beard on his sleeve as he raised his chin to the West. 'The king wants us to move on.' They all turned to look across the valley. The first wagons were already on the road, the drivers tugging at the reins as the oxen began to drop down into the vale. A swarm of horsemen were thundering through the brook heading for the rapidly widening gap as they moved forward to scout the road ahead, and Eofer's face broke into a smile as he recognised the blond mop of hair on the leading rider.

Spearhafoc had taken herself across to the North, tagging onto a group of bowmen who had been sent to stamp out the last embers of resistance from the small group of survivors there. As Danish shields came up and the shafts began to fly a great cheer rent the air, and ash shafts stabbed the heavens in acclamation as the king strode to the crest of the ridge and crossed to his thegn.

'Eofer, my eorle!' the king cried as he approached.

Eofer beamed in return; 'lord.'

'You did it!'

Eofer spread his arms to encompass the men of his battle troop. '*We* did it lord. I could not have asked for a better group of men. Everyman here is an eorle, you have my thanks.'

The horsemen had gained the ridge, and the pair looked across as the leading rider reined in, his face a picture of happiness: 'Eofer!'

'Haystack,' he grinned in reply.

Icel slid from his mount and clasped Eofer to him. Stepping back the ætheling looked at his father, smiling from ear to ear. 'Where would we be without our very own king's bane?'

'Fighting our way uphill,' the king replied, his features hardening once again as the worries of kingship returned to pick at his mood. 'But as we are not, I want you to scout the route ahead until you reach a wide valley.' He looked at Eofer, and the smile fled the thegn's features at the change in the king's demeanour. 'I have that right?'

Eofer nodded. 'Yes, lord. It should be roughly three or four miles ahead of us, certainly no more than five.' He pulled a face as he attempted to judge the distance in his mind. It had been nearly a month since he had sailed the coast on the *Hwælspere*, usually at dawn or dusk, but he was certain in his own mind that he had the distance fixed, despite the jagged nature of the coastline. 'There is a wide grassy valley, perhaps a mile across, with a large estate on the far side.' He frowned as he thought back to the last time he had visited the place. 'We were intending to burn it, but the night was too far advanced and the distance too great to regain the ship before daylight so I abandoned the idea. The coastline takes a northerly turn nearby, it will be on your righthand side, just over the ridge,' he said, flicking a look at Icel. 'There is a path there which leads directly over the ridge and on down to a wide bay.' He looked at the king. 'Despite the fact that the farm escaped that night I scouted out the valley, in case we returned another time. It should be ideal for our needs, lord.'

The king clapped his son on the shoulder. 'Have you anything to ask our eorle?' Icel shook his head. 'Go on then, get going. Despatch a few riders north and send word to me when they discover the whereabouts of King Hrothulf and his army. From what Eofer told me last night they should be nearby, and these men,' he glanced across to the place where Ubba and his Danes were clustered behind a wall of shields and spears, 'were obviously expecting help to arrive sooner rather than later.'

Icel nodded as he vaulted into the saddle. It was a mark of his strength that he was able to do so in mail shirt and helm, and the men around him beamed at the prowess of their prince as they put back their heels and galloped away with a noise like thunder.

A cry of victory went up from the northern part of the ridge line, and the pair, king and thegn, looked across. The bowmen's work was done, and the men, distinctive in their tawny coloured clothing were trotting happily across to bring their bows to bear on the larger group of Danes to the South. Spearmen were moving among the knot of bodies, ash shafts rising and falling as they dispatched the wounded and sent them to the gods. Spearhafoc was among them, and Eofer drew in a breath to call the youth back to her hearth companions when he thought better of it. The girl looked as happy as he had seen her, back among her kind, and the first doubt that she would become a duguth came into his mind. King Eomær was speaking again, and he forced the thought away as he switched his attention back to his lord. 'I have a mind to leave them,' the king was saying. 'Without horses they pose no threat, and I am keen to move the wagons forward to this valley of yours and recall the fleet before we are intercepted, strung out on the march like peas in a pod.'

Hemming and his duguth were standing nearby, and Eofer caught the look of dismay which washed their features as the men realised that their tormenter, the man who had led the chase across Scania, might escape to fight another day. Before he was aware that the words were forming, Eofer was speaking again. 'Lord, the leader of the Danes is Ubba silk beard. This is the man who led the huscarls against us in Scania, who oversaw my brother Wulf's captivity, last winter at Heorot. He ran from my blade once, on a beach near here. It is a matter of family honour that he comes under my sword now.' The king hesitated as he weighed the conflicting needs of integrity and expedience and Eofer spoke again. 'Lord, this is the man who led the raid on Engeln last autumn, you yourself chased his war band down The Oxen Way. I have already repaid the debt owed to the Jute who aided them. Let me settle the score in full, here and now, before we leave these lands forever and he regales Danish halls with tales of daring in the war against the English for years to come.'

Whips cracked as the first of the oxen huckled their charges to the crest of the rise, and the king pursed his lips. 'We cannot wait, Eofer. Strung out on the march we are too vulnerable to a devastating attack.'

'There is no need to wait, lord,' Eofer replied. 'Lend me my brother and we will follow on. There is a small island in the brook which you have just crossed, a flash of lightning revealed it to me on the march down to the coast last evening. Let me take him there.'

The king raised a brow. 'A holm-gang, you mean?'

Eofer nodded. 'Thunor sent a fire bolt to show me the place, lord. I am certain of it.'

The king snorted with amusement. 'Well, Eofer, I am just a king. If the thunder god wills it, who am I to argue?'

Eofer's lips curled into a smile. 'Thrush, grab my *herebeacn*, Octa and Osbeorn find my brother and bring him here. Finn,' he said. 'Take the youth back to the beach. Retrieve our friend with the broken leg, and make a quick search for any of the others who went into the sea. Get him onto a wagon before they all leave and follow on. We will catch you up later.'

King Eomær remounted, the morning sun painting his finery the colour of gold. He looked back as the gesith moved their own mounts to his side. 'Don't take too long, Eofer. You have about an hour, then the rearguard will have to hurry onwards.' He indicated the men in Ubba's skjaldborg with a jerk of his head. 'Don't let our new friends cut you off.'

The king moved off as Octa returned with Wulf, the gesith's features a picture of delight as he pushed through the crowd. As Eofer wiped the blood from fang tooth, Wulf came forward to clasp him by the shoulders. 'Eofer,' he said excitedly. 'You do what you want with Ubba, but if there is a man with him called Hrok, he's mine!'

NINETEEN

Following the storm the water level was higher than the previous evening and the island looked far smaller than he remembered it; but the rune sticks were cast, and he collected his thoughts as Hemming worked the retaining pins free from the shoulder clasps and prised the war shirt apart. Raising his arms Eofer leaned forward, wriggling his body until the mail shirt followed with a metallic swish. Nearby Wulf was ready, his own armour folded neatly at his side, Eofer's brother rolling his shoulders as he loosened muscles for the work to come.

Ubba and Hrok were standing on the riverbank opposite deep in conversation, the Danes stealing glances their way as they discussed their own tactics in the death fight. Hemming's face appeared before him, and his mind came back as the duguth lowered his own helm onto his head and moved to fasten the strap beneath his chin.

'He'll be good, lord,' he was saying. 'You don't get to live long enough to become a huscarl without becoming handy with a blade. Watch that sword blade, not his eyes. And the shield, don't forget the shield. Oh, and keep your own feet moving and don't let him...' Eofer forced a smile, despite the nerves which were building within him. 'Thrush,' he said calmly, the levelness of his voice surprising him.

'Yes, lord?'

'Shut up.'

'Yes, lord.'

Eofer threw his weorthman a wink. 'I am going to win, huscarl or not.'

Hemming's face broke into a smile. 'Yes, lord; you are. The gods of war wouldn't let these bastards take you from me twice.'

Hemming held up his shield with a look of pride and Eofer wound the fingers of his left hand around the handle, hefting it, feeling the weight. Retrieving his sword from the pile Hemming turned the hilt towards the eorle, and Eofer paused to admire the workmanship as the morning sun broke free of the tree canopy to breathe life into the crimson cells. The pommel sparkled as the sunlight reflected from gold and garnet, the grip itself, alternating bands of horn and whalebone polished and worn by the hands of his ancestors, only accentuating the beauty. Curling his fingers around the grip he drew the sword with a satisfying swish as Hemming stepped aside and Eofer glanced across to his brother. They were set and, with a steely look and a slight nod of acceptance, they strode forward to the edge of the bank.

Ubba glanced across, and the Danes straightened their backs, drawing apart as they saw that the time had come. A dozen English spearmen had come down to guard the pair and they moved forward, shepherding the men towards the river bank as Ubba threw the brothers a contemptuous glare. 'We meet again, Eofer,' he said with an icy smile. 'Somehow I always knew that we would.' The huscarl dropped his eyes to the island midstream and cocked a brow. 'There is not much space, especially for four. What happens if a foot touches the water?'

'You lose. Either lay yourself open to a killing strike or my friends will see you on your way.'

'The same rules for all of us?' Ubba asked in surprise. Eofer nodded, and the Dane's face broke into a smile. Wulf was bristling at his side, and Eofer watched as the Dane, Hrok, visibly shrank under his baleful gaze. His brother had told him of the treatment which the man had meted out to him during the time of his captivity in Heorot. His honour besmirched, the chance to take his revenge had been too good to miss.

'Let us start,' Eofer said. 'There will be no breaks, no replacement shields. Only the men, or man, of one nation will leave the island alive.'

Eofer splashed into the channel, wading across to the islet as Wulf followed on. Within a few paces they were there, and the pair took up starting positions at the southern end as Ubba and Hrok, their shields and swords held clear of the stream, moved across.

Eofer's eyes took in the surface of the small island as the Danes began to haul themselves back onto dry land. Up close it looked even smaller than it had from the bank, there would be little room for fancy footwork, despite Hemming's exhortations. Six paces by six, the centre and southern end of the teardrop shaped area pretty much matched the dimensions used when there was no nearby island on which to stage the ritual fight known as the holm-gang, the island-way. On land a woollen sheet would mark out the area of the fight, its dimensions fixed by withies of hazel driven into the ground. Like the island-way itself, a foot which strayed from the blanket would mean instant defeat, in many cases death. The islet rose slightly at its centre, the widest point, where a scrubby bush clung to a precarious existence flanked by rounded pebbles and stones of varying sizes, before tapering away to the North.

The Danes were set now, and the two groups glared at one another as they shifted their grip on shield and sword and awaited Ubba's first attack. As the man who had issued the challenge to holm-gang custom dictated that Eofer receive the first strike, and the thegn raised his shield, his eyes fixed on the point of Ubba's sword as it began to snake this way and that above the ragged bush. Ubba moved slowly into a fighting stance, his own eyes fixed wolf-like on the Englishmen opposite as he prepared to attack, but the heavy silence was ruptured as Wulf spoke for the first time. 'How is Signy?'

Ubba blinked in surprise as the simple question shattered his concentration, and he looked at Wulf as if he were mad. 'Signy? You want to know how my wife is?'

Eofer snatched a glance at his brother and recognised mischief in his expression, a cunning which he knew well. He had suffered his brother's taunts and jokes for a lifetime, but he knew that his kinsman was no fool. There was a reason for this madness, and he looked back to the Danes and redoubled his concentration. Wherever the question was leading Eofer knew that it was intended to provoke a response, one which would give the English pair an edge. Wulf wasted no time in landing the killer blow to their enemy's cohesion, and Eofer watched as

Ubba's expression changed from incomprehension to fury as he realised the meaning behind the words.

'No,' Wulf said, as he switched his gaze across to Hrok. 'I was asking him.'

Ubba's nostrils flared as he saw the look of horror cross his companion's face and, although Hrok quickly set his expression into a snarl, the truth was out, the damage done. Already wounded before a blow had been struck, Wulf's words struck home again as Ubba reeled. 'Thræls know everything that goes on, Ubba, especially the women. Just because you choose not to see them does not mean that they are not there. As you know,' he smiled, 'women like nothing better than to discuss which ploughman is working which field, especially if that field belongs to another farmer. I turned over a few furrows myself while I was King Hrothgar's guest and got to know the girls quite well.' He shrugged and pulled a face. 'Forget that I mentioned it, Ubba,' he said before throwing the Dane a mocking smile. 'It was probably just women's talk after all; tittle-tattle.'

Eofer had been watching the exchange keenly and moved to seize his chance, pouncing as Ubba's thoughts whirled. Darting forward he made to land a blow but pulled the strike at the last moment. As he had expected, caught off guard, Ubba reacted by swinging his own sword across in a desperate attempt at parrying the blow. Eofer rolled his wrist, sweeping Gleaming aside as he took Ubba's counter on the face of his shield. The blade slid across the leather facing, gouging a runnel before clattering off the shield boss and away. It would count as a first strike and, the demands of honour satisfied before gods and men, Eofer moved to attack in earnest. As the

Dane's body was dragged forward by the momentum, Eofer swept Gleaming down and back as Ubba's eyes went wide at the realisation that the wild lunge had opened his flank to a counter stroke. Off balance and pulled across by the weight of his shield, Ubba's mouth gaped in horror as Eofer danced past. In a flash the Englishman's sword was slicing through flesh, scoring the bones of the huscarl's ribcage as he drew the blade up and away in a mist of hot blood.

Ubba staggered sideways as a red furrow opened in his side, blood sheeting out to soak his midriff and trews. Wulf was there, and the gesith drove the edge of his shield into the Dane's mouth as he swept his own blade across to drive Hrok back. Ubba staggered back under the blow, shattered shards of teeth mixing with the bright blood flowing from the ruin of his mouth. Forced back on the stony ground Ubba stumbled and fell, but he had not survived a score years and ten on the battlefields of the North to die so easily. As the huscarl rolled and jumped back to his feet, Eofer switched his attention to Hrok. The Dane's eyes were flicking from side to side as he watched the English brothers, desperate to see an opening before he found himself facing them alone. Wulf's attack had opened up a fleeting opportunity for a counter strike of his own and Hrok seized it eagerly, leaping forward to stab his blade at the Engle as he moved into the gap made by Ubba's fall. As Eofer watched in horror the Dane's sword blade cut towards his brother's thigh, but just as it seemed as if it must pare flesh from bone the blade was stopped dead as it became entangled in the thicket. Hrok desperately tugged at the hilt as Wulf recovered, sweeping his shield across. The metal edging of the board cracked

213

down, and Eofer watched as the sword juddered under the impact of his brother's attack, the tremor of the strike travelling up Hrok's arm to throw the Dane back.

Ubba had recovered enough now to face his opponent and the pair, thegn and huscarl, glowered above their shield rims as their eyes searched for an opening. The last attack had taken Wulf across to the far end of the island, splitting the English brothers apart, and the Danes put aside their differences to move back-to-back as the Engles took up positions at either end of the islet.

Eofer snapped a look at Gleaming, flinging a pearl of blood from the tip with a contemptuous flick of his wrist before moving his head to look at the gaping wound in the Dane's side. 'Nasty,' he winced. 'It looks like the happy days spent burning Englishwomen and children in their halls are at an end.'

Ubba's head had turned aside, his eyes fixed on Eofer as he whispered an instruction to Hrok. Eofer saw the merest hint of acknowledgment enter the Dane's stance, and a quick look down confirmed what he already suspected, that he was on the very tip of the spit of land. The water was burbling past only inches away from each foot, and he knew then what the big Dane had said.

A heartbeat later Hrok was spinning, the pair charging forward as they sought to drive the eorle into the waters before his brother could come to his aid. Eofer held his stance until the very last moment as Ubba raised his sword high to bring the great blade chopping down, but the attack was a feint and the Dane pulled the strike at the last moment as Eofer had known that he would. As Hrok drew his sword arm back ready to thrust into the eorle's face, Ubba drove his fist forward, hooking the cross guard

214

of his own sword over the lip of the Englishman's shield; tugging it down with all his strength. As the rim of the board tilted Hrok's arm shot forward, the Dane's sword flashing in the sun as it cut the air only an inch above the rim.

Hrok yelled out in triumph, but the cry was cut short as Eofer dropped to one knee, launching himself forward and upwards like a charging bull. As Eofer shouldered Ubba aside with the boards of his shield, Gleaming came up like a thunderbolt. Eofer knocked Hrok's shield aside and came on, all the power in his legs and shoulders concentrated on adding to the sword's punch. His own sword arm overextended by the stab at Eofer's face, Hrok's breath exploded from him as Gleaming slammed into his belly. Eofer stepped up, driving the blade upwards, slicing through liver and gut, powering up to cleave the Dane's heart in two. As Hrok's death rattle sounded and his eyes rolled upwards, Eofer spun away from Ubba's avenging sweep as it whistled past his ear. His momentum carried him back to the wider part of the island, and it was Eofer's turn to gape in surprise at the sight which met his eyes as he swung back to face his foe and Wulf came back to his side.

As Hrok bled out into the stony soil, Ubba stood staring at the English pair from beneath the rim of his helm, a look of resignation painted onto his face. The gash in his side was still sheeting blood, soaking the left side of his trews before the waters of the brook flowed to wash it downstream. Ubba levered himself back onto dry land, shooting them a wry smile as the English spearmen came across and prepared to throw.

'It's not the end to keep the skjald's in gold and silver,' he said in heavily accented English, 'but at least I have a sword in my hand.' As the men on the bank hefted their weapons and sighted, the Dane raised a bloodstained hand to indicate they hold. 'Can I ask, Eofer? You have been a worthy adversary, here and elsewhere. Would you show me honour by sending me onwards? I will tell your ancestors of the prowess of the sons of Wonred; that one of their kinsmen is the eorle who burned my king's hall, the other is a loki-cunning gesith.' The Dane lowered his head, rapping the forward plate of his helm with his knuckles as he did so.

Eofer had already seen that the Dane carried the design of the dancing wolf-men above his left eye, he would have been surprised had he not, and he called on the spearmen to lower their ash shafts as he came forward. His own battle helm shared the design as did Wulf's, every warrior of note in the North had passed the ritual to enter the brotherhood. He would give his enemy the death due a warrior, true to his vow the night that he had danced the dance and taken the oath. As he did so Ubba switched his gaze. 'Wulf, you were named after the wrong animal, you are fox-cunning.' Throwing his shield aside with a clatter, he snorted at his own stupidity as he pointed the tip of his sword at the stony ground, opening himself to Eofer's death blow. 'I know that Signy would never betray me, but it sowed a seed of doubt in my mind just long enough for you to seize the initiative and win the fight.'

Ubba inhaled deeply, raising his eyes to the sky as he prepared to pace the rainbow bridge. The beginnings of a smile lifted the corners of his mouth as the sleek lines of a tern drifted into his vision, its underside washed red by the morning sun as Gleaming clove the air.

The roadway exited the tree line and the riders reined in, gasping at the sight which lay before them. A vast bowl of land stretched away to the horizon, the grassy valley sides awash with the tiny figures of men and horses. Below them the English camp stretched for a league or more in a great curve along the flanks of the escarpment. A mile to the North the land rose in a gentle slope, a great green ocean roller capped by the dark mass of the Danish army. Points of colour flickering above the dun coloured host showed the banners of the jarls of Daneland and, at the centre of the encampment, the great hart battle flag of the Scyldings curled lazily in the gentle spring breeze.

'It looks like the Danish scouts found us then, thankfully not before the army reached a gentler part of the coastline,' Eofer said. 'Ubba and his men died for nowt.' Eofer shared a look with his companions and clicked his tongue, the horse moving out into the warm sunshine as he glanced towards his brother. 'You never did say if there was any truth in the accusation you made to that Dane.'

Wulf chuckled as a party of horsemen detached themselves from the army's flank, cantering across beneath the white dragon of Engeln. 'Hrok, you mean? The man was a bastard,' he spat. 'He was always in the slave quarters tupping the women.'

Eofer shrugged. 'So? Most men do.'

Wulf flicked a look and his face creased into a frown. 'Not like Hrok, he liked to play rough.' Wulf spat into the dust to clear the memory. 'The girls said that he killed more than one, just for the fun of it; and not quickly either.' He shook his head. 'Sometimes paying compensation to the owner is not enough. If a *deofol* gets into your soul you will end up below in Hel's frozen hall, and it will be a good thing too. He will realise the error of his ways by now,' he added with a smile of satisfaction, 'now that king's bane has spitted him like the yuletide hog.'

They shared a smile as they recalled Eofer's victory, and the eorle stitched his brow as a thought entered his mind. 'You have still not answered my question. What about Hrok and Signy, Ubba's woman?' Wulf let out a snort of derision. 'Signy had far too much pride to look at a man like Hrok. And he was a braggart, she would have found herself back at her father's hall before she could have splashed her arse clean in a bucket.'

Eofer cast a sidelong look as the pieces of the tale began to fall into place in his mind. His brother had taken on a familiar air of smugness, and the eorle began to suspect why he seemed to know so much about the woman: 'you didn't?'

Wulf put back his head and laughed, the twinkle in his eye as good as any confession, and a smirk lit Eofer's face as he reached his own conclusion: 'you bastard.'

TWENTY

The king glanced across from the knot of caldormen and thegns, and Eofer was gratified to recognise the warmth in his smile. The king's advisors followed their lord's gaze, booming their approval as the sons of Wonred approached. King Eomær made his excuses and strode across, visibly checking his warriors for injury as he came: 'a bloodless victory?'

The brothers exchanged a look, and Wulf answered his king with a smile. 'On the English side, lord. The Danes…' He gave a shrug, 'not so much. It was a victory for English brains and brawn, lord,' he smirked. 'As ever, my brother supplied the brawn.'

The trio shared a laugh as the king's attention switched to the army of King Hrothulf across the valley. 'As you can see, we have been overtaken at last. Well, we had a good run,' the king said distantly, 'we should be thankful for that. Another day and we would have been away. Wulf,' he said brightening, 'I have an important task for you and your hearth brothers. Rejoin the gesith, they will fill you with meat and ale; we have a long night ahead of us. Eofer,' he said, plucking at the eorle's sleeve, 'walk with me once again will you? I have a favour to ask of you.' Intrigued, the brothers exchanged a look as they parted, and the king led Eofer towards the lip of the ridge line. The war flag of Engeln flew proudly from the summit, and if the white of the dragon looked a little less bright after a month in the field, the red background looked no less bloody. The ash men guarding the banner moved away as the pair, king and eorle, paused and turned their eyes to the South.

'You returned just in time Eofer. The bay is as you described it, perfect for our purposes; we are leaving tonight.' Eomær shielded his eyes as he looked out across the waters of the Beltic Sea, the sun low to the south-west painting the wave tops the colour of steel. 'If you look closely,' he murmured as Eofer followed his gaze, 'you can just make out a cloud of sail on the horizon. Beneath that haze lies the hulls of our fleet.' The king instinctively peered skywards as he sought out the position of the sun. The orb lay low down, away to the West beyond the land which was already becoming the old country; the day was drawing on. 'The ships are making their way here, Eofer,' the king said, 'our work in Daneland is done. The last of the English will have left Engeln for Anglia by now, it is time that we followed on.' The king laid a hand on Eofer's shoulder as he indicated that they return to the others. 'There was one more thing that I would ask of you,' he said as they walked. 'Not every man wished to follow us to the new land and I respected their wishes, despite the pressing need for spearmen across the sea. I left them back at Sleyswic, moving the earthly remains of my ancestors from their barrows and reinterring them in secret places throughout Engeln. There is one though which I wish to carry across the sea to Anglia.' King Eomær turned to his war thegn and smiled. 'You have shown yourself to be loyal, shrewd and brave Eofer,' he said. 'Can I ask you to do one last thing for your people, before you too leave our motherland for the final time?'

The shingle scrunched underfoot as Eofer moved about the beach. Thousands of men were filing down the steep sided Combes which cut the coastline, a silvered snake as the light of the full moon reflected from helm, mail and spear point. His brother was shepherding the first arrivals into orderly groups as the first dark outlines of curving prows and snarling beast heads moved into the shallows and mooring ropes flew the gap to shore. Eofer gave a small chuckle as he saw the exasperation written on his brother's face, struggling manfully to form the disparate groups of warriors into ship-sized batches ready for loading. Wulf looked his way and a snort of amusement came as he noticed his brother's grin. 'Come to help?'

Eofer shook his head. 'I have a much easier task. Keep the Danish army at bay while the lucky ones slip away into the night.'

Wulf was about to answer, but a movement caught his eye and he turned his head and called into the gloom. 'Where are *you* going?'

A mumbled reply came from a dark shape there and Wulf snapped back in irritation. 'Well, go where you are! Your group is next to board, we promise we won't look.'

Eofer clapped his brother on the shoulder. 'You are busy, I will let you get on. I just wanted to wish you gods-luck for the voyage.' Wulf was about to protest but the words were stillborn as a figure appeared before them. 'A ship has run aground Wulf,' the man said. 'We need someone with authority to organise a party to push it clear.' The warrior glanced at Eofer and blanched as he recognised the eorle, the hero who had shattered the Danes at the ridge and saved the army from a far bloodier fight. 'Sorry, lord, but the ship is blocking the anchorage. It is mayhem down there.'

Wulf nodded that he would be along, and the warrior pulled an apologetic smile before melting back into the gloom. 'That's what you get for being a gesith,' Eofer said with a smile. 'The king's men always get the hard jobs.'

Wulf snorted but fixed Eofer with a stare. 'You know which one of us always gets the toughest jobs and it isn't me king's bane. You take care,' he said, prodding his brother's chest with a finger. 'And don't hang about in Engeln. Astrid and Weohstan will need you in the new country.' The brothers were about to embrace when a cry of warning caused them to jump back.

'Watch yourself, lord!'

A man came past holding a burning brand before him, the details of his face and chest picked out a dull orange by the flickering flames. The torches had been set at high points on the beach, guiding the ships ashore. Their work now done, they were being led through the crowded anchorage to be doused in the surf in a hiss of steam. Eofer turned again and opened his mouth to call a final farewell but his brother had already gone, swallowed by the lines of shuffling warriors.

Disappointed he made his way inland, past the lines of anxious faces as the English army made their way to safety. Everyman knew that discovery by their *fiend* now would very likely mean the death of their nation. Caught, disorganised, strung out with little hope of forming a cohesive defence, the cream of English fighting men could very well be supping their ale in Valhall before the horses pulled the sun into the sky to the East. Anglia would be stillborn, their women and children sold to *thrældom,* the proud name of Engle a byword for defeat as the over-proud Danes sang their victory songs and piled high their plunder.

Eofer paused as he gained the crest and looked back at the cove. The waters were choked as ships entered the bay, loaded their precious cargo and exited at the northern spur. He snorted to himself as he recognised the value of his brother's work there. The dark mass of men littering the shoreline were already draining away like ale from an upturned cup, and his hand went under his shirt to the small silver hammer which hung there, thanking Thunor that the weather god had looked kindly on the Engles in their time of greatest danger. High above the spring Moon, huge and white, frosted the sea and hilltops with its pale light, lighting the way for the ships of the English fleet. By sunup King Eomær and his army would be through Eyrarsund, putting the cliffs of Daneland behind them as they sailed away to Anglia.

Eofer's shield strap was irritating him, biting into the skin of his shoulder, and he shifted it with a grimace as he hefted his spear. A last look and he turned his back on the mayhem, edging past the last column of warriors as he recrossed the ridge line.

Osbeorn's face showed red in the light of the flames, the worry obvious for all to see. 'Is it time to go yet, lord?' Eofer cast a look across the vale towards the high ground where King Hrothulf had set his standard. The South facing slope was bathed in a silver sheen, the campfires of the Danish host winking in the still air like a hundred suns, but the valley floor was still as black as pitch. The thegn chewed his lip as he thought and cast an anxious look up at the hillside to the rear. He had expected Grimwulf to be back by now, bringing the welcome news that the army was aboard the ships and clearing the headland as they put their prows to the North. 'Don't worry,' he quipped in a futile attempt to lighten the mood. 'Our foemen are not on the move just yet, I can't smell bacon.'

Osbeorn attempted a smile but it was obvious to them both that his heart was not really in it. 'They will be cooking *our* bacon if they realise what is happening here.' He jerked his head towards the valley bottom as Crawa sauntered past between the Danes and the flames. 'It's all right us walking around all night, hoping that they think that the *sciphere* is still here. What if they twig that they are not? That dip could hold an army and we wouldn't know anything about it until they came up the hill towards us.' He grimaced. 'What if they send horse Danes?'

Eofer blew out through his mouth as the tension of the moment finally breached his defences. 'Well, if that happens Ozzy, then we will all die. Unless of course,' he snapped, 'the guda are still looking for volunteers to walk the blood-winding I told you about, then of course, we will wish that we already *were* dead.'

Osbeorn looked at the floor as Eofer cursed. They were all tired and anxious, longing for the days to return when they could sit and share meat, ale and the companionship of their hearth mates in safety once again. It had been so long now since they had sat in Eofer's hall that they could scarcely recall it. The hall itself now was little more than a dark scar on a field in Engeln and two of the men who had shared the last night there were dead, Imma Gold and the youth, Oswin, cut down by Jutish swords as the year of fire and steel had begun. The eorle moved on, clapping his duguth on the shoulder in an action which needed no words. A quick glance to the East told him that no glimmer of light yet showed on the horizon, but a glance to the South confirmed that the moon was on the wane.

As he contemplated herding the last of the horses together, preparing to make a desperate ride to the West, Grimwulf appeared at his side with the news they had all been longing to hear. 'They are all away, lord,' he panted, his eyes bright with excitement. 'The last two ships are ready and waiting.'

Eofer grinned despite his weariness as the cares of the night fell away. 'Tell the others,' he replied. 'Let's get away from here as quick as we can.'

A thought struck him as the youth turned to go, and he called after Grimwulf who stopped and cupped his ear. 'Tell everyone to gather around their senior man and report to me as they leave the camp, I don't want to leave anyone behind. I will be standing by the main path.'

Eofer shot Osbeorn a grin. 'About time. Come on then, let's get going.' The pair trotted up to the crest of the escarpment and within a few moments the first of the rearguard were up with them, grateful smiles flashing their way as Eofer counted them off. 'Keep going lads, straight down to the beach. The *scipthegn* will tell you which ship to board.'

As the last of the invading army melted into the shadows a young warrior approached him and inclined his head. Eofer looked the lad up and down, and his brow furrowed as he realised that he should not have been among them at all. King Eomær had left only five score warriors to form the rearguard under Eofer's command. If not the cream of the army, each man was an experienced spearman, a fighter proven to be skilled at weapon work, steadfast in the face of danger. Clad in a battle shirt and helm of toughened hide, the youngster was struggling manfully under the weight of an oversized shield and spear; Eofer doubted that he had ever campaigned before. The boy hesitated to speak as if overwhelmed that he stood before an eorle, a man of reputation and renown, and Eofer smiled as he attempted to put him at ease: 'you look lost.'

The boy raised his eyes and shook his head, but his voice came strongly as he replied. 'No, lord, I have a favour to ask.'

Eofer exchanged a glance with Osbeorn as Hemming and Octa gathered his own youth in and waited for them by the track: 'ask it.'

'My father was killed beside me in the battle at the ridge.' He lowered the tip of his spear, pointing it towards the thegn as he spoke.

In a flash Osbeorn swept his own spear across, knocking the point aside as he shouldered the boy to the ground. Before the shocked youth could recover Hemming was there, and he gaped in horror as the duguths' own spears stabbed out, twin spear points nicking the skin of his throat as Eofer's hearth men braced to drive them home. Gleaming was already in Eofer's hand, his eyes flicking from one abandoned fire to the next as he sought out any hint that this might be a prelude to a surprise Danish assault.

As the clatter of shield on shield came from Eofer's youth, the eorle, satisfied that no Danes were about to rush the hillside, lowered his gaze. 'Was your father Engle or Dane, lad?'

The boy's eyes looked as large and white as the spring moon above them as he answered in a voice far less confident sounding than before. 'Engle, lord. He was a metalsmith, he plied the lands around Hereford.' Eofer called into the gloom as he checked the valley again for movement: 'Grimwulf. Down here.'

As the youth came up Eofer questioned the boy again. 'Did your father shoe horses?'

'No, lord, the *hoefsmith* did that.'

'But he made horseshoes, bits and other pieces of tackle. He visited the horse farms in the area?'

'Yes, lord.'

Grimwulf quickly realised why he had been summoned and he added a question of his own. 'What was the name of the horse thegn at Bedricsweorth?'

The boy was beginning to recover his composure, and they all shared a grin as he spat a reply which could only come from the mouth of another Englishman. 'There is no horse thegn at Bedricsworth, or any other kind of thegn. The place is a shit hole.'

Eofer looked across to the East as the snake ship edged out of the cove. As he watched, a thin line, dove grey, grew by the moment until it flared to light the undersides of the clouds. As the snaca left the shelter of the bay the great prow beast bucked and rolled as if sharing the happiness of its crew to be safely away from avenging spearmen, and Eofer's thoughts turned to the weeks just gone by.

He had added greatly to his reputation, both by his bold attack on the Danish camp and shield wall and the following duel with Ubba silk beard. If he had felt shame at his capture, despite the fact that all had assured him that it had been unavoidable, the reaction of his hearth men had more than made up for any humiliation.

Thrush Hemming had thrust himself manfully into the breach caused by his loss, and Eofer had been as thrilled as any as he listened to his big friend recount the tale of that weeklong dash through the forests of Scania before the king and his gesith. A warlord was judged by the quality of his following and his, he knew, had shown that they possessed a potent mix of independence, intelligence and aggression.

A ripple of laughter broke into his thoughts, and he peered aft as the rowers slowed their stroke, pausing to crane their necks as they looked back towards the land. The sun was a milky smear on the horizon now and the Danes had discovered to their fury that they had no enemy left to fight. The ridge line which they had so recently crossed was shimmering, the dawn light reflecting off polished helms and spear points as the first of the avenging Danes swept down to the beach.

Their quarry, the men who had risked all to see their countrymen safely away, were now huddled into their cloaks, crammed into every available space, unseeing and uncaring whether their enemies had been made to look fools or not.

The boy, Anna, had been the last Englishman to leave Daneland as had been his wish. The blood of the Dane who had taken his father's life still stained the lad's spear blade and he had promised never to point it at a man again unless he intended to use it. It had been a lesson learned the hard way, but the men had taken to him in the short time he had been with them and even Grimwulf appeared to have forgiven him for the less than flattering description of his home village. He had no family to return to, Eofer would let him tag along for a while; get him across to Anglia at least.

The steersman hauled the big paddle blade to his chest as Eofer settled in beside his troop. Yes, he thought as a wave of drowsiness washed through him, Anna could tag along for a while, a smith was always useful. As the sea slapped gently alongside, he hunkered down into his cloak as his lids became lead weights.

TWENTY-ONE

A glimpse of Hel and then another as Hemming reined in and spoke, his words a breathless blend of horror and wonder. 'Shit. There it is.'

Eofer guided his own mount across to the side, out past the tree line which had obscured his view and looked. For a moment he too sat stunned by the enormity of the sight which lay before them, but he put words to his thoughts as the others moved up into a line. 'The gods know that I never thought to see such a thing.'

He realised that his hand had moved unconsciously to the hammer which hung at his neck, and a glance to left and right told him that he was not alone. At any other time the sight of a troop of battle-hardened warriors gaping at a hillside, rubbing gods-luck pendants between thumb and forefinger would have looked preposterous, amusing even, but not today, not here.

Hemming spoke again. 'We could go north, lord. Skirt the town and swing back south down The Oxen Way.'

As Eofer shook his head he was aware that most of the men strung out to either side seemed to think that he had made the wrong choice. 'No, we have to go through,' he replied. 'I have a duty to perform there. Besides,' he added, 'the *seith* is not aimed at English hearts.'

Eofer clicked his mount on, the horse walking forward as Hemming mumbled a reply. 'I hope that you are right, lord. Seith is bad *spellweorc*, as powerful as it gets. I doubt it can tell the difference between folk, even if it had a mind to.'

The hillside disappeared from view as the road took a dip, curving around the bole of the ancient oak which all Englishmen knew so well. The riders stretched out a hand as they passed the great tree, letting their fingertips run across the age-cracked runnels which marked the bark like the timeworn features of an old man as the story came into their minds. Every man, woman and child in Engeln knew the tale of the Woden Tree, it was one of the first they were ever told, a favourite of children all across the land back to the time of the first settlement by English folk. The god in his wanderings had hunted in the very woods which still stood hard against the town of Sleyswic as he matched his cunning against the great boar, spear-bristle. Brought to bay at this very spot, the pair had fought a death duel which lasted a day and a night. Finally Woden prevailed, but as he had torn the dagger-like tusks from the giant, an acorn had fallen from its mouth. To mark his great victory, the Allfather had buried the nut beneath the head of his foe at the scene of the fight, and the Woden Tree had been born. The lower branches were festooned with offerings to the god, tiny wood carved ploughs and phallus for fertility swayed gently alongside representations of the ships which would carry the last worshippers across the sea.

Clearing the Woden Tree, the road straightened out as it hugged the bank of the Sley and approached the desolation which had been Sleyswic. Eofer gave a gentle tug at the reins, halting the mount as his gaze wandered across the devastation.

The town, the jewel of the nation, had been systematically destroyed, piece by piece, building by building by the departing army, the fire-scorched beams crisscrossing the ground where they had fallen. Crowning the hilltop to the North nestled the broken frame of the king's hall, *eorthdraca*, the earth dragon, a hall of ghosts defended by a spectral army.

Hemming spoke in a gasp, the shock and fear in the big warrior's voice unnaturally loud in the stillness which lay on the ruins like a thick winter cloak. 'There are folk moving up there!'

Eofer gave a slight nod of acknowledgment. 'You stay here,' he called as he slipped from the saddle. 'I won't be long.' Fastening his boar helm, the eorle retrieved his shield and hefted his spear. Rolling his shoulders he turned to them with a confident grin. 'How do I look?'

Hemming drew himself up, the pride in his lord's bearing reflected in his eyes. He had recognised the warrior on the hill now and understood. 'Like a victory-thegn returned from war, lord,' he said in admiration. 'An eorle in his battle-glory.'

Eofer snorted at his weorthman's flowery praise, the words incongruous from his bluff companion. 'Thanks, Oswin,' he said with a smile, the action reflected on the faces of the rest of the hearth troop as they recalled their dead friend.

Taking a grip of his shield, Eofer started up the hill as the men began to chatter, swapping memories of the desperate fight in which the young lad had fallen on the field beside the smoking remains of another hall. He inhaled deeply as he paced the ground towards the meeting, his heart beating with the enormity of the moment as his eyes took in a sight he knew deep down that he would never witness again.

The Ghost Army stood before him, the massed ranks braced and ready for battle. At the crest, beneath the white dragon battle flag of Engeln the Ghost King sat astride his mount, the thin spring sunlight shining dully from polished mail and spear point. Raised above the level of the army as any good king should, Osea's cadaver had begun to take on the waxy sheen of a spit roasted hog after a month facing the sun's daily transit. Eofer gave a snort as he thought back to their last meeting, on the field outside the blackened remains of Jarl Wictgils' hall. He had wondered aloud then how many men had killed two kings in battle and, although he had not slain the king himself, he had played an important part in it. He took a last look before his gaze moved on, taking in the details of the Iron Helm of Juteland, the wolf-grey dome mirroring the darkening clouds above.

Arrayed before the king was his army, four ranks deep with a reserve placed at the high point, ready to bolster any part of the shield wall which came under intolerable pressure. With further mounted riders anchoring the flanks and a line of sharpened ash stakes driven into the hillside before them, the war line had clearly been arrayed by an expert in battle craft. A guda, the priest's face and torso ash-whitened to mirror the army, walked among the ghosts, mumbling spells and incantations as he prepared his charges for the spiritual fight to come.

The figure came forward as he approached, his weorthman faithfully at his side. As the grizzled warriors wove their way through the lines, Eofer saw that the thing which he had promised the king he would carry on to Anglia was safely tucked in the crook of the leading man's arm. A grin split the ealdorman's beard, the action echoing the drawn back rictus of the dead which surrounded them. 'King Eomær is safely away?'

Eofer nodded. 'And the army; we barely lost a man.'

Wonred laughed as the worry which had been gnawing at his guts for the past few weeks finally left him, Penda beaming at his side. Embracing his son, the hoary warrior gripped Eofer by the shoulders. 'Did we get old Hrothgar?'

Eofer gave a snort of irony, the old man's face a mask of shock as he shared the news from Daneland. 'The Danes got there first. The ætheling, Hrothulf, killed his uncle before we arrived and took the king helm for himself. And that is not all,' he added as the men shared a look of incredulity. 'The king of Swedes was killed at the same time.'

Wonred shook his head. 'The world is changing even faster than I thought. I was right, this new age holds no future for old men. Did you see your brother before you left?'

Eofer nodded. 'I left Wulf on the beach as the army was embarking to leave Daneland. The fleet should have rounded the tip of Juteland by now and be safely away.'

Wonred cast a glance across his shoulder. 'What do you think of my army?'

Despite the power of the spellcræft which surrounded them, Eofer felt relaxed in his father's company. It would be, after all, the last time that they would meet on Middle-earth. 'They don't say much,' he replied as he ran his eyes along the front line, 'although they were not so quiet when they thought that they were about to overrun us at The Crossing.' A picture of the men before him as he had known them in life flashed into his mind then, the snarls and taunts which had cut the air when they had come like a storm to take the lives of the little English force. The arrival of Ætheling Icel with the main invading army had saved Eofer's raiding party from that fate, but not before the Jutish jarl, Heorogar, had treacherously killed his duguth Imma Gold and the youth Oswin silk-tongue.

Despite the mutilation and the ravages of time, Eofer's eyes fixed on one of the ghost warriors and he walked across. 'I recall this one,' he said in wonder. 'I gave him a barrel of ale, in the stockade the night before the sacrifice.' Most of the ghost warriors wore leather battle shirts, but this one was shirtless and Eofer looked the cadaver up and down as he marvelled at the guda's work. The Jute's belly had been sliced open from groin to ribcage before the priest had reached in to scoop the entrails onto the hillside below eorthdraca in a bloody mess. Stuffed with straw and grass and roughly stitched together, the bodies had then been dressed and carried by thræls down the hill to the waiting line of ghosts. Rammed arse first onto a sharpened stake, the ghost warrior had been armed with shield and spear as the spirit army slowly formed their spectral battle line. Eofer raised his spear and flicked at a pendant which hung from the withered neck by a leather thong. 'A Christ cross,' he said with a chuckle, 'I would have kept the ale myself if I had known.'

A finch landed, plucking a strand before flying off with a beat of its wings. Wonred sighed. 'The bloody birds have been at it ever since the shield wall was formed. It is a shame that it is nesting season,' he added with a frown. 'Some of the ghosts will start to sag like those old coots with me if the Danes or Jutes don't get here soon.'

The comment brought their minds back to the finality of the moment and the pair exchanged a look as they both realised that Eofer must move on soon. Below them, beside the waters of the Sley, a hundred English warriors were staring their way. Soon Eofer's battle troop would say their farewells as they made their way to the western coast, stepping aboard the ships which would carry them away from Engeln for the final time. Looking back upslope, the thegn raised his spear in salute to the men who were moving about further up the hillside as Wonred sighed at his side. 'My last hearth troop,' he explained. 'Old men mostly, men like myself, men who are too long in the tooth to drag their old bones across the sea. Proud men though,' he added with a smile, 'good men to cross the rainbow bridge with.' The old man, a folctoga of the English, leader of the king's armies, slipped a golden ring from his arm and passed it across with a smile. 'Here,' he said, 'give this to Weohstan. Tell him about his grandfather, when he grows to manhood. Tell him…' he said as his expression took on a distant look, 'tell him that the ring came as *máððum*, a special gift from old King Engeltheow. Given to me on the field of battle from the hand of the king himself, the day we forced the ford together, shoulder to shoulder, king and thegn, and the Brondings fled before us as deer would from fire.'

Eofer nodded as he slid it upon his own arm and turned to Penda with a frown. 'It is still not too late to change your mind. The king asked me to tell you that the offer of a place within the ranks of his gesithas is still open to you. Likewise you could follow the rest of my father's hearth troop into service with Cerdic strongarm in Britannia. I know that they will be well received and shown honour if they come with my recommendation.' He looked at the duguth, willing his old friend to accept. Penda had fought at the centre of the shield wall, the place of greatest honour, in the fighting at The Crossing only a few months earlier. Both men knew that it was no exaggeration to say that without the bull-like defence offered by the man and his warriors that day it was unlikely that Eofer would be standing before them now.

Penda shook his head, and Eofer was surprised to see a smile light the big man's face as he pulled himself upright and spoke a verse:

'Oft to the Wanderer, weary of exile,
Though woefully toiling on wintry seas,
With churning oar in the icy wave,
Homeless and helpless he fled from Fate.'

Penda continued, as pride at his weorthman's words shone in Wonred's eyes. 'I have no desire to escape my wyrd, Eofer; to live an exile's life, an *eardwræcca*. I would not die on a British field or wait for old age to rot me in my bed while my lord's bones lie in a land made foreign. Your father has my oath and I mean to keep to it; I will not break it now.'

The conversation was becoming maudlin and Eofer knew that it was almost time to take his leave. 'Come on,' he said, as he slipped the ale skin from his shoulder and twisted the stopper free. 'Share my ale, and I will tell you of the war of fire and steel.'

A horse snickered softly as Osbeorn moved up, and together they peered down into the vale. 'We could wait awhile,' he suggested 'they are bound to move away soon.' He shot his eorle a wicked smile. 'But you don't want to do that, do you lord.'

Eofer and Hemming were silent for a moment longer as they took in the mayhem at the foot of the ridge. 'No,' Eofer said finally: 'I don't.'

'Still,' Hemming added. 'We could have done with the other lads, eh?'

Eofer raised a brow as he glanced across to his weorthman. 'We could, but they are not here. It looks like we will have to go on alone.' As the men of Eofer's war band closed up and tightened chin straps, the eorle moved his horse forward with a squeeze of his knees. 'Leave your shields covered and strapped to the saddle, but those of you without swords I want spears in your hands,' he said. 'Let them see that are ready for anything.'

It was true, he mused, as the stallion cleared the tree line and broke out into the full light of the afternoon, they could very well use the men who had so recently left them. Mercians mostly, they had taken The Oxen Way earlier that day, travelling south to Porta's Mutha where the last ships were waiting to carry them across the sea to Anglia. A hundred spears would soon put the rabble in the valley to flight, but a dozen? He untied the peace bands which secured Gleaming in its scabbard as he prepared to find out.

The sun was past its zenith in the sky to the South, the weak rays of the northern spring raking the pasture with its light as the first faces were turned their way. The call of a cuckoo drifted across from the woodlands and Eofer wondered at the omen. Good or bad it was too late now, his course was set. As the mournful wail of a horn sounded from the pasture below, hundreds of men, women and children raced to form a line across their path.

Eofer spoke steadily as the horses descended the slope and Hemming moved closer to his side. 'Try to keep calm and avoid eye contact if you can, whatever the provocation. Let me do the talking. If I strike, go in hard. I doubt that they will want to lose their newfound freedom so soon.' Further up the vale a barn, one of the last buildings left standing in Engeln, was in flames, the greasy column of smoke shrouding the view northwards as the light airs smeared the sky. The track dipped into a bracken covered hollow, and when they emerged Eofer could see that the enemy were now fully assembled only a hundred yards ahead. Slowing the horse to a walk, the thegn gave a curt nod in greeting to the man who stood at their head. 'We are moving to the coast, where are you heading?' he asked brightly.

The leader of the group exchanged a look of glee with a companion and Eofer studied the man as he approached. The freed slaves were a motley band, mostly women, but with upwards of forty men of varying usefulness. The man who blocked their path had obviously taken on the mantle of leadership and looked to be of warrior class, certainly a man who had experienced battle. Taller than any of his newfound companions and broad shouldered with it, the man sported a thick beard as black as pitch. Although his hair had been cut short in the manner of ceorls and thræls, Eofer could see that an attempt had been made to twist what little there was into a knot on the righthand side of his head, a distinctive feature of the warrior class among some of the Saxon tribes. His clothing was workmanlike but of good quality for a man of his station, a thick leather jerkin above blue woollen trews and a sturdy pair of knee length boots, and Eofer noticed immediately that although he gripped a sturdy boar-spear in his right hand, no sword hung at his wide leather belt. Several silver arm rings shone from his forearm, so they had been killing and looting, but if the leader carried no sword then Eofer felt confident that they had none among them.

Eofer let his horse come to a halt half a dozen paces from the group as the Saxon replied to his question, and a smile of fox-cunning curled within that great beard.

'All the ships are gone, you have missed the boat.'

The men around him laughed dutifully, and Eofer sensed Hemming's hackles rise at the lack of respect shown to his lord. He hoped that they could keep their tempers in check, but his right hand moved across to rest on his thigh, as close to Gleaming's hilt as he dare. 'It's lucky that we are all good swimmers then,' he replied in a lighthearted tone. 'Where are you moving to?' He raised his chin to look deliberately at the leader's knotted hair as he spoke, 'back south?'

The man's hand went to his head and he snorted. 'It's still a bit short yet, but it will regrow. Yes,' he said with a disarming smile, 'we are going home.' He indicated the horses with a nod of his head. 'As you are about to take a long swim anyway, we could use your fine horses.'

The crowd were beginning to wrap around Eofer's small group and he sensed the tension in the air as the horses began to shift nervously. He fixed the man with a stare, levelling his voice but keeping the hard edge. 'I can see that you are an experienced warrior and I can understand the elation you feel that the gods have seen fit to grant you your freedom Saxon, but we both know that you will never take my horse from me. You can try of course,' he added with a menacing glare. 'But even if I die here it will not benefit you in any way because you will have travelled on before me, on that you have my word.'

The air crackled with tension and the nearness of violence as the two leaders regarded one another. Eofer was aware that many of the men, the weaker and more timid, were shifting slowly away as the confrontation reached the point where one or other of the leaders would have to back down and lose face. It had, as his father had always said, separated the chaff from the grain, and Eofer saw that although the numbers who stood against them were intimidating at first sight, the actual number of fighting men that his opponent could rely on were far fewer. They would be outnumbered maybe two to one, but his own men he knew were well fed and well armed, familiar to each other and experienced in war. The odds were acceptable, and he was about to draw his sword to strike the Saxon down, confident that the cordon would scatter before their onslaught, when he heard a choking sound to his right. The Saxon's mouth had opened in surprise and Eofer risked a glance to see the cause of the interruption to his plan. One of the slaves, a troll-ugly oaf, his face pitted with the scars of a childhood disease, was rising slowly into the air, his feet leaving the ground as they swung in small circles beneath him. Eofer stifled a laugh as he watched the man's face redden, his eyes bulging like eggs as Hemming tightened the grip on his neck. Hemming spoke slowly and deliberately, as the man's tongue lolled from his mouth and his breath came in a rasping wheeze. 'If you lay a hand my reins again, I will snap your neck like a dry twig. Got it?'

Eofer's hand moved instinctively to the hilt of Gleaming as he shot a look back at the runaways to gauge their reaction to the throttling, but he was surprised to see that the men seemed to think it even funnier than he did himself. A look passed between the two leaders then, and both men knew that the confrontation was over. Once men begin to laugh together fighting sprit dissipates like smoke in a gale, and Eofer told his weorthman to drop his victim before he lost consciousness. As the sound of a deadweight hitting the ground came to them, the Saxon moved aside to let the group through. Eofer kept his hand close to the hilt of his sword, but the man smiled as the horse walked on, reversing his spear to show that the moment of danger had passed. 'There are other horses,' he said with a smile. 'Travel well, lord.' It was the first time during the encounter that the man had shown respect to his rank, and Eofer watched as the Saxon's hand went to a hammer pendant lovingly fashioned from bone. Reaching up, he gave the thong which held his own silver hammer a sharp tug, tossing the pendant across as the leather parted with a crack. 'I am Eofer king's bane of the Engle. May Thunor bring you good fortune on your own journey.'

The warrior snatched the hammer from the air and shot the eorle a nod and a grin. 'I am Wulf shield breaker of the Long Beards,' the giant replied, drawing himself upright and raising his chin with pride. 'A free man.'

TWENTY-TWO

A gentle gust lifted the hanging, offering a glimpse outside before the wind moved on. It had been pure chance that he had been looking in that direction, but Eofer saw that the light had almost gone from the day and he made his excuses and rose from the hearthside. Ducking through the door he walked out onto the quay and gazed out to the West. It was, he decided, just about the least impressive dusk that he had ever witnessed, and he wondered with a smile how the scops could weave the scene into a stanza fit to grace the gravity of the moment. The sun was not a ball of fire as the horses dragged it down below the horizon, the lower edges of the clouds were far from a blaze of red gold nor the surface of the whale-road a sheet of beaten bronze. It was, he decided, a pretty underwhelming send off as the last of the Engles prepared to leave their homeland for the final time.

Astrid slipped her arm through his own, resting her head on his chest as the sound of merrymaking carried from the fireside. 'What did you expect?' she asked as she traced a pattern with her finger. 'Fiery dragons cavorting about the *heofons*, the stars falling?' She gave his ribs a poke making him jump, looking up with an impish smile. 'Thunor's goats trundling his chariot across the sky as he waves his hammer in a final farewell?'

Eofer chuckled. It was good to have somebody on hand to bring him back to earth, someone who did not look to him to take every decision. His wife gave a sudden start and reached across to grab his hand. Placing it onto her belly she waited for the next kick. Suddenly it came, and the pair shared a kiss at the thought of the life which would come soon after they reached the new land. Astrid had carried the child for nigh on seven months now and her belly was full and hard, the bairn within kicking and pushing as it grew stronger each and every day. He had hoped that she would stay safely at her mother's hall in Geatland to bear the child, but he had not been surprised to see them as he had led the war band into Strand that evening.

Hemming had already told the tale of his meeting at Skansen with young Weohstan of course, and Eofer had listened to the tale with pride. Astrid had left the boy with his uncle despite his tender years, and Eofer had approved wholeheartedly. Although it was still two more years until the lad turned seven winters, Heardred had begun his training early and, by all accounts, done so magnificently. Eofer was grateful to his kinsman and over-proud of his son, sure now that the boy would be accepted as a full foster of the king when the time came.

Astrid wound her shift tighter as another gust came. The warmth of the day, never very great, was seeping away by the moment as the sun finally set in a smear of washy greyness. 'It's getting chilly,' she said and gave him a nudge as she cradled her belly. 'There are still ways, you know,' she murmured, 'if you are careful. Come inside and warm me up, lord.' Eofer laughed gently and dropped his hand to cup the curve of her buttock. 'You go inside, I will follow along soon.'

He ran his eyes across the anchorage as she moved away. The sleek outline of his scegth, *Skua*, was still visible near the last of the boat sheds, resting on its keel as the waters of the Muddy Sea stilled on the cusp of the flood. On the next ebb tide they too would be away, the very last ship to leave the harbour which had been a home to every English fleet since Sceaf had washed ashore, and the foundling had grown to become the first to wear the king helm of Engeln.

Twin figures stood outlined by the flames of a brazier, the slim shafts of their spears shining red in the reflected light of the fire, and Eofer sauntered across to check on the guard for a final time before he turned in. A scraping sound drew his attention as he passed the open doorway of the boat shed and he turned aside, peering into the gloom. 'Osric! What are you doing?'

The master shipwright looked up from his sweeping and threw the eorle a sheepish grin. 'Oh,' he replied, clearing his throat. 'You know how it is, lord. A lifetime of habit, I always sweep up the shed before I close up for the night. Dangerous places boat sheds, lord.' He glanced about, his face already beginning to bloom as he realised how foolish he looked. 'Wood shavings, pitch, tar, all manner of things which can cause a blaze in here.'

'Good,' Eofer replied. 'Chuck the broom down and go and drink with your son. We want to be away at first light, and this is being fired before we leave.'

Osric hesitated but Eofer insisted. 'Go on, it will all add to the kindling.'

The shipwright tossed the broom aside and pulled a wry smile. 'My father worked here, lord, and his before him. I learnt my own craft at his elbow as my son did at mine.' Osric looked about him as he spoke, and Eofer could see that the man could not have been happier if he had been in the king's hall. He clapped him on the shoulder and grimaced. 'We have all had to make sacrifices, Osric. I burned my own hall and reburied my ancestors. This very morning I left my father to face whichever king arrives to claim these lands, fighting at the head of a group of old men and a spell army.' He indicated the hall with a toss of his head. 'Go and make the most of your time remaining here, I promise you that Anglia is worth the loss. Recall your father and others who have worked hereabouts; keep their memory alive, here,' he said, tapping his chest, 'and here,' as he moved his finger up to tap the side of his head. 'That is where their spirit lives on, not in dusty old boat sheds and gull haunted strands.'

Osric gave a snort. 'You are right of course, lord. I see my father in my own son each and every day. I guess,' he said as he closed the shed door for the last time, 'that we are never truly dead until those that loved and knew us in life have moved on themselves.' The shipwright gave a self-conscious chuckle. 'Listen to me, I am going soft in my old age. You are right, lord. I do need a drink!' They shared a laugh and Osric strolled away to his ale, whistling a tune without a backward glance. Eofer came up on the sentinels as a rectangle of light appeared on the wall and the quayside filled with the ribald sounds of drinking. 'Anything going on?'

Hemming had organised the guard while his lord had been making the final preparations for the voyage and Finn had drawn the first watch of the night. Anna had been told to accompany the youth and Eofer had approved of the choice. It would do the boy good to become more accustomed to the feel of an ash shaft, despite his heroics during the fight at the ridge. He had already shown his worth, teaching a few of his new companions how to fight with the hand axe which he carried hooked in his belt. He had made the head himself and it was a fine piece of work, balanced, vicious; deadly in the hand or thrown. Spearhafoc and Grimwulf had taken up the axe with gusto and Eofer had been pleased to see the seriousness with which they had applied themselves to the lessons. An axe would be an invaluable weapon to both youths. Whether it was a result of her womanhood or Welshness, Spearhafoc was far shorter than the boys and she struggled to use anything but a cut down spear once her arrows were spent or the fighting had become hand-to-hand. Grimwulf sometimes found himself detached as a foot messenger from the war band. It was a dangerous task which often forced him from roads and tracks in his need to dodge past enemies. Swords tended to catch in his legs as he ran and spears were continually fouling on tree branches and undergrowth. The axe was a perfect weapon for both youths, a deadly supplement to their short seax.

Finn shot him a welcoming smile and answered as he came up. 'Only the distant fires, lord. There are none closer than Husem, I doubt that they will bother with the island, especially if they know that we are still here.'

'I am sure that you are right,' Eofer replied. 'Still, light the brazier at the far end of the causeway. It's the only patch of firm ground which leads to Strand.' He looked northwards as the rhythmic croaking of frogs came to them from the marshlands there. 'It's the only way in, and we have got the only ship here for miles around.'

Anna trotted off into the gloom as Eofer turned to go. 'Keep a good watch, Hemming will send replacements soon.'

The sun had fully set now, somewhere beyond the murk the stars would be shining bright. He snorted softly as he thought on Astrid's words and double checked, but no dragons tail chased through the clouds and there was still no sign of goat drawn chariots.

Retracing his steps, the noise and warmth bathed his face as he entered the hall and took his place at the hearth. Hemming handed him a pot of ale as laughter rolled around the room and Eofer looked from face to face as the firelight lit their smiles. They were a good bunch, as good as any. He was proud to be their lord.

Hemming leaned in as a remark by Osbeorn caused Spearhafoc to roll her eyes in mock disgust. 'Astrid turned in, lord. She said to tell you that she was cold.'

Her parting words came back to him then and he swilled his drink and downed it in one. Looking across the hall he saw Astrid's old *thyften*, Editha, with a cup of ale in each hand, belting out a song alongside Octa who looked suitably pained. Eofer shared a laugh with his weorthman as the maid warbled away. 'It looks as though someone is enjoying the last night in Engeln,' he said, 'and it's not Octa.' They both chuckled at the sight and Hemming shot his eorle a knowing look. 'It took me a while to get her to drink lord, but she seems to have rediscovered the taste now. It was her mistress' idea, and she did make me promise to tell you that she was *very* cold.'

Eofer snorted as a twinkle came into Hemming's eye. 'You're right, maybe she caught a chill,' he replied, wiping his beard on his sleeve. 'Best I go and check.'

Osric and his son bounded down the beach, reaching up as willing hands hauled them aboard. Behind them the hall and boat shed were already twin torches, the conflagration alive as the flames roared skywards. Petals of light still winked away to the East as the gangs of thræls moved south towards hoped-for freedom, the first columns of greasy black smoke just hardening into distinct columns as the very last day broke upon the Kingdom of Engeln.

Last to leave, Eofer crossed the beach and clambered aboard without hesitation. Sæward stood at the steering platform of the little scegth, the handle of the great paddle blade of the rudder gripped tightly in his hands as he awaited the command. A curt nod and the shipmaster sprang to life. Within moments the crew were poling the ship, digging their long pine oars into the soft mud of the bay as they sought deeper water. Soon they were in the channel and oars slid into thole-pins as the great curved prow swung around to the West.

Sæward's eyes came alive as the oarsmen turned expectant faces to his, their bodies braced and ready to go. The timing had been perfect, the tide already drawing the little ship seaward as it ebbed away, and the shipmaster responded to Eofer's nod with the command; 'on my mark...' He held them in thrall as the prow edged around before his voice boomed and he called the stroke.

'Row!'

The oars dipped together and the oarsmen curled their backs as the first stroke bit the waters, the ship becoming a living thing as it gathered way. Within moments the sleek scegth had speed, the silty waters of the Muddy Sea edging its flanks in a foam capped wave. The crew found their rhythm and a look of contentment came to the steersman's face as the weight of water pushed against the steering oar and the ship surged ahead. The scegth was moving fast now, the waters sluicing alongside as the rowers put their backs into their work, lifting their heads with excitement as a salty tang came on the air.

The cloud of the previous evening had cleared away overnight and the morning air was crisp; overhead high torn clouds hurried away to the South, their undersides painted pink by the returning sun. Astrid moved to his side, her eyes rolling skyward as she clasped his arm for balance. 'Was this more like the send off you had in mind?' He chuckled in reply. 'Still no goats or dragons.'

The ship's lads Edwin and Bassa were leaning outboard, white knuckled in the spray, clasping the shroud lines as they hooked the last of the withies and dragged them to destruction. The woven markers had guided ships in and out of the harbour for generations, marking out the deeper channels from the deadly shoals and mudflats which surrounded them. Scattered haphazardly about skeletal ribs broke the surface, the age blackened beams testament to the danger which lurked unseen only feet away. Soon the oarsmen were relaxing their efforts as the draining waters picked up the lithe little ship, the men stroking the tide as it carried them westward.

Within the hour the *Skua* was burying her bows in deeper waters, bucking the waves as she put the wind blown shallows behind her. The sleek hull shuddered as she shook herself free of the land, and oars were unshipped and lashed to crosstrees as Sæward ordered the sail shaken out and sheeted home. Within a league the steersman had hauled the steering oar to his chest, aiming the prow to the south-west. By the time that the sun was a hand's breadth above the horizon they had cleared the shoals to bæcbord, the rocky stack of Hwælness hazing astern as the last ship from Engeln headed south.

TWENTY-THREE

The mood grew more sombre with every passing moment. Bassa shielded his mouth against the blow as he called the news from the mast top. 'No lord it's not a whale carcass; it's too spread out.'

Eofer fought to keep the worry from his face as he replied, aware that all eyes were on him. 'Are there any fishing boats visible? They could have gutted the catch before heading into port.'

Bassa shook his head sadly, the grimace on the boy's face enough to confirm their fears.

Sæward spoke at his side as the crew members craned to see. 'We knew that this could happen, lord. You can't move thousands of folk across a sea without expecting to lose a few.'

They had made good time that morning, the little ship bounding the waves as a following wind drove her on. Spirits had been high as the breeze blew away the last traces of smoke from hair and clothes. The sight and sound of Editha, her full frame draped pathetically across the wale as she spewed more green bile into the sea only added to the sense of gaiety aboard; the giant leap into the unknown had been taken, the rune sticks were cast, there was no going back.

Sæward, high on the steering platform, had been the first to see the clouds of gulls billowing on the horizon. Soon, they now knew, they would be sailing through a sea laced with the dead. Within the hour the first had bobbed alongside, shredded clothing and lacerated backs testament to the savagery of the ever hungry gulls. Eofer turned to Hemming and shook his head. 'What is happening? Why are there so many?' The big man shrugged. 'Shipwreck? It was bound to happen. Osric was saying that the king had to charter dozens of ships to get the last of the people away. Frisian traders mostly,' he said with a frown. 'As you know lord, not always reliable. He couldn't make arrangements any sooner because the Danes would have got wind of what were up to. Every freebooter in the German Sea pitched up for the chance to earn easy silver. The hulls of some of the ships, Osric said, made a month old pear look solid.' The duguth looked his lord straight in the eye as he saw the consternation written on his face. 'I know you feel responsible because of your speech at the *symbel* last year, but it's not your fault, lord. These things happen.'

Eofer's gaze wandered outboard as another body passed along the hull. A child, its long hair swept ahead by the current looked back accusingly, the fleshless face a horror. 'There's more to this than worm eaten ships,' he murmured. Turning to the steersman he snapped out a command. 'Sæward, I want to catch up with the tail-ender as quick as we can.' He called across to Crawa. 'While Bassa is at the masthead I want you to help Edwin on the braces.' As the dark haired boy rushed across to his station, Eofer hauled himself up the mast. Coming alongside Bassa he gripped the spar and scanned the sea ahead. 'Any sign of ships yet?' The youth shook his head. 'Not yet, lord, although I doubt that it will be long before we begin to overhaul the last of the fleet.' Eofer shot him a look. 'Why do you think that? They left almost a week ago.' The boy looked surprised. 'Fat bellied traders, loaded to the wales with people and their belongings.' He gave a thin smile. 'Can you imagine the chaos, lord? Children running amok, the decks slick with puke as the crew try to work the ropes; every hour another ship develops a problem and they all heave-to.'

Eofer gave a snort. 'You are probably right. When you put it like that it sounds like we had the easier time of it in Daneland.' He scanned the horizon ahead as he attempted to pick out any hint of a sail. Apart from the feasting gulls, the sea was clear of any signs of life, unnaturally so, and the thegn rested his hand on the boy's shoulder. 'Sing out the moment that you see anything, hawk eye. I am beginning to fear that we may be in for a busy few days.'

Back on deck, Eofer called the men to him. 'Any thoughts?' He looked at his duguth as the youth exchanged glances. 'Thrush?'

'Maybe a ship did go down?' He sniffed. 'The lads at Strand said that some of the Frisian ships looked older than their owners; ask them yourself, lord.'

Eofer indicated Osric with a jerk of his chin. 'If you have got anything to add, I would welcome it. My lads know that I am always open to advice.' He threw the man a smile. 'Consider yourself one of the boys, at least for the remainder of this voyage.'

'After what I have seen today,' the shipwright replied with a nod outboard, 'it could be even worse than a lone sinking.' As Eofer stitched a brow in surprise, the man explained. 'There were more than a few nasty looking bastards among the men that I saw. It wouldn't surprise me a bit if more than a few of our Frisian friends had no intention of completing the journey.' He shared a look with his own men who murmured their agreement. 'What's more valuable, lord, a handful of silver or a boatful of slaves? Add in the valuables, heirlooms, tools…' His voice tailed away as the temptations to make off with their cargo became obvious. 'I am not saying that it could be helped,' he shrugged, 'not with the need for secrecy and all, but I am glad that the people dear to me are on this ship, surrounded by English warriors.'

Astrid had been listening from her place amidships, and she added a question of her own. The bairn was almost due now and, despite her early protestations, she had finally accepted that it was good sense and not a slight on her own shipboard abilities that she remained safely stowed at the most stable part of the ship. 'Where is King Eomær and the rest of the fleet while this is happening? They must have passed this way by now?'

Eofer shook his head. 'Wulf told me on the beach that they were plotting a course for Anglia as soon as they cleared the tip of Juteland. At the moment the English are landless wanderers, King Eomær nothing more than a sea king ruling over a kingdom of wooden decks. With most of the warriors abroad, Anglia is wide open to an attack by her neighbours. If we took weeks to shepherd the people down the coast of Frisia, across the narrow sea and back up the coast of Britannia it is likely that we would arrive to find a hostile army waiting for us on the shore and the halls which we have already built there turned to ash.' He attempted a reassuring smile as the scale of the gamble which the Engles were taking was reflected in her face. 'Don't worry, we have Woden's blessing for our great enterprise. I spoke with him, last year at the *symbel*. I know that he has a reputation for trickery, but I looked into his eye and saw no treachery there.'

An audible gasp left the lips of Osric and his boatyard workers at the revelation, and Eofer threw them what he hoped was a self-depreciating smile as their hands moved to lucky charms. 'I don't make it a habit to converse with the gods,' he said, 'this was a special occasion.'

Any awkwardness was interrupted as a call came from aloft. 'I can see sail now, lord.'

All faces turned towards Bassa as he shimmied to the masthead and shaded his eyes. The gods had seen fit to endow the lad with the keenest pair of eyes that Eofer had ever known, and they waited patiently as he scanned the horizon. 'There are about a dozen that I can see,' he finally called. 'They look too small to be our people though, more like fishermen.'

Whether they were fishermen or not, Eofer was glad of the distraction. The morning had not gone as planned; the sight of dead children and talk of the gods was more than enough to unnerve any man. What it was doing to Osric and his men was etched plainly on their faces. Eofer called up as his men instinctively went to fetch their weapons. Fishermen or not, warriors who wished to live to see their beards grey treated every unplanned encounter as a potential fight. 'Which way are they headed?'

'South, lord.'

Eofer exchanged a look with Hemming. 'They could be following a shoal or heading home.'

'Or they could be tailing a lumbering fleet, waiting for the opportunity to pick off a straggler.'

Eofer nodded. 'We will soon see.'

T h e *Skua* was leaping the waves, pears of spray necklacing the prow as it dipped and rose in the swell. Eofer cast his eyes across the men of his hearth troop as they conversed in the bows, noting how the new boy, Anna, seemed to have struck up a strong friendship with Finn. Anna had chosen wisely. Finn was on the verge of leaving the ranks of the youth, moving up to share the bench with Eofer and his duguth, and he called the pair to him as he walked back to the steering platform. They hurried up, and Eofer put their minds at rest with a smile as he held out a hand. 'Here, let me see your axe.'

Anna slipped the weapon from his belt and handed it across. 'The axe head is all my own work, lord,' he said proudly. 'It's a Frankish axe, a francisca. It can be thrown or used as a close order weapon.'

Eofer glanced at Finn. 'What do you think?'

The youth let out a low whistle. 'Deadly, lord.'

Eofer tested the weight of the francisca as they spoke, moving his hand along the short haft as he explored the weapon's balance. He spun it in the air, catching it by the head as he handed it back. 'Show me.'

The pair exchanged a look of concern but Eofer chuckled. 'I don't want you to draw blood. I want to see how this francisca fares against a short seax.'

The majority of northern warriors carried the short stabbing sword known as the seax. Stout handled, the blade was typically about a foot in length, broad backed and sharpened on the lower edge, tapering to a wicked point. Unlike the longer swords which were used to hack at an enemy when a shield wall collapsed and the fighting became more open order, the seax was the weapon of choice in the press of shields where men struggled as close as wrestlers, stabbing and shoving as they sought the breakthrough which would lead to victory.

Finn and Anna moved apart as each drew his weapon, threading their way between the thwarts as their hearth companions exchanged looks of excitement and hurried down to watch. Thwarts, the strengthening ribs of the little ship, were fixed as bracing to the hull planking once the shape of the ship was complete. They doubled up as rowing benches for the crew, and Eofer was keen to see how each man, and weapon, performed in the tight spaces which remained. His nod marked the beginning of the contest, and a hush descended on the crowd as the pair took up the fighting stance appropriate to their weapon. Immediately it was apparent that the axe was a weapon of movement. Finn went into a crouch, shoulders swaying, his left arm held out to balance the weight of the sturdy blade whilst Anna writhed like a snake, the axe weaving a pattern in the air before him as his eyes sought an opening.

Finn made the first move, a lightning fast lunge, the point of the seax darting in towards the younger man's heart. Eofer's breath caught in his throat as it looked as if the strike would hit home but Anna twisted away, the axe casually knocking the blade aside as he hurdled a thwart. A murmur of excited appreciation at the skill shown by the axeman came from amidships, and Eofer watched the duel in fascination as the pair circled each other like wolves, hungry at a kill. The axe was moving again, snaking before the boy in wide, mesmerising circles as Finn lowered himself into a crouch, his knees flexing as they rode the rise and fall of the planks beneath them. The pattern of the fight was obvious to them all now, a fascinating contest between training and discipline and the more natural, almost dance-like gyrations of the axe warrior.

Anna struck next. The axe swept up and over, hurtling down towards Finn's shoulder. As the swordsman moved to block the strike it moved out wide, curving in towards Finn's knee, but the youth was keen-eyed, snatching the leg back to safety a heartbeat before the axe blade whistled past.

Both lads had now gone close, and Eofer heard Sæward clear his throat as the shipmaster gave vent to his feelings. It was becoming obvious to them all that the fight was quickly getting out of hand, both boys desperate not to lose the battle of wits and skill before their peers. Eofer looked across to the others and saw the same concerns echoed on the faces there, and he began to worry that he had made a grave mistake in ordering the fight at all.

Finn shuffled forward as the axe resumed its gyrations before him. They could all see that the move was designed to pin his opponent against the hull, denying the axeman the space which was necessary for his fighting style. As Eofer decided that he had seen enough and prepared to call a halt, the fight reached its own conclusion. Finn stabbed again, a low strike aimed at Anna's groin. The boy's feet scrabbled for purchase on the curve of the hull and, unbalanced, all he could do was snatch the axe across in a desperate attempt at blocking the lunge. In a flash Finn stepped in, pulling the strike as his left hand shot forward to grab hold of Anna's arm and drag it aside. A blur of movement and the seax came up to rest against his opponent's flank, and Anna froze as he felt the point of the blade pressing against his ribcage.

The watching men cheered the victory, as much in relief that the fight had ended bloodless as for any other reason, and Finn stepped back, a smile of triumph illuminating his face. 'You need a shield really, lord,' the youth said, still oblivious to the concerns of his friends. 'As I said, it's a weapon for open order fighting, but you can see how useful it would be.' Eofer was pleased to see the pair clasp hands in friendship as the watching men moved in to listen. It was an unfamiliar weapon to most of them, but in the hands of an experienced warrior it could clearly be just as Finn had described it at the start of the contest, deadly.

'Even a shield to hide behind would not help most men facing a good axeman, lord,' Anna panted as he sucked in lungfuls of air. 'Not only is it heavy and cumbersome, it restricts the view forward. With a weapon like this,' he smiled as he glanced down at the blade, 'movement is everything. If you are fighting against a man wearing a helm, even the nose guard can restrict his view enough to give you an edge.'

Eofer nodded that he understood, and he added a question of his own as Anna fought to calm his breathing. 'But it is tiring by the looks of things. How long can you fight effectively with the weapon?'

Anna shrugged. 'Yes, lord,' he admitted, 'it can quickly tire you out if you are a fool. It's no use in a shield wall because you leave your own body open to a counterstrike when you swing, but in the open where its strengths lay you can move out of range far quicker than a spearman can follow and take a breather if needs be. Of course,' he added, casting a look about the confines of the little *Skua*, 'I couldn't do that here, so I was at a disadvantage.' He shot his friend a grin and a wink. 'Next time you'll not be so lucky.'

Finn sheathed his seax, and the others began to move away as Eofer indicated to the pair that they follow him to the stern. 'I would ask a favour of you,' he said as the ship ploughed on. 'I have settled my wife amidships as you know, it's the most stable part of the ship and,' he smiled and gave a shrug, 'you both know that she is with bairn.' The smile fell from his face as he came to the point. 'I think that there is a very good chance that we will have to fight sooner or later before we reach Anglia. I am asking you to pledge that you will hold yourselves responsible for the safety of Astrid and my unborn child when I have to be elsewhere.' He looked from one to the other. 'I already have Finn's oath and know that I can count on his loyalty, but this is a matter of choice for you, Anna. I have seen your worth and you would earn my gratitude if you would agree to do as I ask.'

Anna's face broke into a smile as he recognised the honour which was being shown to him by the eorle. 'I would be glad to, lord.'

Their conversation was cut short as another cry carried from the masthead, and they all turned to look as Bassa cupped his mouth and fought to make himself heard above the following wind. 'I can see larger ships now, lord,' he began, 'about two leagues ahead of us. There seems to be a small knot dead ahead, with a lone sail tacking to bæcbord about half a mile to the east of them.'

Eofer shared a look with Sæward at his side. The shipmaster was the first to offer his opinion. 'Either the singleton is damaged and heading in to make repairs, or a ship has been cut out from the flotilla.'

Eofer nodded as he looked outboard. The wind was still blowing steadily from astern, spindrift was beginning to tease from the wave crests as its strength increased. Gripping the backstay he hauled himself up onto the hull and peered to the South. Sæward laughed. 'You'll not see much stood on the wale, lord; not if they are still six or seven miles distant.'

The *Skua* was surging ahead under a fat bellied sail, sheets singing under the strain as the rising wind pushed her on. 'How long do you think?'

Sæward threw his lord a look of pride as he slapped the steering handle. 'If this wind holds? In this beauty, lord? We will have overtaken them in half an hour.'

Eofer jumped back to the deck and nodded. 'Steer a course to intercept our friends running for shore.' He shot his steersman a ravening smile. 'Maybe we can help.'

TWENTY-FOUR

He stood stock-still as Astrid threaded the silver pin through the clasp and secured it. Moving around to the front, she gave her *bonda* the once over. 'That is the best that I can manage,' she said with a smile. 'Unless an eorle turns up unexpectedly, you will have to do.' Eofer returned the smile and indicated Thrush Hemming with a roll of his eyes. His weorthman was attempting to disguise the irritation which he felt that their pre battle ritual had been interrupted by her presence but he was making a bad fist of it. 'Remember what I said,' he voiced as they shared a smile at Hemming's discomfort. 'Stay amidships with Editha and let the boys protect you both.' He ran his fingertip along her swollen belly, making her start. 'It's not just your own life you have to worry about, after all.'

As Astrid moved back to her place at the base of the mast, Eofer watched as Finn and Anna moved in to cover her with their shields. He caught their eye, and both lads raised their chins proudly in response to his nod of appreciation.

Eofer flexed his arms and rolled his shoulders as he settled into his battle shirt. Made from bullhide, the leather had been boiled in the beast's blood before being cut to shape. Imbued now with spirit of the animal, the shirt was edged by strips of gold and blue. Rectangular clasps joined the twin parts of the shirt at Eofer's shoulder, each gold backed cell flashing as it caught the sun. Gleaming hung at his side and his seax, fang tooth, hung suspended from his wide belt. A vambrace protected the wrist of his sword arm, the only armour to grace his body that day. Many warriors chose to trust their lives to wyrd in a sea fight wearing their mail come what may, but Eofer had seen too many men disappear beneath the waves, dragged down into Gymir's wet-cold hall by the heavy steel, to leave his own life to the whims of the sisters who weaved the fates. He placed his battle helm upon his head, allowing himself a gentle chuckle as he noticed Hemming slyly checking that Astrid's handiwork had been up to scratch. Eofer and Hemming always helped each other arm before an action, and he could sense the discomfort that the change had brought upon his friend. Anything which could play on a man's mind needed to be chased away when a warrior took up his spear, and Eofer called his weorthman across as the war troop began to gather at the bows. 'Thrush! Give me the once over will you?'

Hemming's features broke into a smile as he came across and tugged at the fittings. 'She did a good job, lord,' he said grudgingly, 'not bad at all.'

Everywhere men were checking and rechecking war gear as the *Skua* breasted the waves, the narrow hull seeming to shiver in anticipation of its first action.

Eofer walked the thwarts, back to the steering platform as the hulls of the unknown fleet clustered a mile off the steerbord beam. Sæward was chewing his lip as he thought, his eyes darting from right to left as he guided the scegth on. Eofer noticed his concern and called above the wind as he hopped onto the sloping deck. 'What is troubling you?'

Sæward shook his head. 'There is something wrong, lord,' he answered with a frown. 'This ship up ahead,' he said, indicating the lone ship with a raise of his chin. 'It's not acting the way I would expect.'

Eofer crouched and peered beneath the scegth's sail, still full and taut as the northerly drove her on. The ship, a wide bellied cargo ship which the English called a *cnar*, was edging towards them, wearing sail as it zigzagged closer to a string of low sandy islands off to the East. 'Maybe they are waiting for us?' he offered. Sæward gave a slight nod of his head without taking his eyes from the nearby ship. 'Yes,' he said. 'I think that they are, but not out of friendliness. Bassa,' he barked. 'Back up the mast, quick as you can.' As the youth hauled himself aloft Sæward called the length of the deck: 'Edwin!'

The boy had the for'ard watch, braced within the great upsweep of the scegth's prow, searching the waters ahead for anything which might endanger the ship. A log or floating wreckage would be invisible to the steersman despite his raised position, and they had all seen the damage which even the smallest flotsam could do to the hull of a speeding ship. With Bassa now doing the same he could be put to better use working the vessel. Edwin cocked an ear as he listened to his steersman. 'Leave that, come and work the sheets.'

The concern was obvious from Sæward's tone and Edwin gave a nod and hurried aft, grabbing Crawa to help him as he went. Soon they were pulling the pins, the rakke bracket grating as they hauled the yard about its axis, and the way bled off the little *Skua* as the wind spilled from the sail. Sæward was already hauling at the steer board, the prow proscribing an arc to the East as the ship turned to run parallel with the big cnar.

Bassa's voice came from the masthead as the *Skua* edged ahead. 'There is a sandbank between us, Sæward; a big one.'

Eofer and his shipmaster exchanged a look: 'bastards.' Sæward cupped his hand to his mouth and called again. 'How deep?'

Bassa grimaced and shook his head. 'Not deep enough, even for a scegth to cross. I can see the sand beneath the surface as clear as day.'

The sound of jeering carried across the waves, and Eofer glared across the gap as the *Skua* ran eastwards. 'Find a way through,' he snapped. 'Look for a channel.'

Hemming was there and the duguth turned his back to the others, shielding them from his words as he offered advice. 'Let it go lord,' he said sadly. 'We can't save them.'

Eofer rounded on him. 'The bastards are taunting us, Thrush.'

'Because they feel safe enough to do so,' Hemming replied. 'They know these waters and we don't. If it hadn't been for Sæward's instinct we would be grounded now. Even if the ship had survived undamaged, what's to say that these lads wouldn't have returned with lots of friends before the tide floated us off?'

Eofer ground his teeth in frustration as Hemming indicated the storage hatch on the little deck with a nod of his head. 'Remember who we have along for the ride, lord. I may be being harsh, but the king has entrusted us with someone far more valuable to the English nation than a single boatload of settlers. We have a duty to see him safely delivered.'

Yells and cries came from the cnar, and the trio looked back across. One of the crewmen, his dark hair tied back by a leather thong, was balancing a young girl of four or five winters on the wale of the ship and waving to draw their attention. Eofer and his duguth exchanged a look of despair as they realised what was about to happen. The sound of a hard slap on bare skin cut short a woman's grief-stricken wail as the crew of the *Skua*, impotent despite their fine war gear and weapons, lined the ship's side, looking on in sullen silence.

Eofer removed his helm, letting it drop from his fingers to the deck as the Frisian's hand went up to the girl's throat. The movement had caught the girl's eye and she looked across at a thegn of her nation, the fear and confusion writ large on her pale features. Their eyes locked as the killer drew the blade across the girl's throat, her eyes shooting wide in shock and horror as her lifeblood spurted red. The man gripped her blond hair and tugged her head back, mocking the warriors who had thought they were racing to save her only moments before. As the wound widened and twin jets of blood pulsed from the severed arteries, they all watched in horrified silence as the little body went limp and the life left her. The Frisian seaman let the body fall overboard before deliberately brushing his hands together, grinning as the outraged Engles shouted in anger. Eofer had been transfixed by the girl's gaze, but Hemming's shout of desperation brought him back.

'No!'

He looked and saw that Spearhafoc had an arrow nocked and ready to loose, but at the moment of release Octa's hand, alerted by his friend's warning cry, shot out to send the shaft high and wide.

The Briton turned, her features contorted by rage as the duguth grabbed the bow by the stave and forced it down. Hemming was already striding the thwarts, and he arrived just as the first blow landed, Octa's head flying back as the woman spat a question: 'why not?'

'Because he has just saved the lives of the rest of the captives on that ship,' Hemming said as he arrived. 'That is why.' She looked at him as if he was mad, but Hemming explained. 'If you had killed one of the crew, all they would have done is line up the captives one by one and done the same thing again and again. We can't get near enough to save them,' he explained as the girl bit back tears of frustration. 'All we can do is back off and give the folk over there some sort of future, even if that is a life of thrældom.' He turned back towards the steering platform. 'Isn't that right, lord?'

Eofer was still standing staring outboard at the lifeless form of the girl. Floating face down in the lee of the cnar, the little body was rising and falling as the bow wave caught it and carried at away, the long flaxen hair spread on the surface of the water like fronds of macabre rock weed. He had looked into the eyes of the dying before, most warriors had, and seen the disbelief there as the great door of Valhall began to swing open before them, but this time it had been different. He had been able to sense the girl's trust in him, that he would save her despite the evidence of her own eyes, because that was what she had always been told warriors did. It was why her father had paid scot to his lord, why the proud farmer kept his spear sharp, his shield freshly painted in his lord's colours; attended the muster. But he had failed her, and for the first time ever he felt overwhelmed by the sense of helplessness, of events happening beyond his control, a feeling which, he suddenly realised, must be the common lot of any ceorl.

Hemming called again, and Eofer dragged his eyes away from the body. ' Yes,' he replied distantly: 'what?'

Hemming repeated his conclusion, as the men of Eofer's hearth troop exchanged puzzled looks at their lord's reaction. 'I was saying lord, that we need to let this one go. Back off, and give the folk on the ship a chance of life.'

Eofer nodded, but his mind was still elsewhere. 'Yes,' he said distantly, 'do it.'

As the lads rushed to haul the yard, Eofer pushed through the crowd of silent men, back to his wife and her pale faced maid, aware that his face burned with shame. The fact that he had proven powerless to save the settlers was bad enough, but for it to happen in front of his wife was the ultimate humiliation. 'Here,' he said. 'Help me out of these trinkets.' She shook her head. 'No, you need to keep them on. We don't know what we will find when we overtake the rest of the ships.' He shrugged. 'For what good I do, you may as well wear them yourself.'

Astrid flicked an icy glare at Finn and Anna, still stood protectively to either side of her. Finn took the hint and made his excuses. 'The danger is past,' he said with a hesitant smile. 'We will leave you in peace, lady.' As the boys hurried away, Astrid swept the deck with her gaze. Satisfied that all others were well out of earshot she leaned in to her *bonda* and fixed him with a withering stare. 'Eofer,' she growled. 'What is wrong? Is it the girl?' He cleared his throat, stealing a look to the South where the cnar was making her way to safety as the Frisian crewmen tossed ribald comments at the chastened English. 'She looked me in the eye,' he explained, his voice heavy with regret. 'She was pleading with me to save her even as the bastard drew the knife across her throat, and all I could do was stand and watch.'

She looked him the eyes, her expression deadpan. 'So?'

'She expected me to save her, and I let her down,' he replied. 'I let them all down, and in front of you.'

'A girl was murdered, she was just a ceorl they die all the time,' she spat. 'She was like a cow or a lamb, we have plenty more.'

As Eofer looked at her in shock, Astrid noticed that the men of his hearth troop were stealing glances their way. She leaned in closer as she painted her face with a smile. 'The men are looking to you now for leadership,' she said in a voice which belied the harshness of her words. 'They all saw what happened and they feel as bad as you about it. If you are a leader of men, now is the time to prove it, both to them and to me. Stop feeling sorry for yourself and act like the man that I married. If you feel that you can no longer do that,' she added with a sweet smile for the benefit of anyone watching, 'I will return to my family in Geatland, and my brother can find me a *bonda* who will.'

She stood back and nodded as she looked him up and down, raising her voice so that all could hear. 'There, you look magnificent, lord. Thank you for comforting me, it was a horrible thing to witness. Thank the gods that I have you and your men to protect me.'

The men exchanged smiles that their lord seemed to have recovered his wits, and Eofer left his wife to settle down at the foot of the mast as he ordered his thoughts. It was the first time that she had spoken to him in such a manner, and he wondered as he paced the thwarts how serious her threat had been. He pushed the worry to the back of his mind as Hemming's happy face greeted him, but he knew that something had changed between them in that moment, worries he knew would rise once again to the surface, however deeply he tried to bury them away.

He pulled a reluctant smile. 'How are we?'

'All set, lord. Sæward is bringing her about and we are going after the other ships.'

Eofer looked across as the steersman worked the rudder. 'How long, Sæward?'

Sæward wrinkled his nose, his eyes darting up to the weathervane which graced the mast top and back to the heap of sail in the South. 'Within the hour, lord,' he replied. 'They barely moved in the *last* hour or so, even in this wind.' He nodded towards Astrid and grinned. 'At this pace lord, your new son might be born at sea.'

Eofer chuckled, grateful to be returned to the jocular world of men, and he could sense the concerns of the crew wash away as he did so. Astrid was right, the men took their mood, their very confidence from him. If he appeared weak or indecisive that would be reflected in their own thoughts and actions. Very soon he would have no hearth troop to lead as men drifted away to other lords, victory lords, men who would supply the silver, gold and reputation which they craved. He returned Sæward's grin, the ship shuddering beneath their feet as it turned beam on to the waves. 'A sea king then,' he called, 'a family first!'

As the laughter was echoed in those around him, Eofer looked back towards the coast a final time. The raucous cry of gulls cut the air there as the great grey birds clustered over a tiny patch of white. Astrid caught his eye, and she smiled and threw him a wink. The strong man was back, all was right in her world again, everything neat and tidy and back in its place like a well ordered hall. He pulled an awkward smile in return, glancing away before she could see the frown which replaced it.

TWENTY-FIVE

'They are looking a bit worried, lord.' The men on the steering platform exchanged smiles as the snake ship edged over towards them, pale ovals flanking the prow beast as the anxious crewmen watched their approach. Eofer turned to Sæward. 'Unfurl the white dragon, let's put their minds at rest. I think that they have probably had enough to worry about over the course of the last week or so.' As the steersman sent Bassa hurrying towards the mast with the battle flag, Eofer let his gaze wander across the ships which comprised the little flotilla.

The formation was, he decided, a bit of a shambles. Half a dozen sturdy cnars had been gathered together at the centre, no doubt intended as the focus around which the motley collection of smaller boats which made up the fleet would gather. Even in the relatively calm seas and steady winds which prevailed in the German Sea that day, it was obvious that the steersman were finding the art of station keeping beyond them. Whether that was caused by poor seamanship or something altogether more sinister he would soon discover.

Joyful shouts and waves greeted the sight of the *herebeacn* as it snapped forward in the following wind, and the big snaca heeled over to bæcbord as the helmsman came about and pointed her prow back to the South. The *Skua* bounded up abeam, the ship juddering like a warhorse after the charge as the lads brailed up the sail and took up station within easy hail of the smiling faces turned their way.

A *scipthegn* came to the side, resting a hand on the sternpost as he called a welcome across the gap. 'I am Ælfeah Hearding, it's nice to see another friendly face.' He indicated what, Eofer realised for the first time, was no longer the battle flag of Engeln but the battle flag of Anglia with a jerk of his head. 'And a friendly flag.'

'I am Eofer Wonreding, some men call me king's bane.' He shot the man a smile. 'Could you use a little help?'

'We are just starting to corral our charges for the night,' the thegn replied with a mischievous smile. 'You are welcome to shelter under our protection, Eofer. We can exchange our news then.'

Eofer snorted at the man's humour as the ships drew apart. It was plain from the haggard appearance and drained faces of the crew that the duty which they had been tasked to perform in the name of the king had been anything but easy. The man was right, the day was beginning to draw to a close. Away to the south-west a distinct lightening marked the position of the sun, low now on the horizon behind a veil of ash grey clouds. On the far side of the little fleet Eofer could make out the distinctive silhouette of another snake ship, the slender sweep of its bow and stern posts lending it an elegance at odds with the stubby, workaday hulls of its charges.

Within the hour the ships had been shepherded together, their hulls lashed securely to make one floating community of the sea. Sæward had lain the *Skua* alongside as the shadows lengthened, and the crews had swapped tales of the tumultuous weeks in the history of their nation over a cask of ale, a flitch of salt bacon and the last of the loaves baked in the pre dawn at Strand that morning.

Eofer and Hemming had joined Ælfeah and his duguth onboard the ship he now knew to be the *Hildstapa*, war-stepper, warrior, a snaca out of the Anglian port at Gippeswic, as the first songs had risen to hang in the chill air.

Ælfeah tore another chunk from the bread, rolling it around his mouth as he savoured the taste. 'You don't realise just how good fresh bread can taste until you have gone without,' he said with relish. 'The bacon too,' he mumbled through the mush: 'smashing!'

Eofer chuckled as the man slurped a mouthful of ale. From his salt stained boots to his leather hair tie, Ælfeah was an English *scipthegn* through and through. Tough and dependable, his eyes shone with intelligence from a face almost as dark and hardy as the leather of his jerkin, testament to a life spent facing wind, sun and wave; everything that Gymir and Ran could throw at him, and still he came back for more.

'So,' he said, 'you were the last away?'

Eofer nodded. 'As far as I know, yes. We were certainly the last ship out of Strand. We fired the last buildings there before we left and moved the channel markers. We may yet see a ship from Porta's Mutha but I suspect that they have already struck out for the Anglian coast. Lucky for you,' he said with a look, 'I decided to come further south before making the crossing. I have my *wyf* aboard and she is heavy with child, so the less time spent out on the rollers of the whale road the better.'

Hemming was looking out across the decks of the wallowing cnar tied up alongside, and he lifted his chin and spoke. 'This would be the shipmaster of the other snaca, I am guessing.'

Ælfeah twisted and looked back over his shoulder. 'Aye, that's Leofwine,' he said as he blew salt from the bottom of a cup and filled it with ale. 'He's taking his life into his hands crossing those decks in the dusk. Some of those 'traders',' he said with a raise of his brow, 'would cut your throat as soon as look at you. I am sure that some of the women are having to pay more than the king's silver for their passage, but there is nothing that I can do about it at the moment. I need them to work the ships and the bastards know it.' He spat over the side as he glowered at the dark outlines of the Frisian ships. 'If they think that they are slipping quietly away with their pockets full of English silver at the end of the voyage they are in for a shock.'

Leofwine finally arrived and hauled himself aboard. Ælfeah made the introductions as the man sank his first ale of the night. 'Leofwine, we are honoured,' he said with a nod in Eofer's direction, 'this is Eofer king's bane, come to save us.' They shared a laugh as the ale began to work its magic and the cares of the day receded. 'Killer of kings, burner of Heorot, first man in Juteland, first man in Daneland,' he paused and took an exaggerated breath before continuing as Eofer gave what he hoped was a self depreciating smile. 'Last man *out* of Daneland, last man

out of Engeln, saviour of beleaguered ship thegns.'
Ælfeah cocked a brow and flashed Eofer a look of
mischief. 'Did I miss anything out?'

Hemming grinned, seizing his own chance for devilry.
'Kinsman to the king of Geatland, son of a folctoga, a
friend of the British king, Cerdic, occasional advisor to
the Allfather himself...' Eofer forced a cup to his
weorthman's lips, cutting off the waggery as the thegns
began to relax for the first time in days. The laughter
trailed away as the tired men settled in to discuss the
matter at hand; how to deliver the last batch of settlers to
Anglia without losing any more to the many dangers
which faced them.

Eofer was the first to ask a question. 'How many ships
have you lost so far?'

Leofwine grimaced as the conversation turned back to
weightier matters. 'The one today, the one which you tried
to save, was the third. Yesterday the bottom just fell out of
one old tub under the weight of the people and their
belongings. We managed to save some,' he said sadly,
'but very few of them have ever been on a ship, let alone
learned to swim. By the time we got there it was too late
for most of them.'

Eofer nodded sadly. 'They would be the bodies we
passed this afternoon.'

'The other ship,' Ælfeah added, 'just disappeared one
night. We would have heard if it was in trouble and it
can't have drifted so far that it couldn't see the light.' He
indicated Leofwine's ship *Grægwulf,* Grey wolf, at the far
end of the anchorage. A lantern flickered dully in the
night, the tall mast of the snake ship a buttery rod against
the black sky above. 'After that we started to herd the

ships together at night and rope them together.' The inference was obvious, the missing ship must have been the first shipload of folk to find themselves on their way to a slave market in place of the new country. 'Now, with the one today making a break for it...' He sighed and shook his head as he swilled the dregs of ale. 'It will only get worse as we approach the Ælmere. You couldn't have turned up at a better time Eofer.'

Eofer sensed Hemming flinch at his side. Reaching forward to recharge the cups he shook his head sadly. 'We can't stay with you if you take the southern route. We have been entrusted with carrying a treasure to Anglia by King Eomær himself, something of great value to the English folk. Tell me,' he said. 'Why do you think that that is the best way to go?'

The ship thegns exchanged a look of surprise. 'Because these cnar were the last ones available for charter, Eofer,' Leofwine answered. 'Hence they are generally unseaworthy, manned by cutthroats, and no doubt tarrying to give their friends time to arrange an ambush when we reach the islands off the coast. I think that the ship which ran for shore today will very soon be joined by others.' He looked pleadingly at the eorle. 'If you go Eofer, I doubt that we will get many ships through to Anglia.'

Eofer nodded thoughtfully as Leofwine reeled off the list of problems facing the little fleet. 'I disagree,' he said finally as the ship thegn finished and sat back with a sigh. 'Even if you get the majority of the ships past the Ælmere, you will still have to fight off the pirates based at the mouth of the River Rin and then fight off the Salian Franks. The ships that survive that, and the crossing to Britannia, will find themselves off the coast of Cent. Now,

I don't know how much you boys in Anglia know about recent events in Juteland, but we have just invaded the homeland and sacrificed their king to the gods. I doubt,' he said, with a raised brow. 'That the Jutes of Cent will be too welcoming when you pitch up in their waters.'

Hemming made a fist, belching softly as he pushed it into his belly. 'Don't forget the Saxons north of the Tamesis, lord,' he added: 'tough lot, those boys.'

Eofer spread his hands. 'How long do you think that it will take to get to Anglia at the rate you have been travelling? A month? Two?' He shook his head as the *scipthegns* quietened. 'You don't need me to tell you that we only really have one option open to us, and that is to make the crossing as direct as possible. We may lose a ship here and there to Gymir's hall, but every mile travelled will take you further from danger, not deeper into it.' He shot them a smile of encouragement. 'I doubt that our new friends fancy trying to out sail an English scegth in a fat bellied cnar. Keep your station on the flanks and I will sweep the rear. What do you say? Let's get these people to their new homeland, before more end up as gull food.'

'Ah,' Sæward smiled, 'the dawn chorus; I never tire of it.'

Eofer wrinkled his brow as he answered his steersman. 'Yes, that is one of the disadvantages to bringing up the rear. Don't get too close, if this wind backs suddenly we could end up wearing some of it.'

Finn had the helm, and the youth smiled alongside the pair as they looked out beyond the prow. Eofer dug his duguth in the ribs as he pointed out the bulk of Hemming on the ship ahead. 'I'll bet Thrush is enjoying that.'

The sun had barely climbed into the sky to the East and they were already underway. As the portly hulls of the cnar rolled in the swell, the lines of pale arses had quickly been replaced by rows of pale faces as the English settlers emptied first their bowels and then their stomachs into the choppy waters alongside.

'At least it means that there is plenty of food to go around,' he snorted, 'sick people don't tend to eat much.' Sæward chuckled at the knots of bodies lining the wales of the fleet as he answered his lord. 'And it took their minds off the fact that they were out of sight of land, They probably wished that they *had* been dead for most of the voyage!'

After a hesitant start, the previous few days had gone well. The unwelcome news that they were to abandon the coastal route and strike out across the wastes of the German Sea had been greeted with obvious dismay and outright hostility by many of the Frisian crews. Ælfeah's idea that the warriors which could be spared by the three English warships be distributed between the transports had been a complete success, and the sullen ships' crews had finally bowed to the inevitable and knuckled down to work. Immediately the speed had increased and they had made more progress that first day than they had in the whole of the previous week's sailing. Denied the opportunity to make for a friendly shore, the shipmasters had plainly decided that the quicker they could complete the crossing, the sooner they would be paid, the sooner they were shot of a boatful of landsmen, the sooner they could scrub the decks and strakes clean of shit and puke. Now the coastline of Anglia was a sage coloured line on the western horizon, and every man, woman and child, Engle or Frisian, willed the final miles away.

Within the hour the coastline was a hedge of spears as the gorse of the coastal heathland gave way to tree capped headlands. Ælfeah had dropped back from his place out to steerbord of the little fleet as they put their prows to the South, and ribald comments flew between the ships as the *Hildstapa* bore away, making for deeper water as she formed up on the *Grægwulf*. By midday the sun shone brightly from an indigo sky, and the crew of the *Skua* watched with amusement as children on the ships ahead ran excitedly from beam to beam as the steel grey heads of seals bobbed alongside as if in welcome.

An arm of land, hummocky with grassy dunes, ushered the flotilla towards the entrance to the great bay which received the waters of the Rivers Yarne and Wahenhe as the shipwright Osric sidled up to Eofer with a smile. 'I thank you, lord,' he said, 'for safely transporting myself and those close to me to the new country.' He smiled again and ran his hand along the wale of the *Skua*. 'And in such a fine ship too!'

Eofer clapped him on the shoulder, and Osric flushed at his reply. 'There is no finer ship on Middle-earth,' he said. 'I was given the honour of felling the tree from which it was made by the master shipwright himself. It was a great day, back in the old country. I shall never forget it.'

Osric cleared his throat, the emotion of their safe arrival threatening to get the better of him. As the oars dipped and fell and the ship edged into the bay, the great ramparts of the Roman fort at Cnobheresburh drew wonderstruck eyes to the south-west. 'I made this lord, for the new bairn. I hope that you consider it a worthy gift, whether the child is a boy or a shield maiden.' He produced a wooden sword from behind his back and Eofer took it with delight. 'It's made from the same tree as the *Skua*,' he said proudly. 'We kept a few of the better offcuts with this in mind.' He leaned in as Eofer turned the sword in his hand. 'I tried to copy your own sword, lord. I chose this piece because the pattern in the grain resembles that on your own blade,' he said, his confidence growing as he realised that his gift had been well received. 'I had to do my best with the hilt,' he whistled softly, as he stole a glance at the original which hung at Eofer's side. The thegn had retrieved the blade from the burial mound of his grandfather, Ælfgar, and the gold and garnet studded handle had lent Gleaming its name. 'I managed to find a few shards of red glass to fit into the cells instead of garnets.' He shot Eofer a lopsided smile. 'Not too many garnets laying around in shipyards, lord. Nor gold,' he pointed out with a chuckle. 'That there is paint.'

Astrid had come up, and Eofer showed her the replica as Osric beamed with pride. 'That is lovely, Osric,' she said. 'You have a skill with wood, you should use it more often.' They laughed at the joke as Osric called one of his men across. Slipping an item from a woollen sack the man produced a small shield with a flourish. 'This goes with it, lord,' Osric said as his man dipped his head and backed away. 'It's made from the same wood. The lads made it in their spare time and got one of the artisans in the yard to paint on the front the picture from your flag thingy. 'It is called a *hildbeacn*,' Eofer snorted in reply, 'a war beacon,' Eofer smiled as he examined the boards, the burning hart emblem bringing the events of that night flashing back into his mind. It had been the night that his previous scegth, *Fælcen*, had carried him to war for the final time and he recalled his last glimpse of her, the flames which consumed the little ship mast high, with a wan smile. Later that night, Heorot, the hall of the king of Danes had also met a fiery end, and the image of that attack had been woven by Astrid and Editha into a new war banner for their lord.

Sæward took the steering oar from Finn as the ship entered the calm of the bay. A boat came out from the anchorage, coots and moorhens scattering before it as the oars rose and fell in time, and the men on the *Skua* lined the wale, watching as the *Grægwulf* and *Hildstapa* handed over their charges to the port reeve and stood off to the North. The *Skua* came about, clearing away as the cnar were shepherded to their berths. Hemming was waving frantically from the stern of a trader and Sæward glanced his way. 'We had better pick him up, lord; and the others.'

Eofer waved back at his weorthman with a smirk. 'No,' he said, with a twinkle in his eye as he recalled his duguth's waggishness the night they had joined the little fleet. 'Let's not.' They all shared a laugh at Hemming's crestfallen expression as the ship bore away with lazy strokes of the oars; soon they were up alongside the others, and Ælfeah came to the side as a rope was tossed. Leofwine was already aboard, and the *scipthegn* raised a cup to the eorle as the celebrations began. As the crews began to mingle and the ale began to flow, Ælfeah put an arm around Eofer and turned him towards the South. Beyond a reedy spit of land, hundreds of warships lay at anchor, the curving prows ending abruptly where the beast head had been removed and safely stowed away lest they frighten the land spirits of their homeland.

Eofer's heart swelled with pride as his eyes drank in the sight, and he recalled his speech the night in eorthdraca as, *giddig* with symbol ale, he had stared into the glowing eye of a god and spoken:

'Allfather, guide our people to the West. Let us replace the weeds with a hardier seed. Let us grow strong there together, gods and folk.'

TWENTY-SIX

'Well, spit it out, is it or isn't it?' Eofer craned his neck, the corners of his mouth curling up as Hræfen grinned down at him. 'Yes, I am sure now, lord. It is Wulf, I would recognise that handsome smile anywhere.' Eofer lowered his gaze to discover that his own smile had been replicated on a score of faces around him. 'Well, don't stop work now,' he chided them. 'We will need to get this roofed if it is to shelter a newborn.' As the smiling workmen bent their backs, Eofer crossed to Hemming. 'It must be a boy if Wulf is smiling.' Spearhafoc was nearby, and the Briton glanced up as she stripped another hazel branch of its side shoots. 'It is a boy, lord. I could have told you that before your wife left for Geatland.' Eofer and Hemming shared a look as the woman lopped another twig with the blade of her knife and tossed it aside. 'But that was months ago,' he said in wonder. 'How could you have known then?' She shrugged as she reached across to the pile of hazel at her side, her eyes flashing her annoyance at Rand as the youth dumped yet another load at her side. 'Her belly, lord,' she said finally as another trimmed piece landed on the pile before her. 'It stuck out.'

Eofer and Hemming exchanged a look of bemusement. 'Well, yes. We may be men, but we do understand where bairns come from.' She shook her head in exasperation, leaning forward to rest her elbows on her knees. 'No lord,' she explained with a patience which was so unusual in the youth that the pair had to stifle a laugh. 'Her belly stuck out, you know, at the front. Everyone knows that bellies stick straight out when it is a boy and wrap around when the mother is carrying a girl.' She sighed at their ignorance, giving them a pitying shake of the head as she plucked the next withy from the pile and set to with the blade. Eofer raised a brow, the girl shooting them a parting scowl at his retort. 'Let's go and see if our witch is right, Thrush.'

The pair walked towards the dusty track as they waited for Eofer's brother to arrive with the hoped for good news. Eahlswith, King Eomær's cwen, had insisted that Astrid stay with the royal party for the birth. Artisans had been sent on ahead as soon as the decision to resettle the king and his family in Anglia had been taken at the *symbel* the previous autumn, and the new hall had risen at Theodford in time to welcome the king and his family upon their arrival in the new kingdom. With Astrid safe and comfortable, Eofer and the men of his hearth troop had pushed on to begin the task of raising his own hall during the long days of summer. Osric and his gang had offered to construct the oak frame before they started work on the new boat sheds at Yarnemutha, and the finishing pieces were already slotting into place as news of the birth arrived.

They gained the track and the pair paused as they waited, sweeping their gaze over the lands to the South.

'She is still miserable, lord. Do you think that it is something to do with the bairn?' Eofer raised a brow. 'Spearhafoc? No!' he exclaimed in surprise. 'She ran away from that life, remember? Why should she care about bairns?'

'She's been like this for weeks now, ever since we arrived in Anglia, so it can't be the other thing.'

'What other thing?'

'You know,' Hemming said, narrowing his eyes and jerking his head towards his belly, 'the other thing.'

Eofer laughed as he began to understand what his weorthman was suggesting. He had watched the giant kill men with his bare hands and eviscerate a horse with a single sweep of his sword but he couldn't bring himself to mention "the other thing" by name.

'No,' he replied with all the authority of a married man. 'She has no spots on her face, or anywhere else I am guessing. They always get spotty when "the other thing" is happening. Besides, it only lasts a week and this has been going on for months.'

'Well, if she is like this normally lord,' Hemming replied with a frown. 'I will make sure that I am not around when the other thing does happen.'

They craned their heads to the West but the horsemen were still out of sight. The hall stood at the western end of a long ridge and the road dipped down and rounded a bend as it entered the trees there.

'I still say that we should have built the hall further away, lord,' Hemming said. 'Any trouble and we will have no warning at all.' He turned and grimaced. 'We both know how hall burnings end up for those trapped inside.'

288

Eofer thought as he took in the lands of the Wulfings which lay spread out before him. The ridge on which he had chosen to build his hall overlooked the wide grassy wetlands which straddled the mouth of the River Aldu. It marked the southern boundary of the new estate which he had been gifted by a grateful king, from its source deep inland, all the way to the German Sea only a few miles to the East. With the arrival of the English king and his folk, the Wulfing settlements centred on Rendilsham had become little more than an enclave, hemmed in by Eofer's lands and those of the English settlers at Gippeswic in the South. 'No,' he said finally, 'this place is perfect. The Wulfings are not so strong that they can hope to attack Anglia without inviting annihilation, and even if they were, distance would not save us. Jarl Wictgils thought himself safe deep inside Juteland but we burned him out just the same. Placing my hall here,' he explained patiently, 'says to the people across the river, Look, here we are. The Engles live here now and always will.'

Hemming nodded as he looked around. 'It is a fine place, Eofer. With the *Skua* beached at the foot of the hill you have everything that Cerdic offered last year and more.' His face suddenly broke into a smile as he remembered why they were waiting at the roadside. 'So, as our less than friendly witch is so confident that the bairn is a boy what's the name to be, Wonred?'

Eofer shook his head. 'That would honour the memory of my father, maybe next time,' he smiled. 'No, I decided that the boy will be called Ælfgar after my grandfather. You saw the splendour of his burial chamber with your own eyes Thrush, and heard the tales of his deeds in battle against the Jutes and Myrgings. He was held in high regard, his name deserves to live on within the family. Besides, I wield his sword, it seems like a small thing to receive such a gift.'

The sound of horsemen finally reached them from the West, and they turned together as the first riders hove into view. Wulf rode at the head of the column, and Eofer looked on as his brother raised an arm in greeting, coming on in a smear of dust. Soon they were reining in before the pair, and Wulf slid from the saddle to embrace his brother. 'Astrid is fine and you have another son,' he said with a grin. 'Ugly little bastard, looks like his father!'

A rumble of laughter came from the smiling horsemen as Eofer returned the grin. 'Yes, it's a family trait.'

Wulf placed his hands on his hips as he turned and stared away to the South. The sun was lowering in the West and the Aldu was a silver belt on a sark of green. 'So, this is Snæpe.' He turned back with a frown. 'A bit close to the wolf men, isn't it?'

Eofer snorted. 'It's just fine, the Wulfings will behave if they want to keep their land. Not only does it allow me to control the road junction and river crossing here and collect my dues, but I can walk to my ship whenever I feel the urge to fill my lungs with salty air.' He cocked his head. 'Come and see the hall.' They walked across, and Eofer explained the goings-on as Finn appeared with a tray of drinks. 'Osric and his lads are nearly finished erecting the frame. We are doing the panelling ourselves and I have a thatcher down there in the estuary harvesting the reed beds for the roofing material. That should be on within the week.'

Wulf stopped suddenly and threw his brother a smile. 'It's a good place, Eofer. I am pleased for you.'

'Maybe you should try it?'

Wulf snorted. 'No, brother, it's not for me. I am happy where I am, a king's gesith. I fight for my lord and he rewards me with gold, honour and women. I have all that I need.'

Osric came across. 'You are just in time to see the final rafters slot into place on the ridge beam. You won't see it from the outside of course, not when the thatched ridge goes on, but I will get the lads to batten them up, save your thatcher a job. Would you like a quick tour, lord?' he asked as he leaned in, lowering his voice as he wiped the sweat from his brow. 'It gives me the excuse to take a break, and it *is* hot.'

Wulf took a draught of his ale and pointed ahead with the cup: 'lead on.'

Osric grinned with delight, and the brothers shared a look of amusement. No artisan needed prodding into discussing his work and the shipwright was no different.

'Over here,' he began as they sauntered across, 'are the finest walls in Anglia. Because there is plenty of oak available in the valley, all I have done for the exterior wall is split the trunk in two and sink it in a trench. Normally on sandy soil like this,' he continued as he stamped his foot, 'we wouldn't bother worrying about the damp, but with the coast only a couple of miles that way we dug a foundation trench and filled it with shingle from the beach. It helps to support the frame as well as keeping the damp down in the earth where it belongs. We sunk the vertical posts into the trenches and braced them with the tie beams which you can see overhead. The split trunks, staves we call them, then go in curved side outwards, and the interior walls are finished off with these planks, edge butted horizontally and fixed by tree nails, not clinkered like on a ship. It keeps the wall nice and smooth, ready for mounting shields, tapestries and the like.'

Wulf looked down and exclaimed with surprise. 'And a planked floor!' He glanced at Eofer. 'I shall have to tell King Eomær when I return to Theodford that he has a rival in splendour.'

Osric snorted. 'The truth is that we had so much oak left over it was easier to fit floor joists and plank it over than send a cart to the lowlands to bring back clay for a beaten floor. Up here on the heath the ground is as dry as a bone, so you can't pack it down hard enough to get a good solid foundation, the surface will just skip off when you walk on it. Just so long as you build in a good firm base to the hearth though it's not a problem, and easier to keep clean. The twin lines of posts which run the length of the hall support the weight of the roof of course.' He turned to Eofer as Wulf ran a hand along the sandy coloured wood. 'I will send the same man who did the scroll work on the sheer strake of the *Skua* down to carve any designs that you want on them, lord, as soon as I get back to Yarnemutha. A couple of weeks to dry out a little and it will be perfect for carving, oak's lovely like that,' he added wistfully. 'Like carving cheese.'

'And this must be the ring giver's dais,' Wulf said as he hopped up onto the raised platform. Shouts rose into the air from the youth outside and they all shared a smile as Eofer shook his head. 'It is good that they are so settled here,' he said with a snort as the yells came again, louder this time. 'It is a long way to take them back.'

They all chuckled as they stepped up onto the platform, turning to face back down the hall as Osric completed his tour. 'Entrances at the midpoints of the long walls, crosswise for light and air,' Osric said with a flourish, 'and facing this way at the end, the twin doors leading to the buttery and pantry.' Finally he jerked a thumb over his shoulder; 'and through yon doorway, the lord's private chamber.' He spread his hands wide as Eofer began to frown at the commotion which had gained an edge of anger outside. 'There you have it, a hall fit for an eorle.'

Osric's look of pride fell away as a girl's scream cut the air, and Eofer blew out in irritation as the moment was ruined. 'Give the lads a break, Osric, they have worked hard enough for one day in this heat. 'Show my brother the ale store,' he said as he jumped from the dais, before throwing a weary smile across his shoulder. 'Don't let him drink any, just show him where it is.'

He turned back as he strode towards the door, his anger increasing as he got nearer and the noise redoubled. Grimwulf's face appeared in the doorway, the youth hanging on the doorframe as he squinted into the gloomy interior. Eofer immediately knew that whatever was causing the rumpus would require more than his sudden appearance to quieten.

'What is it?'

Grimwulf finally picked him out from the shadows, and Eofer's stomach dropped as he saw the shock written on the lad's face.

'It is Rand, lord,' he cried. 'Spearhafoc has stabbed him!'

Eofer thought that he had misheard. 'What do you mean?'

'Spearhafoc!' he cried again. 'She's fucking stabbed him!'

Eofer pushed past the youth and stepped out into the sun-washed yard. His youth were clustered around a prone figure which had to be Rand, while, off to one side Finn had Spearhafoc lying face down in the dust, his knee in the small of her back and her right arm twisted back and thrust upwards towards her shoulder blades. The knife which the girl had been using to strip the withies a short time ago now lay at her side, and Eofer saw with consternation that the blade was slick with blood. He hurried across, shoving the dark twins aside to get to the injured boy. Horsa had stripped the belt from his tunic, tightening it around the lad's thigh to stem the blood flow, and he looked up as Eofer's shadow fell across him. 'How bad is it?'

Horsa loosened the belt, and a thick red upwelling ran out to add to the sticky patch of mud at his side. 'It's bad, lord,' he said with a purse of his lips, 'deep. But the blood's not pumping or squirting out, just flowing.' He looked across to Spearhafoc. 'I can stop the bleeding for now, but he needs a hedge-witch. Someone who knows what they are doing.'

Eofer stomped across the yard as Wulf and Osric appeared at the doorway, the shock written large on their faces. He jerked his head to the side, and Finn leapt away as he saw the fire in his gaze. Grabbing the girl by the scruff of the neck, Eofer lifted her bodily off the ground and slammed her against the side of the hall. 'Why?'

If he had expected to see defiance or hatred in her face he was to be disappointed. The Briton looked crumpled, as broken as he had ever seen a person, and despite the rage which had built within him, the sight of her held his desire for retribution in check. This was the girl who had lived with them for the best part of a year, saving lives more than once as her arrows silenced guards throughout the lands of the Jutes and Danes. Horsa owed his life to her leechcraft, there had to be a reason. He tightened his grip on the necking of her tunic, balling it as her feet dangled a foot above the dusty ground. 'Why did you stab your friend?' The girl attempted to answer but all that came was a racking sob. He spoke again. 'Will you save him?' She nodded and he let her drop. 'Get over there, and see to it. We have no sacred groves to drown murderers in the new land, if he dies, you hang.'

The youth moved aside as Spearhafoc dragged herself across. Finn kicked the blade out of reach as she passed, and the absence of trust shown by the action drew another sob of misery from the girl. Anna turned his head to catch her words as the girl spoke in a whisper, pointing away with a shaky hand.

As Anna hurried off to do her bidding, Eofer called to Finn and he hurried across. 'Finn, what happened.'

'I didn't see it lord,' he answered. 'But Crawa and Hræfen said that Rand dropped another bundle for her and she snapped something at him. He said something back and she just lashed out with the knife she was using.'

'So it wasn't a deliberate attack. Just a reaction to something he said?'

'It seems so, lord,' Finn answered. 'You can end up just as dead though,' he added pointedly, 'whether it is done deliberately or not.'

Hemming was there, his face like thunder. 'Kill her now,' he growled.

Wulf was at his side and the words seemed to cut through his bemusement at the drama which had suddenly appeared in their midst. Eofer's brother set his face as he added his voice to Hemming's. 'Thrush is right, Eofer, kill her now. No words should be able to break the bond which exists between men who are sworn to the same lord.' His hand moved to his side and Eofer saw that his kinsman was untying the peace bands which held his sword secure within the scabbard. As the ribbons fell away, silver shone as Wulf drew the blade an inch and fixed Eofer with a glare. 'Say the word brother, and I will take her head from her shoulders.'

TWENTY-SEVEN

The torches guttered as a gusting breeze threw them away to the East, and Eofer paused and scanned the heavens. Away to the West the sky was a wall of fire as the wolf chased the horses on, and an image of the wagon drawn orb of the sun flickered into his mind as the age-old pursuit played out. One day, at the end of the world, Treachery would catch the Golden Mares, devouring them along with their charge. It would usher in the Terrible Winter at the end of time, when the great serpent which encircled the earth would thrash the seas to mountains, gods would grapple with giants and snow and ice grip Middle-earth. He snorted, and the spearmen at the entrance to the Howe exchanged a look, covering their indecision with a smile. 'Come on,' Wulf giggled. 'We are keeping two kings waiting.'

The flames recovered as the wind dropped to a sigh, becoming fire-serpents themselves as the giddiness from the *symbel* ale worked its spell. They were the last to arrive and the sentinels moved away to walk the perimeter of the site, joining their fellows there as the pair propped their swords alongside the others, stepped across the threshold and entered the burial chamber.

King Eomær was seated at the far end of the room, and he raised a drinking horn in salute as the sons of Wonred paused again to allow their eyes to acclimatise to the gloom. 'Join us,' the king cried as faces turned their way. 'Eofer, my grandfather wishes to thank you for his safe journey to the new lands.'

The assembled warriors boomed and stamped their feet in approval, and Eofer smiled his thanks as the brothers began to examine the grave goods provided for the ancient king. Immediately before him an iron cauldron hung from the roof beam by a heavy chain with links as large as fists. Beyond that the priests had gathered together iron hooped buckets and pails containing the foodstuffs which the first harvest had provided his descendants. Fruits and berries, nuts, loaves, flitches of bacon, pitchers of ale and mead to wash them down.

At the head of the chamber carpenters had constructed a stout seat, the final gift-stool of the king men said had been the greatest of them all. The golden urn containing the ashes of Offa, King of Engeln rested upon it in honour, surrounded by shields, spears and swords backed by the battle flag which had so recently pierced the skies of Daneland, greatest of *fiends*.

King Eomær was on his feet, and he showed Eofer honour as he came forward to hand him a horn of ale. Resting his hand on the eorle's shoulder he turned back to face the room. 'Offa, *Engelcyning*, this is Eofer Wonreding, who men call king's bane, the king killer. Know that this man is a hero of your people, a treasured *eorle*. At my instruction he carried you overseas to a new land we now call Anglia, so that your shade shall move among your people always.' The king removed his sword and walked back to the king chair as the warriors watched from the benches in silence. Eomær held the sword towards Offa's urn and spoke again. 'Offa, greatest of Engles, I return your battle blade, *Stedefæst*, to you. It has served me well, drank the blood of English enemies as it did in your own time.' The king rested the sword against the bowl of the chair and turned back. 'Eofer, Offa's shade moves among us in this place. Unlock your word-hoard, show him that men of quality and skill still flourish among his people.'

Eofer's mind raced as he sought to live up to the honour of addressing the greatest of Englishmen through a *giddig* haze, but a familiar voice floated into his mind and he recognised it immediately across the passage of time. Offering Oswin's own shade a small smile of gratitude, Eofer raised his chin and began.

> *'Offa was praised for his victory-lust*
> *by far-off men;*
> *The spear-bold warrior ruled wisely*
> *over the empire of the English;*
> *That was a good king.*
> *Eomær was his kinsman,*
> *grim in war, the son of his son;*
> *Jute and Dane quailed at his name.*
> *Gold flowed from his gift-hoard*
> *to gladden his eorles.'*

Again the assembled warriors boomed their appreciation, the space resounding to the stamp of booted feet as Eofer took his place beside Wulf. The men began to stand, one by one, as they too recounted a stanza for the great king, tales of armies crushed and fleets destroyed, as the Engles stained the ground with the battle-dew of their enemies. Soon it was King Eomær's turn to regale his ancestor's spirit with a tale, and the men listened as they supped from their horns to the tale of the Wide Farer. The chosen heroes hung on every word as the unknown journeyman recounted the heroics of other kings, Theodric of the Franks, Breoca of the Brondings, Helm, King of Wulfings, until the king reached the tale of his own kinsman and he set his face with pride:

'Offa ruled the Engles, Alewih the Danes.
He was the bravest of all those men,
but could not defeat Offa in deeds of arms,
and the noble Offa while still a boy
won in battle the greatest of kingdoms.
No-one of that age ever achieved
more glory than he did. With his sword alone
he marked the border against the Myrgings
at the mouth of the Egedore.
Engles and Swæfe observed it
ever after as Offa had won it.'

The walls of Offa's death hall shook as the warriors roared their acclaim. Ale flowed, boar was eaten, and promises were pledged of even greater deeds to come as the English forged their new land in the ashes and rust of an older civilisation. Wulf beamed at his side, and Eofer thought that he had never seen his brother so happy as at that moment. As the laughter and boasting thundered around him, a melancholy air stole over the eorle, sinuous and wraith-like but difficult to shift all the same. Whether it was the fact of his father's death and the part which he had inadvertently played in it he could not say, but it was a truth which sat ill with him that he had played a large part in the decision to move to the new land. If they had elected to remain in Engeln and fight for dominance of the lands which bordered The Belts his father would still live, would still be a proud folctoga.

Wulf topped up his horn, Eofer smiling his thanks as the noise and mayhem swirled around him, and he forced the sour mood down deep. In his heart he knew that they had made the right decision. The first harvest was safely gathered in, new halls and villages had sprung up almost overnight. Already the first delegations had arrived at the hall of the king, their new British neighbours keen to ally themselves to the power which had come into their midst. Gold and promises had been exchanged and the new year would see English arms carried beyond the borders of Anglia, deep into the heartlands of Britannia itself. New life was replacing the old as it always had, as it always would until the wolf finally chased down the sun; in the morning he would formally name his new son, sprinkle him with water at the Temple Ring and accept him into the family.

A chant got up, and Eofer came back from his thoughts. On the benches opposite, Icel was attempting to down an aurochs horn of ale in one deep draught to the delight of the onlookers, and the thegn joined in the smiles of anticipation as they awaited the ætheling's inevitable soaking.

Soon the evening was over and it was time to take their leave. Arm in arm the sons of Wonred staggered into the night. Retrieving their swords they drew them as one, renewing their pledge to their lord and acclaiming his ancestor for the final time.

As they gulped down the cool night air, Eofer smiled in greeting as the next group of warriors to entertain the old king passed him by with a boozy cry. Wulf was hanging on his shoulder and he let out an ale soaked belch and squinted across. '*Wæs hæl!*' He giggled. 'Drink, brother?'

'So,' Eofer said as the pair rode the final few miles, 'you never did explain how you found me in Daneland.'

Hemming shot his lord a look, snorting softly as the events of that week came back to him. 'Only the gods could have found a way, lord. You truly are Woden blessed.' He shook his head. 'We just asked around and struck lucky if the truth be told. Grimwulf was handy, the lad knew the area well from his time as a slave there. And we wore these of course.' Hemming fished inside the purse which hung at his waist and produced a silver hoop. Giving the disc a huff and a quick polish on his sleeve he held it up to the light. 'Jutish brooches, the ones which we took at The Crossing. I knew that they would be useful,' he grinned. 'Not as quickly as it turned out though,' he admitted with a snort. 'If anyone gave us a funny look we pointed at these and they took our accents for Jutish. They knew all about the defeat and capture of King Osea and his jarls, so they just accepted that we would have a score to settle with the Engles. Once we tracked you down to Hroar's Kilde, it was just a matter of biding our time until the opportunity to grab you back presented itself.'

Eofer shot him a look and a grin. 'So your great rescue plan was to sit somewhere wassailing, while your lord festered in a hole.'

Hemming laughed. 'That was your own fault, Eofer. If you had been patient and not tried to escape, we would have had you out sooner.'

As the laughter trailed away, the easy mood changed abruptly as the pair recognised just how close to home they had ridden. Hemming was the first to break the silence, as he sought to ease the burden from his lord's mind.

'It was a close call, lord,' he said, as the horses picked their way up the final ridge. 'Another few weeks and she might have been a duguth.' Thrush Hemming lowered his voice, leaning across his saddle despite the fact that they were the only living things in sight. 'The hand of Woden was in that too, Eofer,' he said with reverence. 'His name means fury, and that's what Rand got.'

Eofer sighed and looked across. He had been dreading reaching the hall for days, the whole thing had cast a dark cloud over events which should have been joyous. Even if the youth had survived, the Briton would pay a heavy price for her actions that day, despite the high esteem in which she was held.

The king's great hall at the new Theodford was no more than a good day's ride from his own. The air carried a sharp bite after the mugginess of the previous few weeks, the first signs of the winter to come. Leaves were losing the waxy sheen of summer and a murmuration of starlings were washing the sky, the dark waves sweeping to and fro against a sky the colour of blood as the day drew to a close.

Gaining the rise he put back his heels, determined to purge the poison of that day from his hearth troop as the golden Ridgeline of his own hall hove into view.

Finn was at the crossroads, and Eofer saw at once that the news was bad. Curbing his mount, he looked down at the youth as Hemming reined in at his side: 'dead?'

Finn pursed his lips and nodded, the pain of the moment written in his eyes. 'Yes, lord, two days past.'

He nodded that he understood and guided the stallion across to the yard. The others came from the hall at the sound of his approach, but their sullen demeanour and downcast looks drew any of the joy of homecoming from the moment. He was glad then that he had asked Astrid to delay her return; the following moments would be unpleasant enough without providing his newborn with such an inauspicious homecoming.

Spearhafoc was still slumped where he had left her, and despite the anger which the others felt towards the girl, he was pleased to see that she was unmarked. Osbeorn, Octa and Horsa came across, smiling in welcome despite the tension of the moment and he was glad of it. Eofer fixed Osbeorn with his gaze as he sought confirmation of Rand's death, hoping against hope to receive a different answer despite the trustworthiness of Finn. 'It's true?'

Osbeorn gave a curt nod. 'His body has been prepared for the flames lord and the pyre has been built.' He wrinkled his nose as he came across to stand at the horse's shoulder. 'It would be a good idea to do it tonight, lord,' he said with a grimace. 'He *has* smelt better, the leg went bad days ago. She said,' he continued with a nod in Spearhafoc's direction, 'that the sap and mould from trimming the withies had dirtied the blade and let bad spirits into the wound. I had to set a watch over the body every night to keep the wolves and foxes away. The lads,' he said with a flick of his head, 'have been pretty spooked, standing there alone knowing that wolves and the gods know what else had been watching them only feet away in the darkness.'

As Eofer went to dismount, Osbeorn touched his leg. 'The girl,' he said softly. 'She insisted on preparing Rand's body herself. She is pretty grief stricken about it all, and I don't just mean because she is going to swing for it.'

Eofer nodded that he understood as he settled back into the saddle. The evening light was slanting in from the West, throwing long shadows across the yard and turning the thatch to flame. He raised his eyes and took in the vista to the South. The Aldu was a silver serpent as it wound its way to the shroud grey sea. Below he could see the boathouse, *his* boathouse he smiled despite the grimness of the moment, with the long low shape of the *Skua* straining at her mooring rope, trailing her stern to the sea as the tide ebbed.

He dropped his eyes and looked at the girl, and a stab of regret flickered within him as he saw how pathetic she had become, all the life and cheekiness driven from her by a moment of madness. 'Ozzy,' he said. 'Take the slave ring from her neck and replace it with a rope.' Osbeorn's face dropped and he made to speak, but Eofer's glare told the duguth that it would be unwise. Now that the moment had come the other members of Eofer's youth, the girl's hearth mates, looked downcast to a man, tearful even as they recalled the girl they had known and loved. Spearhafoc looked up then for the first time and he saw the depth of her despair, her eyes glassy pools set within pits of jet. Osbeorn handed his lord the end of the rope, and he gave it a yank as he hauled at the reins and pointed his mount's head back to the West. 'Come on,' he said as the girl climbed fearfully to her feet. 'There is no place at my hearth for mad dogs.'

He indicated that Hemming follow on with a jerk of his head, and Eofer walked his mount back to the road without a backwards glance. As Hemming fell in beside him Eofer moved to one side and gave the rope a sharp tug. Spearhafoc staggered to his side, and Eofer kept his gaze straight ahead as he spoke to her for the first time since his return, his voice flat and unfeeling despite the sadness within. 'Tell me why.'

Eofer could see the girl looking up at him out of the corner of his eye, but he kept his gaze straight ahead as she began to reply. 'He told me to stop being so blobby, lord.' Eofer shook his head and Hemming raised a brow as his earlier suspicions seemed to have been confirmed, despite the absence of spots. 'No, not that,' he grimaced. 'Why have you been so miserable since we came here?'

Spearhafoc racked her mind as she attempted to think of a clever answer, one which may yet still give her back her life, but nothing would come so she decided to tell the truth however ridiculous it sounded. 'It was the shepherd, lord…and his family.' She hesitated and tried to curl her lips into a smile, but she was sure that it must have appeared as a rictus as she added with resignation and her voice dropped to a sorry whisper: 'but mainly the shepherd.'

Eofer and Hemming shared a look of incomprehension, and Eofer finally relented and met her gaze. 'What, that gibbering old man? The one nobody could understand?'

She nodded sadly. 'He was speaking a language even older than British, lord. It was the speech they used when the Ringing Stones were built, you remember, within the great stone circle which sang for you when you struck them with iron last year. He was counting the sheep, lord,' she explained: 'yan, tan, tethera. You say one, two three but it means the same thing. The country folk still use it near where I come from.' She shrugged. 'I just felt homesick is all. I thought that it would go away, but it didn't, it just got worse.' Eofer could see that the Briton was attempting a smile, but the rope chafed her neck at that moment and her eyes widened into a look of fear.

The crossroads were ahead, the aged oak patiently awaiting its victim as they walked the final few yards. All hangings were done at the place where two roads met, it was a place where spirits paused in their nocturnal wanderings. Any who had visited such a place after dark would testify to their eeriness, it was not without good reason that one of Woden's names was Hangi. Eofer slipped from the saddle and took her hand. 'Come on, Thrush,' he said with a heavy heart. 'I can't do this alone.'

Hemming slipped from the saddle as the girl shook at Eofer's side. 'Here, take this,' he said, thrusting the hand towards him. 'You know what to do.'

An involuntary gasp escaped the duguth's lips as he realised what help the thegn needed from him, and he dragged the girl's hand up and splayed her fingers on the runnels of the trunk. Spearhafoc began to realise what was about to happen, and she gave them a look which was a mixture of gratitude, fear and despair as Eofer drew fang tooth from his belt.

'Hold it firmly Thrush,' he said. 'The quicker this is over with, the easier it will be for us all.'

The seax moved in, its point pricking the skin above the girl's forefinger as Eofer felt for the joint. A heartbeat later a scream cut the air as the short sword stabbed, and within moments the fore and middle fingers of both hands lay on the grass at their feet. 'Nobody attacks a member of my hearth troop and gets away unmarked,' he snarled as the girl swooned, sobbing with pain and shock. 'I suggest that you start practicing with a broom and ladle, you will never draw a bow again. Tie her on your horse, Thrush,' he said as he opened the ground with the point of his blade, rolling the digits in with a sweep of his foot and pressing the earth flat. 'And point her south.'

As Eofer tore up a fistful of grass to wipe the bloodied soil from the point of his seax, Hemming bundled her into the saddle, slapping the horse's rump to send it on its way. The horse seemed in no hurry despite the smell of blood which hung in the air, and Eofer called after her before she moved out of earshot. 'Spearhafoc, never think to return. You will not be so lucky next time.'

The small figure turned in the saddle, and as the pale face that he knew so well looked back at him he saw the moment when the girl's pride came back to shine through her tearstained features. 'Dwynwyn,' she spat, as her chin raised up in defiance and the old familiar strength came into her voice. 'My name is Dwynwyn, barbarian.'

AUTHOR NOTE

If the historical framework which contained the storyline for the previous volume in this series, Fire & Steel, could borrow from the written records which have come down to us from the former Roman lands, works by Gildas, Nennius and others, the events contained within Gods of War are set firmly within the inky blackness of the dark ages.

That there was a migration from the land still known to this day as Angeln in modern Germany is undisputed, the Venerable Bede, himself a proud Angle writing in the early eighth century tells us so. In the Ecclesiastical History of the English People he writes that the Angles came to Britain from, '...the country known as Angulus, which lies between the provinces of the Jutes and Saxons, and is said to remain unpopulated to this day...' The events of that migration, its timescale and the effects which it had on the surrounding peoples will almost certainly never be known. The Scandinavian and northern German societies were illiterate. Christianity, with its bookish scribes and universal dating system were unknown there; it would be several hundred years yet until the last bastions of heathenism were overcome. In this situation it is understandable that what we now consider as linear 'normal' history did not exist. No written records were kept, so none could come down to us today. Even within the land which became the kingdom of the East Angles, any knowledge of earlier times was destroyed in the viking attacks of the ninth century.

One of the primary sources for the period are of course the written accounts we collectively call the Anglo-Saxon chronicles. Begun at the end of the ninth century, almost certainly by order of King Ælfred, even these 'primary sources' are very sketchy regarding events which were ancient history, even to the scribes who first wrote them down. They were after all dealing with events which were as far removed from their own time as the Tudors are from our own.

Here are the entries in the chronicle which deal with the period within which this series of novels will be set.

A.D. 519. This year Cerdic and Cynric undertook the government

of the West-Saxons; the same year they fought with the Britons at

a place now called Cerdicsford. From that day have reigned the

children of the West-Saxon kings.

A.D. 527. This year Cerdic and Cynric fought with the Britons in

the place that is called Cerdic's-ley.

A.D. 530. This year Cerdic and Cynric took the isle of Wight,

and slew many men in Carisbrook.

A.D. 534. This year died Cerdic, the first king of the West-

Saxons. Cynric his son succeeded to the government, and reigned

afterwards twenty-six winters. And they gave to their two

nephews, Stuff and Wihtgar, the whole of the Isle of Wight.

A.D. 538. This year the sun was eclipsed, fourteen days before

the calends of March, from before morning until nine.

A.D. 540. This year the sun was eclipsed on the twelfth day

before the calends of July; and the stars showed themselves full

nigh half an hour over nine.

As we can see, over a period of twenty-one years very little is recorded, and none at all outside the lands which later came to be known as Wessex. As for the various kingdoms across the sea in and around the Anglian homelands, they may just have well have been on the moon.

In many ways this volume lays the foundation, not only of those which follow, but also for the antagonism which seems to have existed between the Danes and the Angles in particular during the following centuries. At its heart seems to lie the struggle between rival lines of the Danish royal dynasty in the early sixth century, the Scyldings.

Several accounts written hundreds of years apart deal with this time, but all are conflicting to a greater or lesser degree. There is a definite schism, with on the English side principally the poems Widsith and Beowulf, and on the other the various Scandinavian traditions typified by works such as the Gesta Danorum, Skjöldunga saga and of course Hrolf Kraki's saga.

Both traditions seem to take the side of opposing members of the Scylding dynasty. The older English sources, Beowulf and Widsith, concentrate on King Hrothgar and his sons. The much later Scandinavian sources follow the descendants of Hrothgar's brother, Halga, and his son Hrothulf.

It's a witches' brew of conflicting tales, our efforts to understand which are not aided by the fact that the same characters are called by different name forms in each tradition. In this as in my other books I have kept to the English spellings, which are older and closer to the original, in an effort to keep confusion to the minimum.

Hrothulf, the killer of King Hrothgar in Gods of War, was known to the Danes as Hrolf Kraki, one of the heroes of the age, but he warrants only one fleeting mention in Beowulf. Hrothgar's son, Hrothmund, the renegade prince in our tale, is never mention at all in the later Danish sources. However one does turn up in the king's lists of East Anglia, and the Beowulf poem has been convincingly argued to have originated there. Wealhtheow, Hrothgar's Queen and the mother of Hrothmund seems to have been a Wulfing, and the Wealh element of her personal name is the Germanic name for foreigner; Welsh and Walloon for the French speaking part of present day Belgium share this ancient root. She could quite easily represent a British strain within the Wulfing dynasty; it was common practice even as late as the eleventh century for foreign born women to take an Anglo-Saxon name on marriage.

In the Danish tradition Hrothgar is a King in Northumbria (before the kingdom actually existed) not Denmark, but h e *is* murdered by a young relative in a dispute over a golden ring. Could this be the reason for the interest shown in Hrothgar and his descendants in the Anglian lands? If Wealhtheow did come from the Wulfing settlements in Britain, did her son seek sanctuary there after the fall of his father? Could it even be a reason why the Danish Great Army of 865 chose East Anglia to invade rather than the lands to the south of them, Saxony and Francia? The great army was the first to arrive under the leadership of kings, and although heathen armies had begun to overwinter several years earlier, notably on the isle of Sheppey on the Kent coast, this time they had come to stay. Landing in East Anglia the Danes subdued that kingdom, followed the next spring by Northumbria and parts of Mercia, all Anglian Kingdoms. It would have been far easier to move south and settle Essex, the kingdom of the East Saxons. With bases already established on the opposite side of the estuary, this would have given the Danes control of the Thames and its rich hinterland.

Was there a long remembered grudge against the Angles of East Anglia, by then ruled by kings who traced their descent from the Wulfings, which caused the Danes to act as they did centuries later?

As ever when dealing with this shadowy period of our history there are more questions than answers and of course we will never now know the truth, but there does seem to be a long history of conflict between the nations. If that also included a vicious dynastic struggle, the later events could even be interpreted as 'payback' by the

Danish vikings. History in illiterate societies was passed on by word of mouth, often in the form of verse and storytelling. The *scop* or skald would tailor his tale to suit the audience in much the same way as a live performer would today. The story would be interactive as the drink fuelled audience exchanged banter with the performer, who would of course expect payment for his performance from the lord who employed him. If there was a connection between the ruling dynasties in East Anglia and Denmark it would be entirely natural for different traditions to evolve over time in this way, each glorifying the ancestors of the respective royal house. It may or may not be true, but it is certainly a possibility, and a great vehicle for a story which I found too good to pass up in the absence of *any* hard facts within which to anchor my tale.

The situation in Sweden at this time was very similar, with a dead king supplanted by his brother and the old king's sons fleeing for their lives. In this case the new King Onela does seem to have had Danish sympathies and it seems that he was later married to Yrse, daughter *and* unwitting wife of Halga and mother of Hrothulf (Hrolf Kraki).

The Swedish princes Eanmund and Eadgils flee to Geatland for safety, whose king is of course the brother-in-law of our own hero, Eofer. Events there will take a turn for the worse and Eofer will be fully involved, but that conflict is for a future volume.

The Ghost Army at Sleyswic I based on a custom which was prevalent on the steppes of what is now Russia. The Greek historian Herodotus writing in the fifth century BC, tells us that the Scythian people there used the method which I described to ring the burial mounds of their kings with a spectral guard. The image which I had as I read about this was just too evocative, and I stored it away for use in a future novel.

If anyone is interested to read further on this period the most entertaining account is to be found within the pages of The Saga of King Hrolf Kraki. Although written down hundreds of years after the events they describe (fourteenth century Iceland no less), it is a stirring tale of men and gods with many similarities to the Beowulf story. The Penguin Classics edition contains a good introduction which goes into far greater depth concerning these connections than can realistically be discussed within a novelist's historical afterword.

In the following volume Eofer and his hearth troop will fight in new lands. As the first war bands move into the area which will become the Kingdom of Mercia, simmering rivalries between rival British kingdoms flare into open conflict.

Cliff May

July 2016

CHARACTERS

Ælfheah - Ship thegn of the *Hildstapa*.

Anna - A youth.

Astrid – Daughter of King Hygelac of Geatland, wife of Eofer.

Bassa – A youth.

Beornwulf – A youth.

Coelwulf – An English thegn.

Crawa – A youth, twin to Hræfen.

Eadward - Ship thegn on the *Hwælspere*.

Eahlswith – King Eomær's cwen.

Editha - Astrid's *thyften*, her handmaid.

Eofer Wonreding, king's bane – Son of Wonred, brother of Wulf.

Eomær Engeltheowing - King of the English.

Finn – A youth.

Grimwulf – An English *thræl*, freed in Daneland. Joins Eofer's youth.

Gudmund - Geat thegn at Skansen.

Heardred Hygelacson - King of Geatland. Eofer's brother-in-law.

Hnæf - Eadward's steersman on the *Hwælspere*.

Hræfen – A youth, brother of Crawa.

Hrethric Hrothgarson - Brother of Hrothmund, killed by assassins while hunting.

Hrok - A Dane. Killed by Eofer at holm-gang.

Hrothgar Halfdanson– King of Daneland.

Hrothmund Hrothgarson - Brother of Hrethric. Escapes the assassination attempt in which his brother is killed. Flees to Geatland with Eofer and Eadward.

Hrothulf Halgason - Nephew of King Hrothgar. Assassinates the king and usurps the throne of Daneland.

Icel Eomæring – English ætheling, son of King Eomær.

Kaija - A volva.

Leofwine - Ship thegn of the *Grægwulf.*

Octa – Eofer's duguth.

Osbeorn – Eofer's duguth.

Osea – King of Jutes.

Osric – A shipwright at Strand.

Penda – A duguth, Wonred's *weorthman.*

Porta – A youth.

Rand – A youth. Killed by Spearhafoc.

Sæward – Eofer's steersman. A duguth.

Spearhafoc/Dwynwyn – Sparrowhawk, Eofer's British shield-maiden.

Starkad Storvirkson – A viking in the pay of the Danes.

Swinna/Horsa - A captive with Eofer. Later joins his war band.

Thrush Hemming – Eofer's *weorthman*, his senior duguth.

Ubba silk beard– A Danish warlord. Killed by Eofer at holm-gang.

Ulf - Danish guard at Hroar's Kilde.

Weohstan – Young son of Eofer and Astrid.

Wonred – Folctoga and father of Eofer and Wulf.

Wulf Wonreding – Son of Wonred, brother of Eofer.

Wulfhere - Eadward's weorthman. Killed during the chase through Scania.

Yrse - Swedish queen. Mother and sister of King Hrothulf of Danes.

PLACES/LOCATIONS

Ælmere - The Zuyder Zee, the remnants of which are the Ijsselmere in the Netherlands.

The River Aldu – The River Alde, Suffolk, England.

The Cat Gate - The Kattegat.

Cnobheresburg – The Roman Saxon shore fort of Garianonum, now known as Burgh castle, Norfolk, England.

The Crossing – Vejle, Jutland, Denmark.

The River Egedore – River Eider, Schleswig-Holstein, Germany.

Eyrarsund - Øresund, the strait between modern Sjælland and Skåne.

The River Gipping – The River Orwell, Suffolk, England.

Godmey - Gudme, Fyn, Denmark.

Great Belt – The channel between Fyn and Sjælland.

Harrow – *Hearg*/temple, now the Danish island of Fyn.

Hereford – Rendsburg, Schleswig-Holstein, Germany.

Hleidre – Lejre, Sjælland, Denmark.

Hroar's Kilde – Roskilde, Sjælland, Denmark.

Hven - An island in the Øresund strait.

Hwælness – Whale Ness – Sankt Peter-Ording, Schleswig-Holstein, Germany.

Little Belt – The channel between Jutland and Fyn in present day Denmark.

The Muddy Sea – Nordfriesisches Wattenmeer, Schleswig-Holstein, Germany.

North Strand – Nordstrand – Wattenmeer, Nordfriesland, Germany.

Old Ford – Hollingstedt, Schleswig-Flensburg, Germany.

The Oxen Way – An ancient roadway, still known today as the Ochsenweg, running approximately north-south the length of the Jutland peninsula.

Porta's Mutha – Portsmouth, now Friedrichstadt, Nordfriesland, Germany.

River Rin - The River Rhine.

Scania - Götaland, Skåne County, Sweden.

Skansen - Kungsbakka, Halland, Sweden.

Skerkir - 'Rowdy', Stevns Klint, Sjælland, Denmark.

The Sley – Schlei, Schleswig-Flensburg, Germany.

Sleyswic – Schleswig, Schleswig-Flensburg, Germany.

Snæpe - Snape, Suffolk, England.

Strand – Suderhafen, Nordstrand, Germany.

Suthworthig – Eckernforde, Schleswig-Holstein, Germany.

Theodford (1) – Kappeln, Schleswig-Flensburg, Germany.

Theodford (2) – Thetford, Breckland, Norfolk, England.

The River Trene – River Treene, Schleswig-Holstein, Germany.

The River Udsos – The River Ouse, East Anglia, England.

The River Wahenhe – The River Waveney, Suffolk, England.

Yarnemutha - Great Yarmouth, Norfolk, England.

ABOUT THE AUTHOR

Born in London and raised in Essex, Cliff May now lives with his family near the coast of Suffolk, East Anglia.

Discover more about my books on my website:
www.cliffordmay.com
or facebook:
https://www.facebook.com/pages/CRMay/6715583695
24813

Printed in Great Britain
by Amazon